QUEEN GEEKS
in Love

Laura Preble

BERKLEY JAM, NEW YORK

THE BERKLEY PUBLISHING GROUP
Published by the Penguin Group
Penguin Group (USA) Inc.
375 Hudson Street, New York, New York 10014, USA
Penguin Group (Canada), 90 Eglinton Avenue East, Suite 700, Toronto, Ontario M4P 2Y3, Canada
(a division of Pearson Penguin Canada Inc.)
Penguin Books Ltd., 80 Strand, London WC2R 0RL, England
Penguin Group Ireland, 25 St. Stephen's Green, Dublin 2, Ireland (a division of Penguin Books Ltd.)
Penguin Group (Australia), 250 Camberwell Road, Camberwell, Victoria 3124, Australia
(a division of Pearson Australia Group Pty. Ltd.)
Penguin Books India Pvt. Ltd., 11 Community Centre, Panchsheel Park, New Delhi—110 017, India
Penguin Group (NZ), 67 Apollo Drive, Rosedale, North Shore 0632, New Zealand
(a division of Pearson New Zealand Ltd.)
Penguin Books (South Africa) (Pty.) Ltd., 24 Sturdee Avenue, Rosebank, Johannesburg 2196,
South Africa

Penguin Books Ltd., Registered Offices: 80 Strand, London WC2R 0RL, England

QUEEN GEEKS IN LOVE

This book is an original publication of The Berkley Publishing Group.

PRINTING HISTORY
Berkley JAM trade paperback edition / November 2007

Library of Congress Cataloging-in-Publication Data

Preble, Laura.
    Queen Geeks in love / Laura Preble. —Berkley Jam trade pbk. ed.
        p.   cm.
    Summary: In the Queen Geek Social Club, boys have always been strictly secondary to the goal of
spreading "geekiness" to every corner of Green Pines High School, until sophomore Shelby is swept
off her feet by the karaoke stylings of a boy named Fletcher, and Becca and Amber fall for an artistic
computer genius.
    ISBN 978-0-425-21717-7
    [1. Dating (Social customs)—Fiction. 2. Clubs—Fiction. 3. Best friends—Fiction. 4. Friendship—
Fiction. 5. High Schools—Fiction. 6. Schools—Fiction. 7. San Diego (Calif.)—Fiction.] I. Title.

PZ7. P9052Qw 2007
[Fic]—dc22

                                                                            2007027184

PRINTED IN THE UNITED STATES OF AMERICA

10   9   8   7   6   5   4   3   2   1

ACKNOWLEDGMENTS

Great love and thanks to:

• my parents, Richard and Therese Preble, first and foremost, for leaving an indelible mark on my world. I miss them every day.

• my California parents, Helen and Manny Klich, who adopted me and understand the burden and responsibility of graduating from a school with a poisonous nut for a mascot.

• my husband, Chris, and my sons, Austin and Noel, for giving me time and space to write, loving me when I'm cranky, and providing nonstop support.

• my friends (especially Becky and Stacey) for constant inspiration and encouragement. Also my sisters, Linda, Barb, and Ann, for making me laugh so hard I can't keep my Kewpie down.

• the fantastic staff at West Hills High School, where the best teachers, administrators, classified staff, and counselors work.

• Laura Rennert, Jessica Wade, Jennifer Puma, and all the people at Berkley JAM who help make my work the best it can be.

• my students, current and former, who constantly challenge me, inspire me, frustrate me, and remind me that teaching is the most important job in the world next to parenting.

1

THE BIG
DATE—PART I

(or The Drag Queen Medusa)

I'm staring into the glass-smooth surface of my best friend's swimming pool. It is June, the most wonderful month of the year, the month in which school stops and summer begins. June, best friend, swimming pool. How could anyone possibly have a problem?

And yet, I do. And the problem can be summed up in one word: boyfriend.

Let's examine the word *boyfriend*. What are its major components? "Boy"—an immature, underdeveloped youth of the male persuasion—and "friend," a word used to describe a companion, somebody with whom you share mutual affection and trust. Can those two things truly blend together?

Unfortunately, I am starting to find out. But let me start at the beginning: I am a self-described geek, I live with my dad (a *Star Trek* geek and scientist), and I was totally happy to keep to myself, play with my robot, and date any cute boy who thought he could talk me into sin. Most of them figured out that I was better at talking than they were, so the sin didn't happen, which was very frustrating for them and led to some hot rumors about me being a lesbian. This was mostly because I started to hang out with Becca Gallagher, a new girl who spikes her hair and tweaks the nipples of any guy who gives her grief. But the lesbian thing is not true, as my current boyfriend, Fletcher, will tell you. And there's that word again.

In our freshman year, Becca came to Green Pines High School, home of the Puking Panthers football team. I suspected that Becca was unique the minute I saw the huge dragon tattoo that covers the outside of her entire left calf, and I wasn't wrong about that; we started the Queen Geek Social Club because she wanted to "find others of our kind." Why? Because Becca has a thing for global domination, and she thought that if we started a club, we'd be able to amass enough girl bodies to storm the White House and effect great social change—okay, really, it was all about Twinkies. We collected Twinkies to send to super skinny super models, this got us on television, and from there we sort of took over the school dance, which went from being a lame event with papier-mâché palm trees to an unforgettable night of piracy, plunder, and one of those kisses that is simply etched in your memory. The kiss belonged to me and to Fletcher, the aforementioned boyfriend.

I should clarify that the boyfriend thing didn't happen right away. Our relationship actually started with me beating him about the head and shoulders with a pillow. I know that sounds kind of mean, but actually, in context, it makes lots of sense. I had met a Norwegian guy at a bowling alley, dropped a ball on his foot, thought he liked me, but then, when we went on a date, he brought a girl. Fletcher happened to be in the car with all of us; he was just one of those casualties of war they're always talking about. I don't think the pillow thing inflicted any permanent damage, although he does twitch when we sit on the sofa.

My trauma involving the word *boyfriend* begins today, two weeks after senior graduation, two weeks into the official start of my official sophomore year. Becca and I are at Becca's mansion (and I'm not kidding about that), lounging around her pool as the late afternoon Southern California sun peeks out from behind a cloud. It's really too cold to be swimming, but it's the principle of the thing. It's summer vacation. We've gotta swim, even if we look like we're wearing goose pimple bikinis.

"If you want my opinion—" Becca starts.

"I don't."

She ignores me as if her heavy-duty sunglasses block sound as well as light. "If you want my opinion, I think you're afraid."

I rub suntan lotion on my pasty legs even though I feel like I should be looking for a parka. "Afraid of what?"

She takes off the sunglasses, sits up in her lounge chair, and fixes me with an "oh, please" stare. Her short-cropped, bleached hair stands up in lots of individual spikes, and the tips are currently dyed royal blue, one of our school colors. "Afraid of actually being with someone who might be right for you."

"That doesn't even make sense," I mutter, trying to distract myself by vigorously rubbing lotion between my toes. Has anyone ever had sunburned toes?

"No?" She stretches and squints sideways at me. "Here's what I think. You like being a loner. You don't want some perfect guy messing that up."

"Perfect!" I snort. "He's about as far from perfect as—well—as anyone." I don't know how anyone can be expected to defend bad dating choices while wearing a bikini in sub-Arctic weather. Instead of listening, I decide to count the number of tiles on the bottom of her pool.

Becca knocks on my head with a toy shark grabber stick. "Hello! Are you paying any attention?"

"Sure I am." That's a lie. I'm desperately trying not to pay attention, actually. Why would I do this to my best friend? Because I don't want to have this conversation.

Becca grabs my shoulders and makes me look her in the eye. "Where are you guys going on your Big Date?"

I don't answer.

She gives my shoulders a little shake. "C'mon, I know it's tonight. Don't pretend it's not important. You have given me absolutely no details on this. Cough it up."

"What are you, the Spanish Inquisition?" I manage to shrug out of her grasp and think about diving into the pool, but I'm afraid I might hit a layer of ice and break my nose. "I don't have to answer any of these questions. It's none of your business."

"It *is* my business." She huffs back to her lounge chair and plops down in it, disgusted. "This whole Big Date thing has distracted you for two weeks, and I have things to do, and I need you, and you've just been this big, quivering ball of . . . of . . ."

"Sorry if I've put a dent in your fabulous life," I snap at her as I bounce indignantly off the chair.

Becca has given up on the weather and has pulled on a sweatshirt; she tosses me one too. "So, what's your strategy?"

"I don't have a strategy."

"Let's eat ice cream."

Becca is freakishly tall, and can eat pretty much anything without gaining weight. I, on the other hand, have always been pretty thin, but since I've been hanging out with her, I've noticed some unwelcome blobs of fat setting up camp in my butt, so I have to be careful about eating like a giant. "I'm not hungry," I lie. I actually could eat a Baskin-Robbins, all thirty-one flavors plus the ice cream cakes.

She throws a towel at my head and trots into the house, snorting in disgust. She's right. I am pathetic. I always vowed that I wouldn't let a guy ruin my life, no matter what; I did fine too, until I met Fletcher, and then I broke my own rule and now I'm obsessing about him, the very thing I said I wouldn't do. Maybe Becca is right. Maybe creamy fat-induced avoidance is the way out. I follow her into the massive kitchen.

"So, let's decide what our strategy is with this Fletcher Big Date thing," she says as she lifts a gallon bucket of ice cream from the walk-in freezer. Seriously, it's like they have a meat locker next to their fridge. When I first saw it, I asked Becca if they had Walt Disney's head in there, and she actually got the joke, which again cemented our friendship. (And if you don't know, Walt Disney supposedly had his head cryogenically frozen and stored in case he had to come back and sue Mickey Mouse for breach of contract. So far, it hasn't happened. But I'm watching Becca's freezer very carefully.) "Get the chocolate sauce," she says as she dishes out massive scoops of butter pecan into little delicate china dishes. "We really need bigger bowls."

"We shouldn't eat like this." I take the first bowl from her, pour a river of chocolate onto it, and begin to dig in. "Starting tomorrow."

"Sit." She pulls a chair out from the cherry wood table, sits, and scoops spoonfuls of ice cream into her mouth all at once. "Sho, whasch you gonna do about Fletsher?" she asks, her words distorted by creamy goodness.

I shrug, mostly because my mouth is crammed full of butter pecan. "Let's talk about something else," I finally manage to say.

She studies me for a moment, the way a cat squints at a mouse to see which hole the little vermin is going to run into. I feel like the vermin, and there is a distinct lack of hidey holes. "Change of subject." She puts her feet up, crossed, on the edge of the table and leans back in her chair. She cradles the gallon of ice cream in her lap and attacks it with her spoon. "We need a summer project."

"Besides eating ice cream?"

Licking her spoon, she nods. "I don't think this will keep us occupied for long. Not at the rate we're eating. Nope." She throws her spoon defiantly onto the table. "We need to create something. We need to branch out."

"No. Not this again." All last year, Becca insisted that we find other kids at Green Pines who were like us: weird, cool, funny. That's why we started the club. But even then, I could sort of sense in Becca this desire to conquer the world, something I do not share. I just want to conquer my own little corner of it, not the whole thing. Who has the time?

"I know, I know." She tilts the ice cream container toward me, and I signal I don't want any more, so she jumps up and heads for the meat locker. "You don't want to keep the club going, do you?"

"Yeah, sure I do," I lie. Actually, I would be happier if it just sort of faded away, which sounds weird, I know. I mean, we got lots of attention, and I met Fletcher, but besides that, I got to thinking that I wasn't cool enough for Becca and her big ideas. I was hoping the whole thing would sort of go away over the summer, and we could just be normal friends. What was I thinking? Besides, I have a robot and a mad scientist dad, and Becca's mom practices weird Eastern religions and her dad is a movie producer. Could we ever have a normal friendship? About as likely as me eating one helping of ice cream.

"So, I've been thinking." Always dangerous. "And here's my plan. We create a website." Her eyes widen as she waits for me to jump up and down in ecstasy. I don't. "Let me say it again: We create a website!"

"Yawn."

"What? Websites are it. Look at MySpace.com. Everybody goes on there. We could be the next MySpace!"

"Great. So we spend the whole summer cooped up in your room or mine, designing a website? Gee, that does sound fun."

She smiles slyly. "Of course, we'd need help."

"Oh no. I see what you're doing—"

She grabs my shoulder. "But he's perfect! Fletcher knows all about computers and web design stuff. You don't have to marry him. Just ask him to help us design it!"

"Listen." I carefully place my spoon on the tabletop and align it so it's parallel to the napkins. "Fletcher and I—we've had a great time since the dance."

"Right. You've been together almost every weekend, he calls you when he says he will, and he can even help you with homework. And now it's summer, and you know what that means!"

Oh boy, do I. That's the problem. Summer. That's when the dating thing that starts in high school either flops totally or becomes totally entrenched, like a virus that cannot be killed. Either way, it's deadly. She does not understand this. To Becca, having a boyfriend like Fletcher is the ultimate fulfillment of destiny, right up there with being famous or having a sandwich named after you. She's really independent, of course, and being a Queen Geek, knows that boys are merely a distraction most of the time, but when it comes to a "serious" relationship, Becca totally does a 180 and sounds like somebody's matchmaking mother. She buys into this whole idea that a guy can be your partner in life, despite the fact that her mom and dad are divorced and spent more time arguing over who got custody of the Warhol prints rather than who got custody of Becca.

"And so tonight, you're supposed to have the Big Date." She says it so matter-of-factly, like it's nothing, like it's having a pedicure or an orthodontist appointment. "Right? So, where are you two going?"

I stare down at the floor, perfect and crumbless, unlike my life. "I thought we changed the subject," I mumble.

Becca grabs my chin in her monster fingers and tilts my head so I'm staring straight into her maniac eyes. "I know you. You are trying to sabotage this thing because you think you don't deserve it or something."

"You've been sitting too close to your mom while she's doing her weird psychic yoga," I spit out, yanking my chin away. "All that far-out Far East stuff is fermenting your brain."

"So you can honestly tell me, after we've solemnly bonded over the sacrament of ice cream, that you are not planning to somehow ruin this evening and then blame Fletcher for it?"

"Ha!" I laugh a little too loudly. "Fletcher is great. Why would I mess it up?" Even as I say it, an evil little voice behind my ear is whispering something about guys and control and heartbreak. "You are making way too big a deal out of this. We're just going out for dinner, you know. Everybody eats."

"Ah, but not everybody eats at Old Sicily. And especially not everybody who can barely drive."

"How do you know where we're going?"

"Gotta pee." Becca squeals as she jumps up and scampers to the bathroom down the hall. "But Old Sicily! It's so exciting! I just know he's going to do something special there. Oh, but I've already said too much. . . . Never mind!" The door slams and I'm left alone with my nagging, whispering evil twin behind my ear and a feeling of deep gray dread lumped in my stomach.

Now, admittedly, most normal girls don't flip out when they're asked to dinner. But two weeks ago, I saw Fletcher at the graduation ceremony, the last big event for the school year (everybody goes, even if they're not graduating). All of us were there, Becca, all our friends from school, and Fletcher and me. He and I sat next to each other in the hot sun, out on the football field, and he held my hand, and it felt totally normal. When I looked down at our intertwined digits lying innocently between us on the bleachers, I felt this cold fear, because I couldn't tell which hand was mine. Well, I mean, I could, because I had on pink nail polish and stuff, but the point was that it felt like it was one big hand.

So then Fletcher looked up at me, really serious, and he said, "There's somewhere special I want to take you in two weeks. I mean, if you're free. I'll have the car! And I think"— he grinned then, and nodded knowingly, like I was supposed to understand some secret code of the hand stealers—"I think it will be well worth your time."

When guys say stuff like that to girls in public, it's like all the other girls in a ten-mile radius suddenly pick up a signal, stop what they're doing, and become huge ears with one solitary purpose: to butt in on your conversation and then gossip about it. Becca had immediately squealed and said "Where are you going? You've got the car!? Wow!" and then Amber and Elisa, two of our friends, picked up on it. Amber made a disgusting leering face and then graciously replayed our conversation with Elisa, sprinkling it generously with wet, disgusting kissy sounds.

Becca returns from the bathroom, humming some '80s love song (I think it's Blondie, "Heart of Glass". How appropriate). "Much better. Now. What time are you going out tonight?"

"Seven. But listen. I don't know if this is such a good idea. He shouldn't be spending all his money on dinner at some fancy restaurant. I mean, he has to save for college and pay for his car—"

"Right. One plate of pasta will probably keep him from going to Stanford." She checks her watch. "Well, it's four now, so we'd better get to your house so you can start getting ready."

"It's three hours from now!"

"I know. We should've started earlier," she mumbles as she grabs my arm and yells for her mom, Thea, the only pierced parent at our school. Thea is also the only mother I know who is called only by her first name. It fits her, though; she's like an artsy beatnik from the '60s who got stuck in a time warp and doesn't realize the years have marched on.

Thea runs dramatically into the kitchen, blobs of blue and green paint covering her arms up to the elbows. "Mom, take us to Shelby's. We have date prep."

"I'm right in the middle of *Water Torture*." When I frown at her kind of strangely, she laughs and says, "No, that's not what I'm doing. It's the title of my piece. It's for a client in Palm Springs."

"Well, that's fantastic and all, but Shelby has the Big Date tonight, so *Water Torture* will just have to drip without you for a couple of minutes." Becca is shoving her toward the sink so she can wash her art off.

Thea frowns at me and then at Becca as she scrubs. "Is this a Big Date?"

"The biggest," Becca says, nodding.

"Hmmm." She wipes her arms with a towel, and then grabs her keys from a hook on the wall. "Well, love is almost as important as art. Let's go."

All the time we're riding in the gut-grinding bumpy Jeep, I'm wondering if my stomach hurts because of the ice cream, the bad suspension, or the nerves.

We get to my house and thankfully Dad is not home. Euphoria, my robot, is home, though, and that's almost worse. She hovers.

"Oh, Shelby, this is so exciting!" She squeals as she rolls after us into my room.

"Euphoria, could we be alone?" I ask. I immediately regret it, because if a robot had a face and that face could fall, hers just did. "Oh, never mind. Come on in."

She emits a high-pitched squeak-whine indicating, I guess, joy. "Can I help pick out her dress?"

Becca rolls her eyes and throws open my closet door. "I'll narrow it down first." She swishes through my wardrobe, rejecting one outfit after another. "Too black, too old, too loose. We need something that says, 'alluring,' 'unavailable,' and 'expensive.' "

"Does your clothing talk?" Euphoria's green face lights blink, puzzled.

"No . . . forget it. Here." Becca pulls a cobalt blue jersey minidress from the closet, then grabs a gauzy fitted bolero top in a lighter blue to go over it. "This will make your eyes like the ocean," she says poetically.

"Wet and polluted?" Euphoria pipes in, then snickers. Robots shouldn't be able to make jokes. It should've been one of those prime directives or something.

"Go dance with the lawnmower," Becca snaps at her. To me, she says, "Now, try this on. I think it's going to be perfect. Then we'll worry about accessories, hair, makeup, shoes. Plus, we need to do your nails. Oh, and your toes! We should've scheduled a pedicure."

"I've got to take a shower first." I grab the dress and jacket and stomp off to the bathroom. I don't want to go on this stupid fancy date. I really prefer sitting at home with Fletcher, watching bad science fiction movies or eating pizza or playing games or something. I realize that any dream I never had of becoming a high fashion model is absolutely not going to happen. The fact is, I don't like getting dressed up.

After a long shower during which I fantasize about turning into a bug and disappearing down the drain, I start to turn pruny, so I get out and towel off. I pull the dress over my head, adjust it, then tie the little jacket. I look good, actually; the blue sets off my eyes, which look like dark-blue marbles with white swirls in the center. My hair needs to be brushed, but I figure I should wait or Becca will just do it over. She's kind of a control freak.

The clock reads 6:00. How did time go so fast? We just left her house. Sixty minutes until D-day. Why does it feel like I'm heading to prison or something? I must have some deep psychological issue. Anybody else would be excited and happy about it. I'm kind of excited, but I am not happy. I'm terrified. Why? What is my stupid problem?

"Hey." Becca knocks on the door. "Did you fall in?"

"No, sorry." I open the door and smile weakly. "My hair looks like red seaweed."

"We can fix it, no problem!" She grabs my hand and pulls me into my room, where Euphoria is set up to be a hair dryer.

"What's this?" I tap on the chrome dome fastened to one of her inputs.

"Surprise!" She sends off static. "We rigged this up just for tonight. I'll dry while Becca styles. Isn't that great?"

"Great," I mumble as Becca leads me to a bar stool they've dragged in for the great beautification ceremony.

"Geez, you act like you're going to a funeral or something," Becca complains as she pulls a brush through my tangly hair.

"Maybe I am. Ow! Euphoria, please don't touch me with the metal parts. It burns!"

"Sorry, honey." She blips in remorse. "I'm still kind of new at this."

This torturous effort continues until my hair is done, my makeup is done, my jewelry is chosen, my nails are done, my toes are done, and I have shoes on. By that time, it's nearly seven.

"Wow!" Becca wipes sweat from her forehead. "Some effort, but totally worth it. Check it out!" She hands me a mirror, and I check it out.

I am stunned. My hair is looping around my head like Medusa, and my makeup looks like a drag queen with palsy tried to make me the living image of '70s Cher. "What did you do to my eyelashes?" They're sticking together like centipede legs and I'm having a hard time opening my eyes.

"Well"—Becca smiles apologetically—"I've never really done anybody else's makeup. It's kind of different when it's another face."

"Well, this is definitely another face." There is a big black spot on my chin. "Why is this here?" I ask, pointing to the big black spot.

"It's a beauty mark," Euphoria says proudly. "I read some magazine about fashion, and all of them said a real beauty queen has to have a beauty mark."

"Yeah, what year were those magazines written?"

"Um . . ." Euphoria whirs for a moment. "The 1940s."

The whole weird hairdo, makeup thing kind of makes me feel better, actually. Maybe I can pretend it's somebody else having dinner with Fletcher. Cher's 1940s male cousin who likes to dress in drag and pretend to be a dead Greek monster. Yep. This is surely a fashion statement that is going to work for me.

2

THE BIG DATE—PART II

(or Pasta and Panic)

The doorbell rings. We all freeze as if we expect the SWAT team to parachute in through the skylight.

"It's him," Becca whispers, as if he might hear her.

"I'll get it!" Euphoria hums some formless tune as she rolls down the hall toward the front door.

Becca sighs, smiles, then puts her hands on my shoulders. "Okay. Now, I know you've gone on lots of dates. But tonight is going to be different."

"Let's not start this—"

"No, hear me out." She fluffs some of my Medusa bangs and squints at my eyebrows, then dabs a bit of spit on her finger and rubs.

"Yuck! Don't groom me!" I bat her hand away.

"Just trying to help," she mutters, a bit hurt. "Okay. Just stay cool, but also try not to insult him. You've been very difficult the last couple of weeks, and I know it's because of this date. But listen, it's not that major. You're just going to eat dinner. Don't get all worked up about it."

"Thanks," I say, feeling just a tiny bit better.

"And," she says as I walk out of the bedroom, "if he asks you to get married or something, just tell him he'll have to wait until you can drive."

"Not helping," I yell back at her.

He's standing in the hall looking as awkward as I feel. Why? We're never awkward together. We've had more than a month of great times, no stress, no pressure, just fun and games. Why is it suddenly so important? Why do things have to get messed up with seriousness?

"Look, Shelby, your gentleman caller is here!" Euphoria practically bubbles with excitement. I'm afraid she might blow a gasket or something. Plus, with her faux-Southern accent (Dad programmed her that way to remind me of Mom, I think), she sounds like a community theater Scarlett O'Hara.

"Hi," Fletcher says shyly. Shy? He's never been shy. God, this is torture. Maybe I can talk him out of it. Maybe I should tackle him. Maybe we could just go play Zombie Taxi Driver and forget about dinner.

What do I say? "Hi." Brilliant.

"Ready?"

"Yep." Boy, this is going to be one sizzling evening of high-level conversation.

"Bye-bye!" Euphoria shakes her claw at me as I follow Fletcher into the yard. "Don't stay out too late!"

"Nice to know someone will be waiting up," he says as he opens the car door for me. *He opens the car door*. He has never done this. Sure, I guess that indicates that he has terrible manners, but it also indicates that he's seen me as an equal, whereas now he sees me as somebody whose limbs don't work, I guess. Or maybe he figures I'm not strong enough to open the door myself. Or—

"You in?" He's waiting to close the door now. I just nod dumbly.

He goes around, climbs into the driver's seat, and sticks the key in the ignition, flashing me a very empty grin in the process. I feel like I'm being sent on a robo-date with an android version of Fletcher. He looks the same: red hair, green eyes, handsome. For a nanosecond I consider that perhaps aliens have kidnapped the real Fletcher and replaced him with this super nice, considerate, traditional gentleman Fletcher, just to see what I'll do. As he steers the car (a Volvo, a lot like my dad's) onto the road and then smoothly glides into highway traffic, I sullenly stare out the window as if I'm being dragged to a dentist appointment. Finally, he says, "Hey, are you okay?"

"Of course." Except for the mind-numbing panic that is squeezing my stomach like an empty toothpaste tube.

"Hmmm." He sensibly settles into the pace of the traffic (again, something he doesn't usually do), and I feel him glancing at me, puzzled. "You just seem distant or something."

"Do I?" I say distantly.

"Yeah, you do." He sighs heavily, then shakes his head. "I thought you'd be all excited about a real, formal date. I mean, all we've done so far is just watch movies and stuff at your house. If nothing else, I thought you'd be thrilled to be alone with me without your electronic surveillance system chaperoning our every move."

"Euphoria is not a surveillance system."

"Well, whatever. But this is about the first time we've really, truly been alone together, doing something without anybody else. . . ." His voice trails off, and I imagine I hear the loud gong of realization whacking him in the head. "Oh. Hey, maybe you don't *want* to be alone with me."

"That's silly," I say lamely.

"Is it?" He laughs. Yes, I said he laughs. I'm in the middle of potentially the biggest crisis of my dating life, and this monkey is laughing at me!

"What is so funny?" I snap at him.

He is still laughing, almost to the point where I expect him to wreck the stupid car. I can see the headlines now: "Promising young adults become victims of excessive jocularity!"

"Oh, c'mon, Shelby. That's it, huh? You're afraid to be alone with me. Wow." He seems pleased with himself, which further infuriates me.

"For your information, I am not afraid to be alone with you."

He snickers. "Right. Well, then why are you being so weird?"

"It's just a genetic thing, I guess. Weird is in my DNA."

We drive silently toward Point Loma, the part of town where the restaurant is located. It's a gorgeous area, really, lots of swaying palm trees and a sapphire-colored bay with this sort of tiki-torch theme throughout. Old Sicily is on a side street, and Fletcher pulls his car into a spot right in front.

"Let's just try and enjoy a good dinner," he says, neglecting this time to open my door. I'm secretly kind of hurt by this. Why would I want him to open the door, but *not* want him to open the door? As I said, weird is in my blood.

We go inside, and the place is dazzling. It's decorated with elegant ivory-colored candles everywhere—in the chandelier, around the fireplace, in sconces on the walls, on the tables. The candlelight spreads in golden pools over everything, making even the little bottles of Parmesan cheese and red pepper flakes look elegant. "Wow, this place is a fire inspector's nightmare, huh?" I say.

Fletcher frowns at me, then shakes his head. "You really are a romantic at heart, aren't you? Two, please," he says to the hostess, a snooty-looking girl with that tri-toned hair that looks like somebody went nuts with a dye-filled spray gun. She marches us to a booth in the corner in the back in the dark; as I slide onto the leather bench, I feel that gurgling wave of dread rising up in my stomach. I immediately open the menu and prop it up in front of my face.

Fletcher taps on it with his salad fork. I peer over the top of the daily specials. "Yes?"

"Could you put that down, please?"

"Why?"

"I'd like to talk to you." He slowly guides the menu back to the table. I'd really like to dive under the tablecloth, but I'm afraid I might tip over the candle and start a fire. Come to think of it, that wouldn't be a bad way to get out of whatever conversation we're going to have. . . .

"Shelby, we've been going out for about a month now," he says, sounding like someone who is about to give a lecture. "I just think it's time we talked about some stuff. Put some stuff on the table."

"What stuff do you want on the table besides silverware and sugar packets?" I ask calmly as I stack the pink and yellow and blue sweeteners. I can only stack about five before they slide off each other, but if I don't use the actual sugar packets, which are thicker—

"Okay." He sounds annoyed. Meanwhile, my little packet experiment is coming along nicely. Up to seven if I only use Splenda and NutraSweet. Those are the yellow and blue ones, respectively, in case you want to re-create my research. "Hey. Don't I at least deserve as much attention as the condiments?"

"I'm not sure sugar is a condiment," I answer. He sighs deeply and opens his menu rather violently.

A waitress with that same tri-tone hair comes over to the table. "Welcome to Old Sicily. Can I take your order? Appetizers? Something to drink? Our specials today are Chicken Parmesan and our chef's prizewinning Fusili Alfredo."

"Silly Alfredo?" I know it's a really bad joke, but I cannot resist. "I never thought of Alfredo as silly." Fletcher rolls his eyes. The waitress just stares at me as if tarantulas are crawling out of my ears.

"Never mind her," Fletcher says, patting my hand. "It's her first night away from the asylum. She doesn't really remember what it's like out here."

Now the waitress, whose name is Typhanee (if I am to believe the atrocious spelling on her name tag), is sort of studying me, fascinated with my obvious issues. "I'll come back," she says, slowly backing away from the table.

"Why do you have to be so difficult?"

"I'm not being difficult."

"You just scared the waitress." He snaps open his napkin and spreads it over his lap.

"*I* wasn't the one talking about asylums."

"Well, *I* wasn't the one stacking sugar packets like an obsessive-compulsive diet junkie."

Grrr. Okay, fine, I guess I have no alternative but to have some sort of conversation with him. "Why are we here?"

He gestures to the table, the menu, the people dining nearby. "To eat?"

"I don't think so." How can I explain to him about the thing in the football stands, about how I couldn't tell our hands apart? How can I tell him what I really think when I don't even know what that is? I wish we were all dogs, and we just sniffed each other and that was the end of it. But I guess they never get taken out to dinner, really. Unless you count table scraps.

"You want to know why I brought you here."

He clears his throat, and seems kind of serious, so I have to make a joke. I can't help it. "To tell me that the butler did it in the ballroom with a lead pipe?"

"Arghghg!" He gurgles in frustration, throwing his napkin on the table. "I'm going to the bathroom. When I get back, I expect to be able to have a conversation with you that doesn't involve puns, board games, or mental illness."

"That's a pretty tall order," I answer lamely as he walks away. "Crap."

Typhanee is standing at my elbow, as if she just appeared from the misty steam heat of the kitchen, a serving goddess. "Here's your bread," she says, tossing it onto the table. Little butter pats fly out as if trying to escape. "Do you want anything to drink?"

"I'd like a coconut drink with a little umbrella and some rum."

She arches an eyebrow at me. "Do you have ID?"

I search my nonexistent pockets for it. "Oh, wow, no. I must have left it back at the nuthouse. Never mind. It probably wouldn't mix well with my medication anyway. Just some ice water. Thanks."

She's still hovering, despite my obvious brush-off. "It's none of my business, but I think you should stop acting so childish. This guy obviously cares about you or he wouldn't be springing for dinner, you know." I am speechless. I've never been psychoanalyzed by someone whose primary function is grinding pepper and Parmesan onto people's dinner plates. "I'm just saying. I've done what you're doing. It doesn't work."

"What doesn't work?" I reach for the bread. Might as well eat.

"You're trying to keep him away, keep it distant. You were probably hurt, and you have abandonment issues."

As I butter, I try not to stab Typhanee with the knife. "Do I have to pay you extra for this?"

"I'm a psych major." She gestures awkwardly at the order pad. "I'm just doing this to get through school. Sorry. Can I take your order, or do you want to wait until he gets back?"

"Hmmm. Let me see. I'd like an order of abandonment issues with a side of damaged self-esteem, well done. Oh, and do you think you could bring extra dressing?" I'm a bitter, bitter girl. Typhanee sighs and walks away.

Fletcher has returned, somewhat calmed. "So. Ready to order?"

I laugh in spite of myself. I wish I could share with him the conversation I had with Typhanee, but that would be pressing my luck. "Sure. I think I'll have that silly Alfredo."

He smiles at me, then motions toward Typhanee, who studiously ignores us. "Huh. Wonder what's up with that? She acts like she didn't even see me."

"Don't know," I mumble as I shove another piece of bread into my mouth.

"Okay. So. Here's why I wanted to bring you here. I think we've been getting along great, and I really like you, and—"

"You going to eat that last piece of bread?"

He stops abruptly. "What?"

"Are you? If you're not, could I have it?"

He frowns at me, puzzled. He says nothing. I mangle the bread like a hungry piranha. Finally he sighs, frustrated, and says, "I can see that this is going to go nowhere." Part of me wants to scream, to jump up on the table and say, "Yes! I like you!" but I can't. So, I guess I win. No deep, meaningful, intimate conversation. Yippee.

Eyes focused on the table and the silver and the water glasses, he says, "It's not really major, or anything. I just wanted to tell you that I like who you are, and I like that you let me see who you are. . . . I . . . just like *you*."

Some ice wall inside me melts with a big gush of warm air. This results in major flooding in the region of my eyeballs. I grab for my bread-crumbed napkin and dab carefully at my eyes, hoping not to create graffiti streaks with the centipede mascara.

"Why are you crying?" He shakes his head. "I thought that would make you happy!"

"It does," I mumble, trying not to sob like a big baby into the bread plate. Typhanee chooses this fantastic moment to reappear.

"Well," she chirps, "seems like someone had a break-through. Free breadsticks." She scurries away, leaving Fletcher looking after her, baffled.

"What did that mean?"

I continue dabbing. "I didn't want to say anything, but while you were in the bathroom, she confided in me that she's actually a real mental patient. She sort of felt like we bonded."

We both laugh, and it feels good. I feel like I've had clenched fists balled up inside my stomach and they've finally let go. Even with the Medusa hair, it's starting to look like it might be a nice evening. When the waitress/therapist comes back with the breadsticks, we are still laughing and she flashes me a little victory sign, as if she had something to do with our reconciliation other than bringing baked goods.

We order food, and since I've stopped feeling tense, I instead feel incredibly hungry. For a vegetarian, Italian restaurants are great, because you can actually get great food with no animal parts (except cheese . . . I mean, I figure the cows have to get rid of that milk anyway, so what's the harm?) When my Fusili Alfredo comes, and Fletcher's Angel Hair Marinara, we both dig in like starving Marines.

Between bites, we talk about stuff. We talk about Becca, about the website, about Amber and Elisa and my dad. Then he says, out of nowhere, "I think we should date each other exclusively."

Luckily, I had just swallowed. Otherwise, it's very possible I would have choked, needed resuscitation, and probably died, because if either Fletcher or Typhanee tried to give me mouth-to-mouth, I probably would have resisted. "Huh?" is all I say.

He bites the head off a breadstick. "I said, I think we should date each other exclusively. I mean, we are anyway, right? I just want it to be official."

"Why?"

He frowns, puzzled. "Because I just want to date you exclusively."

"Well, if we're already doing that, then what's the problem?" The balled fists are regrouping in my stomach. Tears are on red alert and ready to burst forth.

He sighs, exasperated. "I guess I just want to know that you feel the same way I do about it. I don't want to commit to something if you don't feel the same way."

The word "commit" causes me to panic. I consider several options: setting my hair on fire, setting Fletcher's hair on fire, throwing food, or foaming at the mouth like a rabid dog. None of these sound appealing. I opt for my traditional favorite: avoidance.

"This is fantastic Fusili Alfredo," I say rapturously, rolling my eyes as if it's the best food I've ever eaten. In reality, it tastes like the back of a cereal box with grated cheese and pepper.

He stares at me, crosses his arms, and I half expect him to wag his finger and scold me.

Instead, I say, "Is your pasta good?"

"Fine." He stabs at the noodles with his fork, punishing them severely for my behavior. Nothing is fair. "You obviously don't want a serious relationship with me. We can just be friends, I guess."

Okay, now that was really unfair. He's giving me what I think I want, which isn't what I want, and that just sucks. "Wait," I hear myself saying. "I'm sorry. This is just so sudden."

He snorts. "I'm not asking you to get married, Shelby. I just want to know that you're not interested in other guys."

"I'm not." There, I said it. Out loud.

"You're not what?"

"I'm not interested in other guys." I want to bite my tongue. Traitorous tongue!

My reward is that he relaxes, smiles, and doesn't seem at all mad. "Great. See, that wasn't so hard." He twirls his pasta onto the end of his fork, now more gently. I feel like I am those noodles—wimpy, shapeless, and easily manipulated.

I pretend everything is totally normal for the rest of the meal. Typhanee only comes over one other time, to see how we're doing, and again she gives me a thumbs up and a wink. As we finish our dinner, I say, "Hey, don't tip the waitress. She spit in your water when you were gone."

All the way home I am numb, but pretending to be carefree and witty. When he pulls into my driveway, I bolt from the car before he can kiss me, pretending that I get my shoe caught in the seat belt. "Good night!" I wave frantically as I hop to my door, one shoe askew.

Standing next to the car, he waves, then shuts the door and trots up next to me. "Hey, let's seal the deal with a kiss."

Before I can protest, he has gently pulled me toward him, and he's covering my mouth with his. Immediately I melt inside, and forget everything I was thinking at dinner. Was there a problem? No . . . all I know is that I feel comfort, warmth, electricity, and some weird buzzy vibration that starts at my feet, shoots out the top of my head, whooshes back in and then settles in my lips. He pulls away, and I'm staring deep into his eyes, diving into an ocean with no life jacket. "Hey. See you soon. I'll call you tomorrow." He dances a crazy jig to the car, and as he backs it down the driveway, he honks the horn in a pattern that I think is supposed to be the Beatles' "She Loves You". Or it could have been Handel's *Hallelujah Chorus*. I don't think Fletcher's very musical.

3

POST-DATE FALLOUT

(or Nuclear Con-Fusion)

It's nine o'clock, and just getting dark, so everything has a golden glow about it. The scent of jasmine fills the air, and far away, someone is playing the piano. I ease myself onto my porch swing and rock slowly. I feel like I've been jumbled up, a puzzle whose pieces don't quite fit, and suddenly, with that kiss, all the pieces magically fit together. And I feel happy.

Dad comes out to the porch too. "So, you're home?"

I just smile. I imagine I look pretty dopey.

He sits next to me and picks up the rhythm of the swing. "Have a nice time?"

Again, the dopey smile.

He laughs and puts his arm around me. "I guess you did." We just sit like that, together, for a few minutes. Finally, he says, "Want to talk about it?"

"About what?"

"Your Big Date."

I usually do talk to my dad about a lot of stuff. Ever since my mom died, we are sort of each other's support system. But I still don't know what the rules are concerning teenage romance and dads. I also don't want to worry him. Dads worry about their daughters. "We went to Old Sicily and had some good food. I got psychoanalyzed by a waitress. Fletcher said he wants to date me exclusively."

Dad frowns and stops the swing. "Date you exclusively? What does that mean?"

"I don't know. I guess it means that we don't go out with anybody else." I try to continue the motion of the swing, but he stops it.

"I don't want you getting serious, Shelby. You're only fifteen. You're much too young to be in any exclusive relationship."

Great. So now I have to defend a choice I didn't want to make to my dad, and even though I wanted what he wanted, I got what he didn't want, so everybody's going to be mad. There's no way out of it. "Look, Dad, it's no big deal. It doesn't mean we're getting married or anything—"

"I should hope not!" he says, all flustered. "Maybe you should stop seeing him. He *is* older than you, you know."

"It's not like he's in a retirement home, Dad. He's only a year or so older."

"Well, in high school, that's a lot. Boys his age . . . have needs."

Oh, gross. Now we're going to have the sex talk. I *so* do not want to do this. I don't want to do the talk, and I don't want to do the sex, and so we really shouldn't have to discuss it. Of course, I will never be able to convince my dad of this. All dads assume their daughters are wild tiger sluts ready to shinny out the bedroom window on a bedsheet at the first sign of interest from a guy. Even my dad, who's a pretty intelligent guy, thinks this. But that makes me really mad because it's like he doesn't even know me, so I have to torture him a little.

"What does that mean, 'boys have needs'?" I bat my eyes innocently.

He turns red. "Uh . . . you know what I mean."

"No. No, I don't."

Dad sighs heavily, looks at his watch, and then stands up. "It's getting late. I think you should go to bed. Why don't you talk to Euphoria about this?"

"Ask Euphoria about what?"

"About this Fletcher thing." He leans over, kisses me on the top of my head. "I'm going to my studio. I'll be up late, so don't wait on me for breakfast."

I walk into the house and go directly to my room. Euphoria is hanging out there, sitting on her charger, listening to Mozart. "Hey, Shelby!" She whirs. "How was the date?"

"Wow, you'd think that I had no life before this dinner happened." I kick off my shoes and throw them carelessly into a corner. "Why is everybody so concerned about my eating habits?"

Euphoria clicks disapprovingly. "Now, now, sweetie. You know everybody just wants you to be happy. Maybe we should go mow the lawn. That might take your mind off of things." Euphoria has a crush on Fred, our lawnmower. She'll use any excuse to do yard work.

"It's getting too dark to mow the lawn. Besides, didn't we just mow it Tuesday? The grass doesn't grow that fast."

The phone rings, and Euphoria, who is directly tied into our Internet and communications system, answers. "Chapelle residence. Who may I ask is calling?"

"Euphoria! It's Becca. Put Shelby on and take her off speaker phone!" Euphoria harrumphs and pushes the appropriate button, then hands me the phone. She hates being left out of a conversation.

"Hey."

"So? How was it? Did he ask you to elope? Get married? Have his baby? Do his homework?"

"Wow. All of the above, and in that order. You are so good." I throw a shoe at Euphoria, who keeps turning the lights on and off in protest.

"Well, listen, you can tell me tomorrow. We're having a meeting with Amber and Elisa to talk about our summer plans."

"Do we have summer plans?"

"For the club. I've got lots of ideas."

"You? Ideas? Naw." I yawn and consider how nice it would be to get a shower, wash the makeup off my face, and put on my favorite super-soft cotton jammies. "What time is the meeting?"

"My house, noon tomorrow. That way you can dream about your date for several hours. He'll be here too, by the way."

"Who? Fletcher? Why?"

"He's helping us with our website, remember? Just be here. Amber and Elisa will be here too. Tell Euphoria we just got satellite cable and the dish is really hot."

"You're evil." I switch the phone off and change into my pj's as Euphoria clucks around me.

"Shelby, you seem preoccupied. Do you need anything? Hot cocoa? Want to watch a science-fiction movie?"

"I really just want to go to bed, to be honest. Let me get washed up and I'll be right back."

It doesn't take me long to get to sleep. As soon as my head hits the pillow, I can feel myself drifting off. And then . . .

I'm on an island. The water is cool blue-green, and it washes up on a white sand beach where I sit under a swaying coconut palm. In my right hand is a tall glass full of exotic fruit punch; in my left is a penguin. It does not say anything.

Fletcher is suddenly there, leaning against the trunk of the tree. "Nice penguin," he comments. "Could I have a drink?"

"A drink of my penguin?" I ask.

"No." He laughs, grabbing my glass. "I want some of your blood."

I stare, horrified, at the glass. "That's not blood, is it?"

"Sure." He gulps down a huge swallow, wipes his lips, and goes for more. "It's magically delicious."

"Why are you drinking it, then?"

"I'm trying to steal your essence." He drains the glass, spatters the remaining drops onto the sand where they disappear. "Or maybe it's a low-carb thing. I am getting a little pudgy around the middle."

"So, this is a dream, huh?" I turn toward the penguin, who, so far, has kept quiet. "What does it mean?"

"You think everything is black and white," the penguin answers, sadly lolling its shiny head from side to side. "And a lot of times what you think is true, isn't."

Fletcher now turns into the penguin and walks away, leaving little waddling footprints in the sand. I stand up to chase him, but instead wake up in the dark with Euphoria, my robot, shaking my quilt. "Shelby. Shelby! Wake up!"

"What?" All I see in the dimness is Euphoria's green optical sensors glowing next to the red numbers of my digital clock.

"According to my scans, you were having a nightmare." She fastens one claw around my comforter, pulls it up toward my chin, and attempts to tuck me in. "There, there. I'm sure it was nothing. Can you tell me what happened?" She asks as she tries to perch awkwardly on the edge of my bed. She's not so good at the bending-at-the-waist thing.

I rub the sleep from my eyes and recall the dim vision of a drink, a penguin, and Fletcher. "No. I don't remember. Probably that spicy Italian food."

"Hmmm." Euphoria sounds unconvinced. "I think there's more to it than that."

"Do you, Oprah? Well, let's get you a talk show and maybe we can just dig into it on a more personal level."

Her green eyes flash in the darkness. "No need to get snippy about it. I'm just trying to help." She whirs (and it sounds, I swear, like she's ticked off, which is weird considering she's not supposed to have any emotions), and her lights flash once, then her processors whir again, downshift, and go silent, leaving me with nothing but a lingering memory of fruit punch and penguin sweat.

What did that mean, "trying to steal my essence"? That's what he said, right? Black and white, black and white . . . something about black and white . . . were police cars involved? I roll over onto my belly, punching my pillow in frustration. I know this dream means something, but I don't know what. Dreams are like guys—confusing, enigmatic, and they keep you from getting a good night's sleep.

The next morning, the phone rudely interrupts another dream. This one does not involve flightless waterfowl, but it does somehow make use of Fletcher in a ballerina costume, so I suppose it's best left undiscussed. "Wake up, already!" Becca squawks into my phone.

"Why?"

"We have work to do! I just knew you'd be sleeping in and totally forgetting our meeting. Do you know what time it is? Get moving!"

"Yes, drill sergeant. Want me to scrub your toilet with a toothbrush?"

"Not necessary." She takes a deep breath and drops the bomb. "I wasn't going to tell you this until later, but I think I've just got to get it out there right now. We, you and me and the other Queen Geeks, have got to work with Fletcher to get our website up because we sort of made a promise that it would be up by July."

Now I'm awake. Becca's bizarre plots are more stimulating than a double tall espresso with a shot of battery acid. "Back up a little, and keep in mind I've had no coffee. Somebody promised somebody else something. I think."

"Yeah." She sounds a bit sheepish, and I hear voices in the background. "Listen, could you just come over as soon as possible? This would be better if I explained it in person."

"Are you sure? In person, I could throw something and possibly hit you."

"Naw. You have lousy aim."

So, as usual Becca has me embroiled in some scheme without my permission, and it involves intimate contact with a guy who makes me dream of talking penguins and revenge fantasies. Summer is supposed to be a time of relaxation. But why should the summer be any different from last school year, when Becca had a plot at every turn?

To go to Becca's house I need a ride, and that means my dad. He's nowhere to be found, though, which puts a dent in my transportation plan. "Euphoria, where's Dad?"

"It's not my turn to watch him," she grumbles from the kitchen, where she is belligerently whipping an innocent batch of pancake batter.

"Don't be mad," I say, patting her back panel. "I didn't mean to be snippy with you. I just had another bad dream."

She inclines her metallic head slightly toward me, then turns to flash her green eyes at me. "That's okay, honey," she says. The batter starts bubbling on the griddle. "I think this must be about that young man. Did you have a spat?"

"No one calls them 'spats' anymore." I dip a finger into the glass measuring cup full of maple syrup and lick off all the sugary goodness.

"Well, something happened." The first batch of golden-brown perfect pancakes is ready; I grab a plate. No use standing on ceremony. "And don't eat too many of those. You have to watch your figure."

"Watch my figure?" I slather butter on, then drown the poor cakes in a sea of syrup. Too bad for them. "Why should I do that?"

"Well—" She turns over another flapjack and thinks for a moment. "I don't really know. Why do people say that?"

"Never mind." I take my plate to the dining room and come back for a glass of milk. "Anyway, back to my original point. Dad is gone?"

"He's in the garage." She pours more batter, then an alarm sounds from her midsection. "Time to make more coffee. Could you go out and get your father? He wanted me to alert him when it was eleven."

Still in my fuzzy plaid pajama pants and T-shirt, I pad barefoot outside. For some bizarre reason it's eleven in the morning and a lot of people are awake. I hear Dad in the garage making semiverbal grunts, which means he's messing with the lawnmower formerly known as Fred.

We inherited Fred when an acquaintance of Dad's decided he wasn't working out and planned to turn him into a garbage disposal. My dad rescues crappy machinery like some people rescue pound puppies, so Fred ended up living in our garage. Unfortunately, Euphoria has a big crush on him, even though he's pretty limited. When you think about it, it's kind of like my situation. I've always dated substandard guys who can't communicate, but mine just haven't been as handy as hers. Fletcher, of course, is an exception. Perhaps he actually could mow a lawn with his teeth.

"Hey." Oh, trouble is brewing. Fred is lying in greasy pools on the garage floor. "Is this a punishment or an accident?"

"Hi, honey." He blindly waves in my direction as he turns a wrench and produces a painful squawk from a rusty bolt.

"Euphoria sent me to retrieve you for breakfast. I also think she wanted an update on Fred's condition."

Dad stands up and wipes his hands on his already filthy jeans. "I'm afraid that Fred really should've been a garbage disposal. I think he's chewed his last turf."

"Sorry." He smiles and nudges a pile of parts with the toe of his boot. "Come on in the house, Dad. Euphoria made pancakes, and if you don't come in, I'll eat them all. And she told me to watch my figure."

"She did?" He shakes his head and gestures toward the brick path to the front door. "She doesn't know what she's talking about. Look who programmed her."

"Yeah, you're right." I grin at him and as we reach the front door, I spring it on him. "Hey, can you give me a ride to Becca's?"

"I guess." He wipes his feet on the throw rug and then takes off his shoes. You have to do both, otherwise you get an aluminum tongue lashing from Euphoria. She doesn't allow dirt on the carpet, and she doesn't like to clean dirty shoes.

We sit down to pancakes, coffee, milk, and a bowl of fresh oranges. Euphoria doesn't sit, but she does hover, and has to put in her two cents' worth, as usual. "Mr. Chapelle, I really think you need to speak with Shelby about young men."

"Uh . . . I'm in the room. You can talk to me if you want me to do something."

She ignores me. "As I was saying, she doesn't seem to be thinking about her figure, and you know that once a girl begins to put on a little weight, it just goes straight to the hips."

Dad is laughing quietly, clearly amused about getting fashion and health advice from something that has no internal organs or clothing allowance.

"Dad, will you please tell her that no one cares about my figure?" I viciously stab a golden-brown blob and stuff it into my mouth.

He chews thoughtfully on his breakfast, then takes a sip of coffee before answering. "I think you're probably wrong about that, sweetheart." Euphoria snorts triumphantly. "You're going to be sixteen in January. From what I remember of being a teenaged boy, I'd suspect that most of them are looking at your figure. But who cares? Fletcher likes you for who you are."

"Are you saying I'm fat?" I pour more syrup as Euphoria's red warning lights blink like a neon sign with hiccups. "Could I have a straw with this?"

"Shelby, please!" Euphoria yanks the syrup away. "I'm just looking out for your best interests!"

"No, of course you're not fat. I just meant that—oh, never mind." Dad sighs and cuts a few more pieces of pancake with his fork. "If Shelby wants to eat pancakes, nothing is going to stop her, Euphoria. She's just like—" He stops himself, fork in midbite. "She's stubborn." He puts the fork down and, for a moment, just stares vacantly at a spot on the tablecloth. I know exactly what he's thinking.

Mom.

Even though years have passed, these little moments will pop up now and then, more for him than for me. He'll be going along, having a normal life, and then like a freight train, some smell, or sight or sound will remind him of Her. And when that happens, all the pain and the stuff he's buried because it hurts to think about it, all that rushes at him like a wave, out of control, and he can't stop it. But all he does is pretend it's not there.

It passes; he looks up, smiles, pretends his eyes aren't just a little bit wet. "Just finish up and get ready, honey. I'm leaving in about ten minutes."

We drive to Becca's in silence. I know we're both thinking about Mom, but neither of us wants to mention it, so we pretend to be alone.

When he pulls the Volvo into the circular driveway in front of the Gallagher mansion, he leaves the engine running. "Okay, then," I say, giving him a peck on the cheek. He grabs my arm a little too hard. "Ow."

"Sorry." He lets go and grips the steering wheel. "I just want you to know that—I'm glad you remind me of your mom. It's not a bad thing. I mean, I didn't want you to think—"

"Dad." I do understand, but I can't even tell him what I'm really thinking: that I don't remember everything about her. "Don't worry about it. I knew what you meant."

As he drives away, I pause to watch him before I ring the bell. Nobody ever gives you a rule book on how to deal with a death in the family, and even if they did, nobody's problems would be the same, I guess. And it's been almost four years. Shouldn't we be kind of over it by now? And just as I think that thought, a big rush of guilt hits me in the face, and I start to think that maybe I didn't really love her, if I want to forget about her. . . .

"Hey." Becca pokes me in the small of my back. "Were you planning to come in, or are you just going to become part of the landscaping?"

"Yeah." I grin at her. "Maybe I'll do that." She gives me a quizzical look, and I can't blame her; I'm sure I look sort of wigged out. "Just had a Dad thing. What's up with you?"

"Ah." One good thing about Becca: Whenever I want to distract her, all I have to do is talk about her. She is, actually, her favorite subject. "It's like this. We have to get our website up and running, and it needs to be great because—" she takes a big breath as if she is about to confess that she clubs harbor seals to make furry thong bikinis "—because we are going to be entering a website competition at Comic-Con in a few weeks."

This makes me totally forget my awkward morning. "You are kidding." I stop in the doorway.

"Come in or Thea will be griping about the air conditioning," she says, pulling me into the hallway.

I should explain what Comic-Con is, for people who don't know. It's this total geek fest where thousands of people who love science fiction, comics, movies, *Star Trek*, and that kind of stuff all show up at once and create a huge rift in the geek/normal continuum. You can see famous actors, pretend to be a Klingon, or spend your college fund on little plastic figurines and comic books. It's like geek nirvana. But these are serious geeks, not the dabblers that we are. We will be crushed by the overwhelmingly superior geek quality of the other people who live and breathe this stuff. Becca doesn't know what she's getting herself into, as usual.

"Okay. So, what do you mean, we are going to enter a contest at Comic-Con?" I ask. Becca rolls her eyes sheepishly toward the vaulted ceiling as she prepares to be nagged by me. "There is no way we can enter a contest at Comic-Con. It's full of professional people, and we are not that. Besides, where would we get the money? And why would we do it? I mean—"

"Hey, Shelby." Fletcher's voice in my ear causes some chemical reaction that makes me dizzy and I want to giggle. So, I do.

Becca stares at me, aghast. "What are you laughing about?"

I can't stop. I just shrug and keep on giggling. Fletcher, who is standing in the hall, waves to me and grins. I wonder if he will start giggling too.

Becca glances suspiciously between us. "Okay. Let's all have some coffee. Maybe the effect of whatever you guys are on will wear off before Amber and Elisa get here. Come on."

Fletcher puts his arm around my shoulders, and it feels so good there I consider having it grafted on. We amble down the hall to the room that I refer to as a giant chocolate truffle. It's her family playroom, with these great mounds of cushy brown suede sofas and pillows, and a big pool table, plasma TV, and of course, a killer sound system. She clips her iPod into its dock. Within seconds some kind of New Age whale-mating Celtic music surrounds us.

"Is this elevator music for dolphins or something?" Fletcher quips. He even thinks of the same jokes that I do!

We sit together on the biggest of the chocolate truffle sofas as Becca thumbs a hidden switch on the wall. "Meredith, could we have coffee service for six in the front room? Thanks."

Meredith is what the Gallaghers call a personal valet to the family. She's not a maid, because maids don't get paid well, nor do they wear Prada. I've never seen Meredith clean anything and I've never seen any other housekeepers, so best I can figure, she must coordinate a closet full of gnomes to cook and scrub.

"Okay." Becca takes a deep breath, grins at the two of us, and plops down on the deep-pile caramel silk rug. "As I said, I entered our club in this high school website contest that they have at Comic-Con. I want us to win, because if we win, we'll get lots of exposure for the club."

"Why do we need to do that?" I scooch away from Fletcher just a bit. "And this is about the Queen Geeks, isn't it? Why is Fletcher involved? He's definitely a geek, but as far as I've heard, not a queen."

"Thanks, I think." He arches an eyebrow at me quizzically.

Meredith, her timing expert as always, slides silently into the room with a silver tray full of delicious caffeinated goodness. She's like a smooth-running machine; she never makes a sound. It's kind of creepy. If she didn't have coffee, I'd probably try to knock her down and check for an on-off switch. She smiles at me as if she knows what I'm thinking and pours the steaming beverage into three white ceramic mugs. "Anything else?" she purrs.

The doorbell rings. "Could you get the door?" Becca asks apologetically. Apparently, Meredith doesn't answer doors either. She gives Becca a look that reminds her of this fact, and then she heads wordlessly for the front door. "That must be Amber and Elisa."

"Okay, okay." I take a swig of coffee. "But how do we fit in to Comic-Con? That's all movies and comics and stuff, not school clubs."

"You're right," Becca says. "Comic-Con is for movies, comics, stuff like that. But here's the great idea: We actually do a graphic novel that is all about the Queen Geeks, and we become, like, superheroes in it, and then we sell it and have a website, and then we become sort of these mass-market super media darlings, and then we get people to play us in the movie. I'm thinking for me, maybe Lindsay Lohan."

Stunned, I simply stare at her. Last year was bad enough. We had to start this club and recruit other geeks and then get on TV and work on the school dance, but that was all small potatoes compared to what she's talking about now. "I don't even know what to say."

Fletcher clears his throat. "Look, I know I'm not officially part of the club, but honestly, this is a good idea, even if it sounds kind of out there. You've got to give Becca credit. She dreams big, and that's how things happen. Why shouldn't we do it?"

"Well, first of all, *we* are not you. You are not *us*. We are us. You are you."

"Pronoun abuse." Fletcher whistles through his teeth. "Two-cup penalty. Cut her off."

"Fletcher has been around all through the whole birth of the Queen Geeks," Becca says. "In fact, he's the one who really helped us sell the idea of the dance last year. And that's what really got people to notice us."

Amber and Elisa join us. Amber is the resident goth-poet girl, tall and reedy, and she owns every piece of black clothing they sell at the mall. Elisa's feet barely touch the floor when she's in an SUV, and she's almost as wide as she is tall. She also has a secret love affair with her electronic daily planner Palm Pilot, which I found out she calls "Wembley." If you're dorky enough to name your organizer, you are definitely a geek.

"Hey, ladies," Elisa says as she goes for the coffee. "Oh, and Fletcher. Sorry."

"No offense taken," he answers. "I think of myself as a lady, in the universal sense."

Amber snorts. "Well, you'd better let Shelby in on that little secret. At least you guys could share clothes and makeup tips, huh?"

"Very funny." I jump off the couch to get more coffee from the silver pot. Then the doorbell rings. "I'll get it," Becca screams as she scrambles up off the floor.

"Who's that?" I ask Fletcher.

He sips from his coffee mug. "That's probably Jon."

"Jon?"

"He's the guy who's going to draw you guys for the website and the comic book."

4

THE LOVE RHOMBUS

(or The Geometry of the Heart)

I hear Becca's voice squealing in the hallway, which makes me wonder: I know that she only squeals when her hormones get revved up. So, it's no surprise when she walks into the playroom arm in arm with this guy, and I can see from her face that she's already gone.

"Hey, everybody, this is Jon Conner. He's a computer genius and an amazing artist!" She's gushing. It's so totally disgusting I practically throw up my Starbucks. "Here, Jon, you can sit by me." She drifts to an overstuffed chair where Elisa is sitting, then pokes Elisa with her finger, motioning with wild eyes that she should move to another location.

"Fine, I can take a hint," Elisa mutters under her breath. I'm thinking it wasn't so much a hint as an order, but whatever. Becca parks in the chair that's barely big enough for two people, and Jon sits uncomfortably next to her.

He's tall, like Becca, which is probably one reason she likes him. She's taller than a lot of the guys at Green Pines, and that's intimidating, so she has a hard time finding dates sometimes. But this Jon is as tall as she is, maybe taller, and even though he's said nothing, I can tell that he is totally wrong for her. He has this blue-black hair that's straight as a stick and hangs in front of his face, and he's wearing a tattered black denim jacket scattered with patches from semi-famous punk bands with names like Pus Ponies and Giant Bloody Eyeball. He's wearing leather bracelets with silver spikes sticking out, and even though it's summer, he's wearing studded leather boots with pointy silver toes. What if he was behind you in the lunch line at school? He could totally stab you in the shins and act like nothing happened. I think he's dangerous. And totally wrong.

Becca continues to gush. "Jon is an *amazing* artist. When I saw his portfolio, I practically *died*. I mean, he has such depth and such technique—" When she starts talking in italics, I freak out. "He's going to draw us, as superheroes, and we'll enter our website in the competition, and then we'll win—"

"So, Jon," I say, shooting him the most uncompromising look of analysis I can muster. He barely blinks behind the curtain of hair. "Tell us about yourself."

Becca doesn't even let him talk. "He's a junior this year, just like Fletcher, and he's already got certification in three different computer programs, and he's going to go to work for his dad's company. His dad is like some computer genius too—"

"Yo, speedy," Elisa says, waving her arms in front of Becca's beaming face. "Does he talk too?"

"Oh." Becca blushes. She blushes! I've never seen this in all the time I've known her. "Sure. Sorry." She meekly folds her hands in her lap like some new millennium girl-next-door. "Jon? Why don't you tell them about yourself? Oh, but first, let me introduce everybody. You know Fletcher." She gestures toward him and he flicks a half-hearted soldier salute to Jon. "This is Elisa Crunch—"

"And, just so you know, no jokes about candy bars or cereal. My name is a respected one in many parts of Slovakia." Elisa sniffs indignantly, as if she's waiting for someone to insult her fantastic candy bar name.

"Right. No crunchy jokes." Becca smiles eagerly and turns to Amber. "This is Amber. She's a fantastic poet, and she's extremely artistic." I can see by the look on Becca's face that she regrets saying this. Amber is artistic, Jon is artistic . . . conclusion? They should hook up. Oh no! She's sabotaged her own dream date! "Anyway, Amber is a writer, not so much an artist. And her poetry is very dark."

Amber frowns and swings her curtain of brunette hair from her face. "Well, I wouldn't say it's dark, exactly. I mean, there's no hellish suffering. Unless you count school."

Jon chuckles under *his* curtain of hair. This may be a solution. If I can just get him interested in Amber, then—

"Right." Becca nervously clutches Jon's hand, and he tries to evade her without seeming rude. It's so pathetic. I cannot believe someone like Becca, the original Queen Geek, would go on a drool-fest for some guy! We are going to have a serious talk. I might even have to have Euphoria reprogram her. "And this is Shelby."

"Hey," I say noncommittally. Becca shoots me a purse-lipped, big-eyed stare of disapproval.

Jon sighs and stretches, I think partially to escape from Becca's fawning. "Yeah, so, it's great to meet you all," he says in this laid-back-to-the-point-of-coma tone of voice. "I'm excited about the website thing, and the graphic novel." Graphic novel? That's just a comic book that costs ten dollars. Anyway, Jon does not sound excited. I wonder if he's just being cool, or if he really isn't human. "I've been wanting to submit something to the amateur comic contest at Comic-Con, but I just didn't have a great idea that I could really get inspired about." I see him glance at Amber through his curtain of hair. "So, I'm hoping you'll all inspire me."

Fletcher stands up to get more coffee. "So, anyway, Jon's going to sketch each of you today, just a real quick thing, and then take it back and work on it. Then we can go over the drawings and make any changes before he does the final versions." He looks over at Elisa and frowns, as if concentrating. "We need to come up with names, though. Elisa, maybe you could be Paper Girl."

"What would be my superpower? Filing?" she scoffs. "No, I want to be the Anti-Barbie. I'll wear Keds and have a mask and no makeup, and my hair will be all up in a bun."

"Well that sounds like you *all* the time," Amber says, laughing. Elisa snarls at her and everybody starts chattering. I notice that Jon moves away from Becca, who follows like a sick puppy. Oh, we are *so* going to have a talk.

Amber, who is sitting on the floor with her legs drawn up under her, says, "I want to be the Dark Poet."

"I thought you weren't dark?" Becca says snottily.

"Well, I'm not, but my superhero person could be dark."

Fletcher waves his hands. "Hang on! You have to focus your powers. I mean, you need to be superheroes of geekiness. So, what talents or skills do geeks have that could be exaggerated?"

We all ponder this for a moment. Studying, organization, pranks, creativity . . . none of these things sound to me like the makings of a superhero, even a Wal-Mart, low-budget superhero.

"What about the Geektastic Four?" Becca says. "You know, like the Fantastic Four, only geeky."

Jon's hair has migrated to behind one of his ears, which I guess indicates that he is engaged in the conversation. "Yeah, and each one of you could have a geek power within the Geektastic Four," he says.

"Like?" Fletcher asks.

Becca pipes up, "I could be Smart-tastic. And Elisa could be Organize-i-tastic. Shelby's vegetarian, right? So she could be Vege-tastic."

"Amber could be Art-tastic," Jon says, causing Amber to blush.

"Sounds great," Amber says with a squeak. Well, the conversation goes on like this for probably forty-five minutes, and the whole time I'm sitting there just fuming about this Jon. The girls are fawning, Fletcher is amused, Elisa detaches and jots down stuff in Wembley. Suddenly, with the arrival of Jon, the whole Queen Geek thing seems to be falling apart instead of getting stronger.

"Hey, Becca, didn't we have plans to see a movie tonight?" I blurt out as Fletcher is spouting off about some video game he's been playing. Everyone turns and looks at me like I've grown a third head. "What?"

"Have you been tracking the conversation?" Becca asks, annoyed. "We were talking about Comic-Con. Why did you all of a sudden bring up a movie?"

"I just thought we'd spent enough time on this website thing," I say casually. In reality, I'm trying to find a way to ditch the boys so we can have a real discussion.

Jon stands up and stretches like a black cat. A hairy black cat. "Yeah, I really need to get going. Let me take some digital shots of you so I can have something to work with for the drawings." He pulls a silver camera from his pocket. "Becca? You want to go first?"

Becca flutters and giggles like a moronic junior high beauty queen, and stands up. "Sure. Come over here where the light's good." She takes his hand and drags him into the hallway, where the light is not actually very good. From down the hall, we hear Jon say, "But I can't actually see you. . . . Let's move back to the doorway."

The pair comes back, Becca looking dejected (since her attempt at being alone with Jon has failed) and Jon looking clueless. "Just stand here for a minute," he says, pointing to the doorway and adjusting his camera. Becca obliges.

We all have to try to crack her up while she's being photographed, of course. Jon tells her to look smart (since she *is* Smart-tastic) and she ends up looking more like she's got digestive problems.

"Oooo, Smart-tastic, show us your brain!" Elisa croons at her.

Amber stands up, grinning, and says, "Please, save us from calculus, Smart-tastic! Banish evil theorems!"

After Jon snaps a few shots and checks them out, he motions for Elisa to assume the position. Becca perches on a chair, ready to tease. "C'mon, Organize-i-tastic. Show us your self-sealing envelopes! Remove some staples, baby!"

"I'm trying to look organized!" Elisa hisses through clenched teeth. She brandishes Wembley, her Palm Pilot, like it's a police badge. "Take that, chaos and disorder!"

Jon clicks a few, reviews them, and nods in mute approval. "Shelby?"

I trudge over reluctantly and stand there like a piece of driftwood.

Becca snorts, jumps up, and tries to pose my arms in what I think she must see as vegetarian poses: praying hands, Egyptian hieroglyphic hands, belly-dance hands. I let my arms flop like they're boneless. "Shelby, just cooperate, will you?" she whispers fiercely. "He's almost done."

"Sure. I'll just pretend like I'm enjoying it." I opt for the hands palm to palm above my head, fingers pointing to the ceiling. Jon waves Becca away and starts clicking. I give him my best malevolent goddess stare.

"Okay, cool." He turns and looks at Amber. "Okay, you're last but not least." She stands up, all willowy poet grace, and switches places with me. "Now, I think for this one, you should be holding a paintbrush or something."

"I don't paint," she says doubtfully.

"Right. But you paint with words, don't you?" Jon twitches to get the hair out of his eyes. I swear, I am going to go after him with scrapbooking scissors and cut that mop so it has scalloped edges.

Amber ponders his inane question. "I guess I do sort of paint with words, yeah. Okay. Becca, can we use one of your mom's brushes?"

Clearly annoyed, Becca flounces out of the room in search of photo props. Meanwhile, Jon wastes no time. "So, Amber, what's your sign?"

"My sign?"

He sidles up next to her and brushes a strand of hair from her face. Their eyes meet. I can almost see the Emo sparks arcing between them. "Yeah, your sign. I think astrology is awesome. You can learn a lot about a person from their sign. I'm Aquarius."

"Oh." She is attracted to him, I can tell, but she knows that going after that particular piece of boy candy is going to bring her nothing but grief. "I'm a Libra."

"Awesome. Libras are artistic, creative, a balance of dark and light. Air sign. Just like me." He fidgets with the camera. "You were in Mr. Scott's English class, huh? I saw you every day on my way to art class last year."

Becca has returned with a handful of paintbrushes that she wordlessly thrusts into Amber's hands. Jon totally ignores Becca and focuses on Amber. "Okay, so can you cross two brushes, sort of like the bracelet thing Wonder Woman used to do?"

Amber strikes the pose. Elisa snickers and says, "Go, Art-tastic! Velvet paintings forever!" Becca glares at Amber.

Fletcher has eased over next to me and puts an arm around me, then whispers in my ear, "Wow, looks like it's going to be a summer full of she-fights, huh?"

"Well, if your friend wasn't such a dork, he'd probably realize that Becca has a thing for him, and then he'd stop going after Amber," I whisper back.

"I guess, unless he likes Amber and doesn't particularly like Becca." Fletcher grins. "Ain't love grand?"

Jon finishes photographing Amber, and I notice (and so does Becca) that he has taken far more shots of her than of any of the rest of us. He checks the digital camera, smiles (the first time I've seen him do it too), and says, "Cool. I'll start working on these right away. I think it'll rock. Oh, hey, Amber," he says as he turns to go. "Could you look at something on my car? I wanted your opinion about it."

"What is it?" Becca asks brightly. Jon ignores her.

Amber looks very uncomfortable, her eyes darting between Jon and Becca. "I really have to go . . . wash something. So, I'll see you, okay?" She darts out of the room, presumably to clean the mystery body part or whatever.

Fletcher continues to look amused and smug. "Hey, Jon, I'll go out to the car with you," he says, ignoring Becca's look of death. They walk out, babbling guy talk about some video game they both play, and I'm left in the tiger cage with Princess Pissy.

"What was that all about?" Becca whirls on me and starts to screech.

"What?"

"That whole . . . display of whatever it was!" She is in my face now, and I am feeling very claustrophobic. Elisa sits, eyebrow arched judgmentally, Wembley poised to take a photo of us if things turn violent. "You totally blew that for me. I absolutely have a huge crush on Jon, and you tried to do everything you could to screw it up!"

"Oh, you did a pretty good job of that all by yourself," Elisa butts in.

"I didn't ask you!" Becca plops down on the truffle chair and sighs, all the vicious wind out of her sails. "Sorry. I just really feel like I had no chance with him. And I really like him."

"Look." I sit next to her as Elisa studies us like we're frogs in biology. "I'm sorry I was being weird. But all of a sudden you were this . . . this . . . ."

"Fawning, obnoxious, lust-smitten boy puppet," Elisa offers casually. "I mean, no offense. You were out of control, though."

"Right." I shoot Elisa a silent thanks. I wouldn't have gone so far as to say puppet, but in reality, I had been thinking kind of the same thing. I look Becca in the eye. "I admire you, and I like how you are. When he came into the room, you suddenly started drooling and being this girly-girl whiner who waits for a guy's approval before you make a move! That's not Queen Geek."

"Yeah." Elisa stands and stretches, putting Wembley back in its holster. I guess she figures no disfigurement will be forthcoming. "You were just an emotional noodle. What was that all about? He was skinny, and his hair was in his eyes."

"But—" Becca starts, but then Amber comes back into the room. Becca clams up.

"Is he gone?" She searches with her eyes, as if we're hiding Jon under the couch or something.

"Yes, he's gone," Elisa says, taking her by the arm. "You may return to Earth."

Amber smiles shyly. "Well, he was kind of cute." She's looking sideways at Becca, wondering if they're going to have a hair-puller. "Are you okay?"

Becca absently rubs the little spikes of hair on her head, and leans into the cushy chair. "Yeah, I guess. If you want him, you can have him."

"You make it sound like you're trading a sweater or something," Elisa comments. "Maybe he's gay."

Both Amber and Becca pipe up loudly, "He's *not* gay!"

"Methinks the ladies doth protest too much," Elisa mutters as she stretches. "Anyway, what else do we have to do today other than losing our minds over hairy Emo guys?"

"I say it's time for the Geektastic Four to head for the pool," Becca says decidedly. "You all brought your suits, I assume?"

"Uh . . . bathing suits are against my religion," Elisa says.

"What religion is that? The Cult of the Crappy Body Image?" Becca snipes at her. "C'mon. You owe it to yourself to liberate your thighs. They need to be free!"

"If you'd seen them, you'd know that freedom will be dangerous," Elisa replies. "But if you're willing to put yourself in harm's way, I'm willing to put on Lycra. Got a suit I could borrow?" She sizes up Becca's tall frame. "On second thought, maybe your mom has one I could borrow. Or maybe your mom and your maid could stitch two suits together. . . ."

"Stop beating yourself up!" Becca says, ironically thumping Elisa with a pillow as they trot into the hall and up the stairs in search of swimwear.

Amber grabs a canvas bag from the corner and hesitates before heading upstairs. "Hey, Shelby."

"Yeah?" I already have my own suit on under my clothes, so I pull my T-shirt over my head.

"What about this Jon thing?"

I wad up the shirt and throw it into my bag. "What about it?"

"Do you think Becca really is okay with me . . . and him . . . you know." She is fiddling nervously with the strap of her bag, which I notice has a big ugly picture of Edgar Allan Poe on it. He kind of looks like Jon, actually.

"I don't know, Amber. I mean, she's hard to read sometimes. I think she really has a thing for Jon, for whatever reason, and you know when she gets focused on something, it's hard for her to let go . . . but she did offer him to you."

"Like a ratty sweater," she mutters, swinging her dark hair. "I don't think that was very nice. It's not like he belongs to her."

"True." I hear the other two Lycra worshippers upstairs squealing. "But you know what? We don't want to miss whatever Becca will come up with for Elisa to wear. So c'mon. Don't worry about the Jon thing. It'll sort itself out. I'll race you." We both run like stupid puppies up the stairs. Maturity is overrated.

Elisa is standing in the middle of Becca's bedroom wearing a purple one-piece that tugs in odd places. "It was Mom's maternity swimsuit," Becca says apologetically. "I know it doesn't fit, but it's the closest thing I have to a . . . a . . . ."

"A polyester tent," Elisa offers as she examines her shape in the mirror. "It's okay. It's just going to be us anyway. So,

I'm okay with being Moby Grape." When we finally all have our suits on, we head for the pool.

Today is warm and sunny, the perfect weather for lounging poolside. Becca also has a fridge next to the pool, which is well stocked with diet soda and water and munchies. Her mom also put up this big slide at the deep end, so it's like our own personal water park. After two or three good cannonballs, I find a soda and a bag of cold pretzels, and park on one of the lounge chairs to get some sun.

Suddenly something blocks my rays. "Got sunscreen?" It's Fletcher.

Elisa, who is at the top of the slide, squeals as if she's been hit with a dart gun and clings to the ladder as if she's about to float into space. "Why is he here?" she wails. "Now I can't get down!"

"What, are you swimming naked?" He laughs. Elisa makes an inhuman sound of suffering. "Okay, fine, I'll cover my eyes."

There's a big splash, and Elisa bobs up from the bottom, then dog paddles to the side of the pool. "Okay, it's safe now."

Fletcher crouches at the edge of the pool. "Are you one of those girls who hates how she looks in a bathing suit?"

"That's *all* girls, dork," Elisa says. "But yes. I'm wearing a borrowed suit, and it's kind of unflattering. You're not staying, right? I don't want to get all pruny in here."

Fletcher stands again and blocks my light. "Could you just sit down?" I ask. "I'm trying to tan evenly. I don't want a Fletcher-shaped pattern on my tummy."

"There are so many ways I could respond to that comment, but I'll just shut up." He pulls up a chair next to me and sits. "So, wanna go out tonight?"

"Where?" I continue to sun, acting as if any date is of no consequence, when, in fact, it makes me nervous again.

"I was thinking maybe a movie."

"Well, let me ask Becca—"

"No, no," he says. "Just the two of us."

Here we go again. I am excited at the thought of being alone with him, but it also makes me feel like punching something. I think I must be the most messed-up teenaged girl on the planet. But I also realize I can't avoid this forever unless I just break up with him, so I guess a movie is pretty safe. "Okay. What time?"

"I was thinking seven."

"Seven it is."

"I'll pick you up at six-thirty." He stands, stretches, and waves to the other girls. "See you, Geektastic Four."

As he walks away, Becca throws a towel at me and says, "So, somebody has a date?"

"It looks that way," I answer, stretching like a lazy cat. "Just a movie. We're not getting married or anything."

"Not yet," Elisa adds.

Amber is rubbing sunscreen on her purposefully pale skin for the fifteenth time. She tans but doesn't want to. "Well, I hope you have a good time. It's nice when you have someone to go to a movie with," she says, concentrating very hard on spreading that zinc oxide evenly.

5

THE GEEKTASTIC FOUR

(or Pretty in Pixels)

Dad picks me up and we drive uneventfully home. "I have a date tonight," I say as we pull into the driveway.

"With Fletcher?"

"Yep." I duck out of the car before the interrogation can begin.

"Whoa! What are you going to do?"

"About what, Dad?" I'm to the door, and he trots up beside me.

"What are you going to do? I mean, tonight?"

I give him a kiss on the cheek before I open the front door. "Just a movie at six-thirty. No big commitment."

"Will you be here for dinner?"

"Not hungry. I have to get ready." I bolt down the hallway to my room as my dad calls out behind me, "It's only five o'clock!"

Euphoria is busy making dinner in the kitchen, so I have my room all to myself. Having a personal robot is kind of cool, but honestly, there are times when Euphoria gets on my nerves. She has to get into all of my business all the time. If I'm getting dressed, she offers fashion advice. If I'm doing homework, she wants to do it for me. If I'm talking on the phone, she eavesdrops. It's like having the FBI for a nanny. If the FBI commented on miniskirts and algebra, I mean.

I put on jeans and a blue T-shirt, nothing too dressy. I don't want Fletcher to think I care what I look like, so I have to take extra-special care to look like I don't care. Put my hair up in a ponytail, slap on just a little makeup . . . yeah, I look casual, but good. Perfect. I tackle some boring home-work, and the time goes quickly.

The doorbell rings, and I grab my purse and rush to the door to get to it before Mrs. Nosey Bolts trucks on in. Fletcher's kind of dressed up, no less: tan pants, white shirt, hair actually combed. "Wow, I feel like a slob compared to you," I say casually. I actually feel like I've won a point. He's dressed up, I am not, which gives me superiority in the game of who cares most.

"Well, it'll be dark," he says, closing the door behind him. "Anyway, you look great."

"What are we seeing? Let's go." I grab his arm, turn him around unceremoniously, and open the door again.

He stops me. "Hey, what's the rush? I was hoping I could see your dad too."

"Nope, sorry. He's gone."

"Hey, sweetie," Dad says, emerging from the kitchen munching a celery stick. So much for timing. "Hey, Fletcher."

"Mr. Chapelle." He extends his hand like he's meeting an old friend or a business partner. Maybe they'll trade after-shave tips or something. Gross. "Nice to see you again."

"Gotta go. Don't want to be late!" I say. I shove Fletcher to the door. "See ya, Dad."

Once outside, I can see that Fletcher is kind of ticked at me. "What was that about?" he says as he opens the passenger door.

"What?"

"Don't you want me to get to know your dad?" He hops into the driver's seat and starts the engine on his magnificent orange Volkswagen hatchback. He picked me up for the Big Date in his dad's Volvo, but now that the newness has worn off, I guess, I get to ride in the rustbucket.

"You didn't answer my question," he says as he backs down the driveway. "Some honesty, please."

I take a deep breath. "Look, it makes me feel really weird when you act like you're a . . . a man or something around my dad. Like you guys are going to work out a deal for the smooth transfer of my ownership papers or something."

He laughs. "Ownership papers. Right. We really need to get your head examined. I think there must be some paranoid little gnome living behind your frontal lobe."

This sets me to fuming. "What movie are we going to see, master?" I say through gritted teeth.

"Why don't you decide." He shakes his head, and negotiates the car onto the freeway entrance.

We end up seeing some Adam Sandler movie. It doesn't matter which one, because in all Adam Sandler movies, he plays a guy like Adam Sandler who alters reality, or likes a girl who is far above him, or both. We sit in the middle, which doesn't make either of us too happy. I like the back, he likes the front. Just one more reason he's totally wrong for me.

"Popcorn?" he says, shoving a big bucket of butter-drenched fiber in my face.

"No, thanks. I don't want to have a heart attack before I'm old enough to drive." I watch the stupid movie trivia thing on-screen. Who writes those things? That's someone's job. They must actually sit around and surf the net for stupid trivial facts about movie stars. I wonder if they have another job. Like, they are heart surgeons by day and while they're operating, they're secretly cruising the movie database and stuff. Geez, now I'm really glad I didn't eat any of that popcorn.

"Shelby," Fletcher says awkwardly. "Look, I—" A big shadow falls over Fletcher's face. I turn and see this amazingly tall guy standing next to me in our row. I am literally staring into this guy's knees. I just hope Fletcher doesn't owe him money or something, because I'm right in between them. I plan an escape route that involves throwing the greasy corn at the big dude and then sliding out of the theater on a carpet of Good & Plenties.

"Hey, Fletch," the giant says, extending a huge hand. Fletcher shakes it, and stands up, smiling. Good. No giant wrangling needed today.

"Hey, Carl." Fletcher nods toward me. "This is Shelby Chapelle. Carl Schwaiger."

Carl sits down next to me; now that I can see his head, I see that he's blond all over, blond eyebrows, eyelashes, blond hair, even a little blond wannabe mustache inching across his upper lip. He gives me a lopsided grin. "Hey, how's it goin', Shelby?" He has one of those caveman-jock voices that rattle windows. "I've heard a lot about you."

"Really?" I give Fletcher a withering look. "Don't believe any of it."

Carl shoots Fletcher a confused glance. "Yeah, well, it was all good, but if you don't want me to believe it, okay." He focuses on Fletcher again. I consider moving. Maybe they'd like to be alone. "So, what's up with you, dude? Summer's good?"

Fletcher glances at me before nodding. "Yeah, pretty good. You?"

"Not bad, not bad." He stretches his legs out, and they wrap around the seat in front of him. That's going to totally freak out whoever sits there. Imagine reaching for your popcorn in the dark and instead you get this gigantic Converse with old gum stuck to the bottom. "I'm working at my dad's shop."

"What kind of business is that?" I ask politely, just to show that I can engage in conversation.

Carl looks mildly surprised. "Uh, he owns that sport shop over by school. Makes signs and stuff and trophies." He looks at me, then at Fletcher, then back at me again. "Yeah, so I'll leave you two alone. Nice meeting you, Shelby. Fletch, IM me or something, dude. I have to talk to you about some stuff." Again, he looks at me, like I'll be an obstacle to his deep, intellectual conversation about sport signs. "Later."

I watch him stand up and lumber away. "Wow, Fletcher. You have a secret life, huh?"

"What?"

I nod toward Carl. "I mean, here I thought the jock thing was just for show, but you actually hang out with guys like that! I am totally shocked."

Fletcher stares ahead frostily at the screen as the lights dim. "You're kind of narrow-minded, you know."

"Am I? Well, let me tell you something, I can be—"

"Shhh!" He puts his finger in front of his mouth. He's shushing me! "I want to see the trailers."

When the movie's over, we walk out of the theater, and he grabs my hand.

"I like you. Why does that piss you off?" he says as we walk under the white twinkly lights surrounding the mall's central walkway.

"Well, that's a little blunt. Want to rephrase that?" I don't look at him.

He turns me around and right there, under the sparkly tree decorations, he puts an arm around me, pulls me close, and holds the back of my head with one hand. We are eye to eye, and the light is strong enough for me to see the kalei-doscope whirls of yellow in the center of his green eyes. "I really like you. And I'm going to kiss you now. So get over it."

He does, too. I'm not really sure what happens next, because I sort of have an out-of-body experience. I am float-ing above the twinkle lights, floating above the discarded corn-dog sticks and the movie-ticket stubs, bumping into pigeons and air conditioning ducts. I am full of electricity and could probably light up the neon beer signs at every bar within ten miles of the mall.

He pulls away, and I slam back into my body. That neon-light buzz feeling is vibrating through me, and I feel as if all that bitchy nastiness I was throwing at Fletcher has all gone down a large drain. I melt into his hand, lean into his chest, and I kiss him back.

The next week, we all get together to swim a lot at Becca's (and Elisa finally gets a swimsuit—a black thing with a little skirt on it), and Jon comes over several times to check his drawings against the digital pictures and the real thing (us). I notice that he and Amber seem to be getting a bit more comfortable with each other every time he visits, and Becca sees it too.

Speaking of getting a bit more comfortable, I notice that after that Movie Kiss (as opposed to the Big Date Kiss), something sort of snaps in me, and I can't get my mind off that boy's lips. For about a week, I can't think of anything else but the Kiss. I burn a batch of fudge, I vacuum my sweatshirts instead of my rug, and I keep replaying the whole episode in my head like an on-demand HBO movie. Even Euphoria notices.

"Shelby, I have to ask you a very sensitive question," she says one night as we're finishing up dinner dishes.

"Shoot." I put away the last plate and begin my search for dessert. I have to wait until she's gone, though, or she'll scold me about putting on too many pounds or something.

"I don't know how to say this," she says as her lights blink cautiously. "But . . . are you on drugs?"

"What?" I can't help but laugh like I'm going into convulsions. "Drugs? Where did you get that idea?"

"Well, you've just seemed very strange lately." She reaches out and pats my hand with her claw. "If you are on drugs, it's not a problem. I have some very good deprogramming software that I can use to help you kick the monkey."

"Kick the monkey?"

"You know. 'Bite the horse that feeds you.' 'Get up at the dawn of crack.' Please, Shelby. You must have heard some of these phrases at school. It's what all the kids are saying!" She beeps proudly. "I've been surfing the Internet."

I put an arm around her and steer her toward the living room. "Euphoria, I promise. If I ever do any drugs, you'll be the first to know."

I can hear her processors whirring over that one. "But, what about all this unusual behavior? Your increased blood pressure? Your excessive sweating?"

"Hey. That's kind of personal." I sniff under my arms as subtly as I can. "I'm not sweating excessively."

My dad notices that I'm distracted also. At breakfast one morning, he just sits and stares at me. "What?" I ask between bites of toast.

"Something is going on with you." He leans on one hand and fixes me with this mad-scientist squint. "Are you doing drugs?"

"What, is this a conspiracy to get me to be a junkie?" I throw down my napkin and shake my head. "First Euphoria, then you. Why is everyone convinced I'm on drugs?"

"Well, I honestly didn't think you were on drugs, but you are acting pretty weird." Coming from my dad, accusations of weirdness are very frightening.

I am unable to really express why I'm behaving strangely, even though I know it's true. It's disturbing to me, but I've sort of made peace with it. Here's the deal: I realize now that, at my age, hormones are powerful chemicals that will take over brain function, and when near a male with a specific chemical pheromone makeup (like Fletcher, for example), my complete neural network gets scrambled. It's like when a signal jams radar or something. I cannot be held personally responsible for the fact that I turn into a drooling idiot around Fletcher any more than a radio operator could be held responsible for getting a message wrong when there's an electrical storm.

My theory gets proven again and again over the course of the next few weeks. Fletcher and I have had exactly seven dates now, I mean formal dates, and we've also had several kind-of sort-of dates (that's where he comes to my house and we watch sci-fi movies and Euphoria pops popcorn in her microwave compartment). I won't go into all the boring details of all of these dates, but at about date three, I realize that I'm walking with my head on his shoulder wherever we go. It occurs to me that our bodies might fuse together, and only a medical miracle will ever allow us to be two separate people again. And, oddly enough, I think that's okay. Freaky, I know.

The Becca/Jon/Amber triangle becomes more and more scary as time goes on. Everything sort of breaks loose one night when we're all sitting around Becca's house for the unveiling of the Geektastic Four.

It's one week before the deadline to submit websites to the Comic-Con competition. Jon has even dressed up for the occasion, which means that instead of a torn black denim jacket, he wears a black denim jacket with patches.

Jon has brought his laptop with him and he and Fletcher are hooking it up to a projector in the truffle room. Becca is sitting on the big couch, staring dreamily at Jon while Amber, Elisa, and I pick at a bowl of chocolate-covered almonds. "So, if the website wins, what do we get?" Amber asks. I notice she's also wearing a black denim jacket, even though it's almost ninety-five outside.

"I'm sure it's something really valuable, like the whole first season of the Weather Channel on DVD," Elisa answers as she munches busily.

"I don't think the prize is really important," Becca interjects. Apparently the spell of Jon has worn off momentarily. "It's more the visibility. We want people to know who we are."

"Why is that?" I ask.

Becca sighs and stands up, stretching so her dragon tattoo seems ready to pounce from her long leg. "Oh, this again. I told you last year: We want to find others of our own kind. Websites and stuff are sort of a shortcut way to do that. All geeks surf websites. And most of them read graphic novels." Okay, so now *she's* calling them graphic novels too. Soon toilet paper will be elevated to the status of "hygienic pulp byproduct."

"Okay! Ready!" Jon shouts. I mean, he shouts in his Jon-like way, which means that he sort of flips one hand in a weak wave and then talks above a whisper.

Fletcher plops on the sofa and motions for me to sit with him. I'm tempted, but feel the need to be less like a lapdog called by its master and more like a superhero. A superhero sitting on the floor eating chocolate almonds.

Becca dims the lights, and we all focus on the projection screen that slides silently from the ceiling. (I told you it was a mansion.) Jon clicks frantically at the laptop, until finally an image pops onto the screen, a surface that looks like polished metal with a big insignia in the front, a turquoise star with a big G in the middle. Fletcher's voice booms: "In a world where geeks are an endangered species . . ." A graphic sweeps into the picture. It's a silhouette of a woman, definitely not any of us since none of us have legs that long or boobs that big. The voice continues: "Where computer nerds tremble with fear . . ." Another silhouette zooms in. "Where six-syllable words are outlawed . . ." A third figure pops up. "And where intellectual curiosity means watching *Sesame Street* with the sound off . . ." A final figure joins the first three, and an electric blue flash fills the screen, then fades to reveal the four figures again, glowing faintly blue. "Help is on its way! The Geektastic Four!"

A deafening guitar riff shreds the air as the electric blue gets brighter and starts pulsating. Fletcher's narration continues: "Saving the world, one geek at a time! Smart-tastic!" One of the silhouettes zooms to the front and becomes a cartoon illustration. "That's me!" Becca squeals. Then she frowns and tilts her head. "Why do I have a librarian hairdo? And glasses?"

"Organize-i-tastic!" The shorter figure zooms to the front and resolves into a colored illustration of a superhero clutching a Palm Pilot and a calculator. Her eyes glow green below close-cropped red hair, and the pattern on her skin-tight suit is a checkerboard Excel spreadsheet.

"Is that supposed to be me?" Elisa growls. "I am not that short! And I never gave my approval for spandex!"

Jon pauses the program. "Well, I only had, like, four basic body shapes to choose from. I thought this was closest, and it's different from the other three."

"So, I'm a disfigured troll to you?" Elisa says frostily.

"Let's move on," I say, hoping to stave off a punk-versus-disfigured-troll war.

"Art-tastic!" Fletcher's voice booms, and Amber's superhero expands to fill the screen. Hers is pretty cool, actually; she has magenta hair and a blue beret and this kind of turquoise skin. She's carrying a laptop and a camera, and has on these killer hip boots.

"I want those boots!" Amber says. She and Jon exchange glances. Is it a coincidence that her superhero is the hottest? Of course, I haven't seen mine yet. . . .

"Vege-tastic!" The fourth figure, mine, resolves into a fruit-salad nightmare of organic clarity. I have a big yellow growth branching out from the top of my head, and my weapons of choice are celery sticks and a rather sharply whittled piece of zucchini.

"Where's my weapons-grade juicer?" I ask. Fletcher chuckles and nods at me. I know he must have had something to do with the design. My boobs are bigger than everyone else's, I notice.

The presentation goes on as the Geektastic Four hover, ready for action. "Fighting for the rights of oppressed geeks everywhere, it's the Geektastic Four!" Some synthesized music swells and our alter egos stand there, looking like they're ready to kick some butt. Or correct some papers. Or make a salad.

"Okay, so then, once you get past the intro screen"—Jon is talking faster than I've ever heard him talk—"there's a page to describe the whole Queen Geek Social Club, and then if you click on each of the superheroes, you go to her individual screen. There, you can do blogs, games, statements or purpose, that kind of stuff. Like for Shelby, I thought you could have a kind of battle game."

"What? Peas versus carrots?" I ask, sounding kind of snotty.

"No, I mean . . . like she's going after people who eat bad stuff or fast food or something," Jon says. He looks a little hurt. As Vege-tastic, I don't think it's my job to understand mere mortals. Especially mere mortals who put produce on my head.

"Maybe we could go together and help old ladies organize their produce shopping," Elisa snipes. "Turn on the lights."

Becca, who has been strangely silent, hits the dimmer switch, and we all blink a bit. The Geektastic Four hover expectantly on the projector screen. We all just sit there looking at each other. "Well, I thought it was great," Amber finally says.

"Of course you thought it was great," Becca says acidly. "You looked hot. The rest of us looked like Marvel Comics rejects. What power was I supposed to have? Collecting library fines?"

Jon sighs and looks at us as if we are too dumb to get his brilliance. "The Geektastic Four are supposed to be a joke. If you had real superhero powers, it wouldn't be funny. Your power is doing homework and calculating square roots and stuff. I mean, you can make up anything you want, as long as it sounds kind of weird." He flips off the laptop. "I've almost finished the graphic novel. I don't have the time to do it over, so if you don't like it, I guess we can just scrap it."

"No!" Amber says, a bit too loudly. We all stare at her. "I mean, we want to enter the competition, right? Since Jon has done all this work, the least we can do is go for it. And we can all help write our own content, right, Jon?" I can tell by the way she says it that she loves rolling his name around on her tongue. I check Becca's expression . . . she hears it too. I'm surprised she hasn't jumped off the couch and whammed Art-tastic with her own laptop.

Fletcher pipes up. "I agree with Amber. You guys might as well just finish it. So what if it's not perfect? It's just a goof anyway. You're all taking it way too seriously." He stands up and motions for Jon to follow. "We'll get out of here and let you guys talk it over amongst yourselves. Let us know what you want to do."

He leans over and gives me a fatherly peck on the top of my head and Jon kind of waves half-heartedly at Amber, totally ignoring Becca. I consider stowing away in Fletcher's back-pack to avoid the inevitable cat fight, but then, I wouldn't be a very good friend if I didn't stick around to mop up the blood and smeared lipstick.

We've never had trouble talking before. I mean, usually when the four of us get together, it's a tidal wave of sound.

But now we're all sort of staring off into space or at the floor, pretending to be alone. I realize that I am the only one who can start this discussion, because Becca and Amber are too mad and Elisa likes awkward silences.

"Okay," I say, feeling kind of like a camp counselor for dysfunctional cheerleaders. "Let's talk about this. We can't just sit here and stare at the shag carpet all day."

"We would never have shag carpet," Becca spits.

"Why? Because you can't stand anything average and normal?" Amber says quietly. "Like a guy liking a girl who isn't you?"

"Well," Becca says, laughing nastily. "If you think that's the problem, then you are more dense than I thought."

Amber stands up, and I see fire in her eyes that I've never seen before. Maybe she's channeling Art-tastic. "Look, I've put up with this for weeks, but I am sick of it, Becca. I'm sorry Jon doesn't like you. But I'm not sorry he *does* like me. Why can't you just be happy for us?"

Elisa, meanwhile, is tracking this grudge match like she's watching a championship game of tennis. I'm sure if she had snacks, the whole thing would be perfect.

"Wait, wait," I say. "We can't let a little thing like a boyfriend get in the way of our relationship. Can we?"

That's when the aforementioned tidal wave of sound crashes in like an audio tsunami. Amber and Becca are squawking at each other, making ugly faces and gesturing in threatening ways with their hands, while Elisa stands up between them (although she's quite a bit shorter than either of them) and tries to talk to each one individually. I try to butt in, but every time I open my mouth, I feel like the words are just evaporating in the chaos. So, finally I do what my dad taught me: I let out a real big wolf whistle to get their attention. Everybody stops talking and stares at me as if I've just grown a third head.

"There's no need for that," Becca says, crossing her arms.

"Well, apparently there was, because you were all screaming at each other like rabid parrots."

"Rabid parrots?" Elisa tries to remain serious, but she sort of giggles, and then everyone else does too, including me. "Sounds like some punk band."

"Just sit." I pace a bit, then go to the door. "Now, here's the problem, as I see it. Amber and Becca both like Jon. Jon likes Amber. Becca is mad. Amber feels weird. Jon is oblivious. No fault, no foul." The girls are nodding in agreement. "But the real disturbing part is that we're letting this ruin our friendship. Isn't that something we said we wouldn't do?"

Becca sighs and chews on her lower lip.

"I mean, last year, wasn't it all about what we could accomplish, and how we didn't need guys? And remember all the great stuff we did?" They all nod. "And now suddenly, some scaggy guy in an unwashed denim jacket is tilting the axis of our world?"

"I'm not sure you can tilt someone's axis," Elisa offers.

"Oh, he can tilt my axis anytime," Becca adds, then, seeing Amber's smoldering eyes, says, "Okay, sorry. Inappropriate."

"Right." I put one hand on Becca's shoulder, and one of Amber's. "First rule of Queen Geek: We never let guys get in the way, right? And isn't that exactly what you're doing?"

"What about you?" Becca says accusatorily. "What about Fletcher? You've been a melting popsicle ever since he kissed you."

"What?" I squeak. Amber and Elisa are smiling slyly and nodding in agreement. "I'm not a melting popsicle!"

Amber leans back in the chair, happy not to be the center of attention for the moment. "You've been so unfocused that I'm surprised you remember to brush your teeth."

"On the plus side," Elisa says, "all that kissing is probably really good for staving off tooth decay."

I can't believe I'm getting ganged up on by the rabid parrots! Obviously, I'm not cut out to be the camp counselor. "Whatever. Let's get back to the point. How do we handle this stupid love/hate triangle?"

"Actually, if you include the you-and-Fletcher thing, it's more of a love rhombus." Elisa whips out a small notebook and pen. "I can draw it for you, if you want."

"No, thanks." I grab the notebook and pitch it onto the couch. "Here's the bottom line: Becca, you will give up on Jon. Amber, you will date Jon if you want, but try not to torture Becca with it. Elisa, you will stop trying to do geometry in the summer."

"What about you?" Becca asks.

"Me?" I casually head for the door. "I believe I will be swimming, and you will all be eating my dust as I run to the pool. Last one in is a rabid parrot!"

I take off for the back door, with the other three squealing behind me.

6

HERO SANDWICHES

(or Spandex Becomes Her)

The day before Comic-Con happens is a blur of activity. We're all at my house for a change (Becca's mom is hosting a group of traveling Sufi dancers, and Becca says they make the house smell like baba ghanoush). We're in my room with costume pieces strewn everywhere, doing a dry run with our outfits so we can maximize our departure time. Euphoria is trying to help, but she's actually in the way.

"Explain to me again about Geektastics," she bleeps at me as I try to navigate around Elisa, who is struggling with some spandex-based costume. Even though spandex is Elisa's kryptonite, she's been sucked into the superhero fashion machine.

"It's the Geektastic Four," Becca says again. "It's like four superheroes. Do you know what a superhero is, Euphoria?"

"I should say so," Euphoria answers, clearly offended. I mean, she's been programmed to be the ultimate science-fiction database, so asking her about superheroes is kind of like asking Webster the dictionary guy if he knows how to spell "cat." "I just don't understand which superheroes you are supposed to be."

Amber is adjusting a flowing fuchsia wig and a blue beret in imitation of Art-tastic. "I don't know if I can keep this hair on all the time. It's hot."

"What about this plastic cauliflower on my head?" I glance into the mirror at my Vege-tastic headdress. "You don't think that's going to be hot?"

"Steam it and sell it," Becca suggests. "Great fund-raiser. 'Eat Vege-tastic's head, only a quarter!' "

"I'd want more than a quarter." Really! I'm not that cheap.

Becca's wearing a long blue wig pulled into a prim pony-tail over her normal spiky do, with these retro hornrimmed glasses. She does really look like Jon's drawing of Smart-tastic, right down to the blue-and-white zigzag pattern leggings and gold leg cuffs that cover the front of her calves. She's kind of a cross between the neighborhood librarian and Russell Crowe in *Gladiator*. I'd hate to think what she'd do if you had a late return.

"But superheroes usually have superpowers, don't they?" Euphoria tugs down at the red-and-gold towel thing covering my nether regions. "This is too short, Shelby. It's not decent."

"It's fine." I hike it back up. It's all the way to my knees anyway; the indecent part is the tiny skirt underneath it that clings dangerously to my Vege-tastic thighs. "We super-heroes can't worry about social hang-ups."

"As to our superpowers," Becca says, adjusting her blue-and-white tiara, "we can all do things that all geeks would love to be able to do. For example, I'm Smart-tastic, and my superpower is that I can speed read and calculate pi to its ultimate end."

"The last piece of pi, hmmm?" Euphoria snipes. "No one can do that."

Amber arches an eyebrow at my robot. "Did your dad program her for pun humor?"

"Oh, no. That just sort of happened." I turn to examine my gorgeous costume in the full-length mirror. According to Jon's design, I have a bright red bustier, a green sash, the yellow and red skirt/towel ensemble, and a dark green cape trimmed in gold. My hair in the drawing looks like wilted asparagus, so I have these olive-colored dreadlocks hanging in my face. He also made my skin Green Giant sweet-pea color, and Vege-tastic wears what look like gold Birkenstocks.

"So, are you going to paint your skin green?" Elisa asks as she struggles with her Excel-patterned bodysuit.

"I guess." At the costume shop I bought a big round container of green body paint, just so I could achieve the effect. I'm not putting it on until we go to Comic-Con, though. I don't want green streaks on my sheets. God knows what Dad would think.

Amber strikes a pose in her cool-looking Art-tastic outfit. It's actually something you could wear to an avant-garde dance; she has blue leggings, turquoise calf cuffs, a fuchsia skirt, and a tight top that looks like one of those modern paintings where the guy just lines up little squares of different colors and calls it high art. Her blue beret tops it all off, and turquoise lipstick over pale makeup and dark eyeliner make her look awesome. "I can make art," she says simply. "What more do I need to do?"

Elisa has finally finished wrestling with her leotard, and she plunks on the red wig and mock phone headset that Jon designed for her. She looks at the rest of us. "Why do you guys get to look hot while I look like a reject from the *Bride of Chucky* auditions?"

"I look like the produce aisle at Safeway, so don't complain," I remind her. We then do what anyone in our position would do: We decide to go to the nearby McDonald's to frighten the customers.

Euphoria stands at the front door, waving a handkerchief like my southern nanny. "Y'all be careful! No trans fats!"

I won't bore you with the details of the McDonald's trip. We do stuff like this all the time, really, but I will say that wearing a vegetable on my head and the various wigs and hats (and tight tops) gets us more attention than our usual togas or Halloween masks. I order a Diet Coke, and in my Vege-tastic persona, warn people about the evils of eating hamburger. One guy leaves me a quarter as a tip.

The other Queen Geeks are sleeping over at my house tonight, in preparation for tomorrow's glorious conquest of Comic-Con. Since my room is too small to accommodate all four of us (and Euphoria will not sleep in the kitchen, even though I point out to her how nice the blender is), we all bunk in the living room in front of the TV, which gives us a great opportunity to watch bad sci-fi, one of our favorite things to do.

"What about *Creature from the Haunted Sea*?" Amber asks, holding up a DVD case featuring a swooning woman being menaced by a bubble-eyed thing that looks like some-body's shag rug with arms.

"Oh! I want to see *The Giant Gila Monster*!" Becca yells, seizing a DVD with an oversized lizard sticking its tongue out at the world. "This is an awesome movie. This giant Gila monster terrorizes a small town full of fifties bobby-soxers, and the main character has a crippled sister who needs leg braces, but he's broke, so he has to tow cars for practically nothing, and everyone thinks he's a bum." She takes a deep breath to make up for the verbal diarrhea. "Anyway, it's a hoot."

Elisa stretches out on the floor in her rubber ducky shortie pajamas. "Is Johnny Depp in it?"

"Johnny Depp couldn't be in it," Becca says. "He wasn't born yet."

We agree on the Gila monster movie, and Euphoria rolls in with popcorn and homemade fudge, then parks herself near the couch. "Aren't there any mechanical men in this picture?" she whines. She's developed kind of an obsession with movie 'bots, especially the big muscly kind like Robby the Robot from *Forbidden Planet*. I'm afraid to let her watch *Star Wars*; if she gets a glimpse of C3PO, she might have a meltdown. He's not exactly macho, but that accent might rope her in.

So we're watching this flick, and the Gila monster in question (a vision in pink-and-black pin dots, according to the sheriff) has an appetite for model railroads and drunks. Whenever the locals hit the bars and drive home, this mon-ster appears suddenly in their headlights and spooks them into driving off the road. The last shot of every character is when the Gila monster stomps them with one big webbed foot; then everything goes black.

After yet another town boozer is squished, Amber says, "Maybe he's just trying to keep the freeways safe."

Becca nods as she shovels in another piece of fudge. "Nobody ever understands the monster."

"Speaking of," Elisa says. "What about Fletcher?"

"What about him?" I answer.

"Are you guys just dating or getting serious? Or is it all simply falling apart?" She rolls onto her tummy and strikes a terrified B-movie pose. "It all seemed so romantic, but then it all went sour, like a monster had stomped on her heart!"

"Very poetic," Amber says, laughing. "Keep your day job."

"I don't have a day job. That's why I obsess about the lives of others." Elisa sits up and fixes me with a wide-eyed, manic stare. "Are you and Fletcher going to get really serious?"

"Serious?" I ask. "As in . . ."

Elisa grins and shrugs her shoulders. "As in getting married, having kids, buying a house, going into debt. You know, the American dream."

"I'm a little bit young to be getting a mortgage." I lean into the couch cushions. "What about you, Elisa? Maybe we should work on getting you a guy."

"No, no." She shakes her head vigorously. "There's enough drama in this group already."

Elisa is a funny addition to the group, really; she's kind of nasty sometimes, without meaning to be. It's kind of like when you eat those sour candies, the ones that sort of bite your tongue when you suck on them; Elisa is tart, and brutally honest, but there's something about her sourness that adds the right spice to the group. And without her Palm Pilot skills, we'd be hopelessly disorganized.

Elisa fixes her heat-seeking gaze on Amber. "So, Amber. What about Jon?"

"Hmm?" Amber stares innocently into her bowl of popcorn.

"Are you serious about him?" She waves a hand in front of Amber's down-turned face. "Hello? Are we going to be seeing a double wedding in the spring?"

Becca snorts. "Elisa, what is the big deal? Nobody's getting married. Jon and Amber haven't even gone out on a date." She looks to Amber for confirmation of this, and again, Amber studies the kernels as if a magic answer will appear. "Oh."

Elisa ignores her and continues. "I'm just concerned about all these hormones. Because here's my hunch: If you all get boyfriends, this club will sink faster than a concrete turd."

"Nice imagery," Becca answers. "Classy."

Euphoria, the resident expert on all things romantic, has to weigh in, of course. "All human beings have the need to mate, you know." She buzzes with something like excitement. "It's all part of the need to keep the species going. Mechancials don't have that problem. We can always make more of our own kind."

"Well, so could we, if we hadn't paid attention in health class," Elisa says. "It might just take a little more effort and perhaps a nice dinner."

Eventually, Elisa drops the whole dating interrogation, Euphoria douses the lights, and we curl up in our respective piles of blankets. As I stare up at the ceiling and listen to

Becca snore (she never has trouble falling asleep), I think about Fletcher. Again. It's so annoying. I don't want to think about him, really, but his face pops up in front of my eyelids whenever I have two minutes of downtime. We had that romantic date, I burned fudge and got disoriented, so isn't that what love is all about? I don't know.

We get up so early the next morning that it's still dark out, which is kind of a sin in the summer. But this is Comic-Con day, so we have to get ready, put on our costumes, and go downtown to stand in line with all the other geeks. Dad has agreed to take us, even though he hates getting up early more than I do.

Euphoria is, of course, perky as ever since she doesn't need to sleep. I smell buttermilk pancakes and bacon; Elisa waves her hands frantically. "If I eat anything, this spandex is gonna blow," she says. But I see her sneak a piece of bacon, and I think she probably inhaled a pancake or two. Euphoria is a great cook.

By about seven, we're ready. The whole event doesn't open til ten, but you just have to go early anyway. Somebody once made the point that if you waited til ten-thirty you could just walk right in, but where's the fun in that?

Dad grumbles about taking us, of course. "I don't understand why you have cauliflower on your head," he says over coffee. "What is it you're supposed to be again?"

"Vege-tastic." I swing the asparagus-dreadlock green wig out of my way. It's already hot and I'm not even walking around. "We're all geek superheroes, remember?"

"So why does Elisa look like the Joker from *Batman*? Is her superpower doing bad sequels or something?"

Elisa shoots him a dirty look as she snatches a pancake. "I just hope the graphic novel doesn't make me look like an idiot. I never did get to see it. Did any of you?"

Amber waves, embarrassed. "I did."

"You did?" Becca says sharply. "When?"

"Uh," Amber stutters, then accidentally-on-purpose spills maple syrup. "Oh, let me get a paper towel. Sorry about that."

"Was it good? The comic book, I mean," Elisa continues, oblivious to the fact that Amber is trying to avoid the subject.

"Yeah," Amber mumbles as she blots at the brown, sticky blob on the table. "It's actually a really funny story. I think Jon should do pretty well at the amateur table. Maybe he can make some good connections."

"Sounds like he already made at least one," Elisa says loudly.

We all get our stuff together, get our badges (Dad picked them up early . . . what a sweetie!) and we truck down the freeway, four cosmetically perfect superheroes crammed into a Volvo. "Make sure your vegetation doesn't dent the ceiling," my dad cautions as my cauliflower headdress pokes into it.

When we finally get to the convention center, we all tumble out of the car proudly wearing our badges. "I'll pick you up right here at seven," Dad says. Knowing Dad, that means more like eight, so I know we have a lot of time. "Right here, by this potted plant," he says, motioning to a planter.

"I'll be sure to wear a carnation or something so you recognize me," Elisa says, waving as she scampers across the street with Becca and Amber close behind.

I lean in to give Dad a kiss, leaving a green streak on his face. "That's actually a good color on you," I say, dabbing at the makeup with the hem of my tea-towel skirt. He grabs my wrist as I try to leave. "Listen," he says. "Be careful in there."

"It's not like I'm going to the prison open house." I try to retrieve my wrist, but he doesn't want to let go. "What's up, Dad?"

He stares up at me, squinting into the sun. "I'm kind of afraid to let you go to someplace like that all by yourself. It's easy to get lost."

"I have my Geektastic sisters. They'll protect me. We have a circle of power." I laugh, but he doesn't. "Oh, c'mon. You aren't seriously afraid about me going in there, are you?"

He laughs nervously. "I know it's silly. You're just . . . young. I worry."

I kiss him again, and this time I leave the green streak. "I promise I won't run away and get married or anything."

"Deal." The other girls are waiting for me impatiently, so I run across the street (carefully checking for traffic, of course). Dad stays at the curb, watching us cross at the light with a sea of other people. I look back once we reach the convention center; he's still sitting there, watching me.

I don't want to think about my dad, or his issues, so I just let myself bask in the glory of weirdness that is Comic-Con. To get a sense of this event, picture every quirky/strange/bizarre person you ever met. Now picture them all mixed together into a stew of weirdness and shiny plastic. That's Comic-Con. There's a great feeling when you're walking in with a tidal wave of other geeks; it's like you're not alone in the world. It's okay to have a burning need to collect action figures even if you're an accountant with three kids, or to strap on a lightsaber even if you're an Eagle Scout, or to have a Magic card slap down with your gym teacher. All geeks are equal here. Geek-qual, if you will.

We get quite a few looks because of our costumes, which is great. If you can get someone to look at you at Comic-Con, you've done something right. We scurry up the stairs and into the center, where the exhibit hall beckons. This is where everybody with geek wares sets up shop and sells everything you can imagine. Clothes, jewelry, art, comic books, toys, everything from the free (what they call "swag") to the incredibly cheap (six dollar anime posters) to the massively expensive (I see a teeny piece of paper framed that costs $500. No kidding. Some lithograph thing . . . pretty, but it's still paper, come on!)

The greatest compliment comes about ten minutes in, when a total stranger asks us to pose for a picture. That means our costumes are awesome, or at least so weird that someone notices. Becca sort of takes the lead in walking us around the exhibit floor. Walking, by the way, is a great challenge, because there are so many bodies in this place that no one moves very fast, and there's so much to look at that you can't watch your feet or where you're going. This results in quite a few bruised heels and scuffed up Stormtrooper boots.

We scan the program and map, and locate the amateur graphic novel table, which is planted at the far end of the cavernous hall. It takes us about twenty minutes to walk there, and in that time, I calculate that I stab at least six people with my cauliflower head.

Jon is sitting behind the table, talking to a scruffy-looking guy in a flannel shirt. "Jon!" Amber yells and waves. He lights up when he sees her, which I know is going to result in a Smart-tastic/Art-tastic showdown at some point. Oh, well.

"Let's see the book," Becca says, all business.

"Good morning to you too," Jon says sarcastically as he hands her a copy of *The Geektastic Four*. It's printed on thin paper, and the cover is only three colors, but it still looks pretty good. I have to admit that it feels pretty flattering having my face on a comic book, even if I do look like a green salad.

"I'm gonna hang out here for a while," Jon says. "Fletcher's meeting me here in an hour, and then we can all go to the website contest."

"Sure," Becca says coldly. "We'll see you then." She stalks off, a giant pissed-off librarian. The rest of us wave to Jon and the scruffy comic guy, and I notice that Amber steals a little peck on the cheek from Jon before joining us.

After nearly three nonstop hours of listening, preening, gawking, and trying to pee without totally undressing ourselves, we decide to break for lunch, another challenge. The food is expensive, and we don't want to spend our money on it. We decide to split a soft pretzel four ways. But we do spring for the extra cheese sauce.

While propped against a wall near the escalator, with my wilty-asparagus dreadlocks dipping annoyingly into my cheese sauce, I notice something odd, even for Comic-Con: a very, very tall somebody in a white rabbit suit. "Check that out," I say, wiping the fake cheese from my chin.

"Hmmm." Becca squints at the bunny, who is trying, without the benefit of opposable thumbs, to open the pages of a comic. "Interesting. Greg the Bunny fan?"

"I don't think so." Elisa fishes for a bottle of water and takes a long chug from it. "I don't think Greg the Bunny is white, is he?"

"Are you a racist or something?" Amber chuckles. "Color doesn't matter. All bunnies are furry on the inside."

"Don't want to know how you know that," Elisa says, brushing crumbs from her spreadsheet tights. "Want me to go ask him . . . her . . . it?"

Becca throws the sad remainders of her pretzel portion into a trashcan. "Naw, let's leave it alone. I want to go check out the sci-fi posters." Like Halloween ducklings, we follow her to a nearby booth.

"I was hoping I'd find this!" she squeals almost immediately. She holds up a reproduction of a *The Day the Earth Stood Still* poster, the one with the robot Gort shooting his laser beam eye at the army while holding some blond woman who's not even in the movie. There's also a huge, mummified hand over the Earth. I never understood whose hand that was. Maybe the movie studio had it left over from making *The Mummy*, so they recycled it.

"If the robot guy and the alien are actually *on* the Earth, how can there be a hand *covering* the Earth?" Elisa asks the guy behind the counter. He shrugs.

Amber sidles up to me and hisses in my ear like a Madagascar cockroach.

"Geez, stop it!" I wave her away. "You're getting spit in my makeup!"

"That bunny guy . . . he's following us!" I start to look and she grabs my chin, jerking it back toward the mummy hand poster. "Don't look!"

"How can I see if he's following us, then?" I whisper awkwardly, since I can't move my chin. She lets go.

Becca, blithely unaware of the stalking rabbit, pushes her Smart-tastic glasses down onto the edge of her nose so she can look smart reading the prices on the movie posters. "*Queen of Outer Space*!" she yells. "Bingo!"

"Shh!" Amber and I both clap hands over her mouth. She freaks and almost knocks us both down. "What are you guys doing?" she yelps, swatting our hands away.

"Come down here," Amber says in measured tones as she slowly, slowly sinks down to the not-too-clean floor. "Try to look unconcerned and casual."

"How can I look casual when I'm crouching in somebody's old gum and discarded bubble wrap?" Becca asks as she conks her head on the edge of the poster table. By this time, the poster seller is starting to look at us suspiciously. Wonder why.

Elisa doesn't see us on the floor, and as she whips around the corner of the table, she stumbles and falls with a squeal on top of us.

"You girls are going to have to move on!" the poster man tells us. I can't blame him. Four squealing superheroes are probably not good for business.

"What are you guys doing on the floor?" Elisa sputters as we all try to stand up with as much dignity as possible while wearing assorted vegetables, capes, and tights.

"We were having a meeting." Amber scans the sea of faces. "Someone was following us."

"Who?" Elisa straightens up a pile of plastic-covered posters that she'd toppled as the poster man shoos her away.

"Some tall guy in a bunny suit." Becca says, laughing. "You guys are seriously paranoid. If you're going to be afraid of anybody here, check out some of the guys with the spiked jewelry and masks. They walk all creepy and mysterious, hiding behind their Sith makeup and stuff. They freak me out."

As we walk on, Amber mutters, "Rabbits can have a dark side."

The day really zips by. We hardly slow down at all, except for a brief rest at the Sci-Fi Channel space, which kind of looks like a giant aluminum toilet set on its side, bathed in cool, blue light. Well, it's roomy and has seats (not toilet seats), plus, they're giving away these cheeseball plastic capes there. I get one for Euphoria.

While we rest with our sore feet propped up, I hear an all-too-familiar voice over my shoulder. "Hey, Vege-tastic. Want to help me make a salad?"

"Hi, Fletcher." Becca reaches a long arm toward him. "Come sit down."

As he rounds the curve of the fake aluminum toilet, I notice that Jon is with him. Fletcher plops down next to me and puts an arm around my caped shoulders. "You look fantastic!" He plants a kiss on my cheek.

"Your lips are green," Elisa remarks.

"A small price to pay to be near the asparagus I love." He gives me another kiss, which makes me giggle. Jon sits next to Amber, and I notice Becca bristling uncomfortably.

"So, how's it been going?" Jon asks, never taking his eyes off Amber. "The table visit went really well. The guy said that the *Geektastic Four* could really work. He especially thought Art-tastic was hot."

Becca says, a little too loudly, "We've had our pictures taken a few times, and I found some great sci-fi posters too. Want to see?" She fishes them out of an oversized yellow bag, and she holds up *Queen of Outer Space* proudly.

Jon totally ignores her and keeps his attention riveted to Amber. "Are you all going to the panel discussion about websites? It's where they're going to announce the winner of the contest."

"Why don't you guys go and then text us if we win." Becca stands, clutches her bag and scans the hall as if looking for something. "We still have a lot to do. Shall we, ladies?"

Amber hesitates and says, "I'd kind of like to go. Maybe I can be there to represent the Geektastic Four. . . ." Her voice trails off as Becca glares at her. "I mean, if you don't want to go."

"Sure." Becca stalks off into the crowd, exuding diva vibes in her wake.

Fletcher shrugs at me, gives me a squeeze, and says, "Want to meet up later for dinner?"

"Yeah," Elisa answers. "All we had for lunch was a soft pretzel."

"Is that part of your superhero diet?" Fletcher asks. "Or were you just trying to scam some cheese sauce to dip in Shelby's hair?"

"Ha-ha." I hug him back and follow Becca, who has already waded out into the stream of people. "See you later." As they walk away, I notice that Jon puts his arm around Amber.

"We better find Becca or we'll never catch up to her," Elisa says, tugging at my sleeve. "How is she, do you think?"

"Hmmm." I scan the crowd for the towering blue hair of the most pissed-off librarian in the exhibit hall. "It's definitely a problem. I'll have to talk to her."

As we elbow our way through various incarnations of Luke Skywalker and try not to get our heels nicked by geeky parents with baby strollers, Elisa bobs up and down at my side as if she's trying to avoid drowning. "I would think she'd be excited about the website and the comic book. But she doesn't seem to care."

"I guess some things are actually more important to her than the club," I say, grabbing Elisa's arm so she doesn't get sucked into a tidal wave of very tall aliens coming our way. "I haven't seen her like this before."

"Hormones," Elisa yells over the noise surrounding us. "Thank God I don't have them."

We finally spot Becca examining strange role-playing costumes (PVC corsets? C'mon, it's made of plumbing!) and maneuver over to her. After forty minutes of shopping and no purchase, she finally agrees to move on. At just that moment, my phone buzzes.

"It's a text message from Fletcher," I yell. "Becca!" I have to yell because we are next to a big mob of people waiting for a free keychain or something. She turns to me, stone-faced, and follows as we swim upstream and get out of the crowd to a relatively quiet spot, but not before I lose a strand of asparagus. People are brutal when it comes to free key chains.

"So?" Elisa is leaning over my shoulder, trying to read my phone.

"Just a minute." I get to my message menu, and click. "It says, 'Sux . . . no win. Hungry?' " I flip the phone closed. "So, that's that. At least we got some cool costumes out of it."

"We're not done yet!" Becca announces. "How could we not win? Our site was awesome. Nobody else had anything like we did—"

"How do you know?" Elisa has taken off the headset and is scratching the spandex neck of her costume. "Can I take this off now? I didn't like this idea from the beginning. I think I'm allergic."

"You could have said something, then," Becca says, on edge.

"How can anyone say anything when you just take over?" Elisa tries to stare Becca down, which is tough, because she only comes up to Becca's chest.

"Listen, if you don't like how I do things, then—"

"Shut up!" I hiss. Everyone stops and stares at me. "The bunny. The bunny man is following us again!" I subtly gesture with my asparagus hair toward a booth behind us.

We all freeze. Becca slowly turns her head, hoping not to be seen. But as she does this, the bunny man ambles up to us, establishing direct contact!

He (I'm assuming it's a he) is even taller than Becca, and with his ears, he is quite imposing. He towers over us, a menacing cloud of white fur with a little pink nose.

"Uh . . . hi." Becca extends a hand, trying to shake paws with it. The bunny man stands totally still, silent. "We . . . we like your costume."

Elisa and I instinctively cluster around Becca, just in case we have to defend her from the stranger. I think about what he could do in the middle of a big crowd: Throw deadly carrots? Use his powder-puff tail to suffocate us? But still, he's scary.

"So, we've noticed that you're sort of following us," Becca says, trying again to open lines of cottontail communication. No answer. "Okay then. Guess we'll be going. Nice to meet you."

As she turns toward us, the bunny man slips a note into her hand and walks away.

7

RABBIT DROPPINGS

(or Euphoria Bags a Boyfriend)

"What does it say?" Elisa stands on tiptoes trying to read the note.

Becca clutches the paper to her chest. "Would you just let me read it, and then I'll tell you?" She holds the note away from her face and squints at it, biting her lower lip in concentration. "Whoever it is, the person definitely doesn't want us to figure it out too easily."

Becca reads:

Sweet Mary Ann, I send you greetings from the rabbit hole.
And hope you have the fur and whiskers writhing in your soul.
More words to come I will impart to others, by and by,
A fan, some tea, a little cake, and oysters as they sigh.

We all stare silently at the note as if it will explode.

"What does *that* mean?" Elisa asks, grabbing the note as if she thinks Becca has made up the whole thing. "I think the rabbit ate carrots laced with LSD or something."

Becca's eyes sparkle. This is just her thing; she loves a good puzzle. I, however, think the whole thing smells like a prank. "Look, that guy must be somebody from school," I say reasonably. "I would almost bet that Fletcher put him up to that."

"Maybe not." Becca has taken possession of the letter and stares at it intently, as if her laser vision will somehow make a secret message appear that will tell her the meaning of life, the universe, and everything, including big sweaty guys in big sweaty rabbit suits. We have to table analysis of the mystery message for a while because it's time to meet Jon and Fletcher and Amber for some dinner. Through some complex text messages, we agree either to meet at the café in the exhibit hall or to fly to Paris for snails in butter sauce. It's hard to tell with text messages sometimes. We opt for the food court.

We get grub and somehow snag a table, which is a contact sport. After we get our delicious food (sarcasm there), we have to actually hover above an Asian family of four that seems to be lounging at the table without really eating anything. After being surrounded for five minutes by the Geektastic Four, the family scurries away in fear of a tasteless makeover.

"So, who won the contest?" Elisa asks as she chomps her way through a wilty salad.

"It was a group from Seattle, a bunch of hip-hop nerds who call themselves Grand Funk Spaceport," Jon answers. "They write lyrics to the *Star Wars* songs and then put it to a hip-hop beat. They wear costumes like the band in the Cantina from the first movie. You know, the buggy-looking aliens?" He's sharing a hoagie with Amber, trying to catch bites of the sandwich between hair flips. Becca glares as if she wants to zap a killer laser beam at the hoagie and all lips touching it.

Fletcher snatches one of my fried zucchini pieces. "Those aliens at the Cantina could not have even played their instruments. They had no lips." He leans over me and gives me a surprise peck. "Unlike you."

"Did anybody comment about our stuff at all?" Elisa snorts, disgusted. "I wore spandex for nothing. How humiliating."

Fletcher, who has laid off my food and is inhaling a bowl of lentil soup from a Greek food cart, says, "One guy thought Art-tastic was sexy."

"Oh, sure, but that was Jon." Elisa chuckles.

"No, it wasn't me." Jon realizes he put his foot in it, and checks Amber for her reaction. She's busy slurping up hoagie leftovers, so I guess she missed the whole sexy exchange, which is just as well.

Becca, who has elected to make her dinner a diet soda and a Mrs. Fields cookie, proudly displays her note. "I got a secret message from a giant rabbit."

"Sure you did." Fletcher arches an eyebrow at me. "A giant rabbit. Right."

"Seriously, she did." I feel I have to defend her because, after all, she *did* get a letter from a giant rabbit, and how often can a person really say that and mean it? "It's a cryptic poem."

"Let's see."

She hands him the crinkled paper, and he carefully unfolds it as if it might explode into a million face-shattering pieces. As he reads the poem, he mouths the words solemnly, as if he's reading the secret of resurrecting the dead and fashion-challenged. Finally, he folds it up and hands it back to her. "Guy's on crack."

"He's not on crack, you moron." Becca stuffs the note into her Smart-tastic bustier. "You don't deserve to read it anyway. Obviously, this guy has a sense of the mysterious, the twisted, the bizarre."

"Perfect for you." Elisa picks through the plastic salad container, looking for one last crouton, but doesn't match Becca's melting stare. "What? I'm just saying, he's a unique individual. I hope you two will be very happy in your hutch."

"I have to figure out what the poem means first." Becca replies.

We all decide to call it a day, and since Fletcher has his mom's van, he offers us all a ride. We change out of our Geektastic outfits too; the body paint is starting to smear and the asparagus dreadlocks are itchy. As we head for the bathroom, I, of course, have to call Dad to be sure it's okay that Fletcher gives me a ride.

"I don't know," he says. "Is he a responsible driver?"

"No, Dad. He frequently tries to hit pedestrians and police officers."

"Don't do that. I'm serious." He sighs deeply, as if to let me know that letting me get a ride home could be one of the biggest decisions of his life. "I guess it's okay. Can we talk later, though? I have some things I need to talk to you about."

"Oooh. That sounds ominous." I'm trying to be light and breezy on the phone, but it does, in fact, sound kind of scary. My imagination always flips out when he says stuff like that: I usually imagine scenarios that are much worse than reality. We need to talk about . . . what? Moving? Getting a kidney transplant? Sex-change operation?

Rather than pollute the phone lines with my paranoia, I just say, "Thanks, Dad. Be home soon." I flip my phone shut and catch up to the group. No one else has to call home, I notice. I think this is because my dad is especially protective of me. Ever since Mom died, he's gotten weirder every year about this; I think he's worried he'll lose me too. If he saw Fletcher drive, he might be even more concerned, but I'm not going to tell him that.

Stopping at the bathroom, we all detach ourselves from our spandex (Elisa is so happy she practically purrs) and get back into our old familiar jeans and T-shirts. I know at that point that I will never truly be a superhero. I can't dress the part, not long term.

When we get into the van, Becca dives into the back seat right after Jon, making sure that Amber can't sit next to him. I climb in the front seat; as girlfriend, I get to ride shotgun. It's one of those things in the unspoken dating code, I suppose. I'm not going to argue; I do not want to see a cat fight break out in the back seat. In that enclosed space, it might pack the equivalent power of a nuclear explosion in a tin lunch box.

Elisa parks herself in the third seat in the row, leaving Amber to sit in the third row back. Smoldering annoyance is radiating from back there. Elisa just seems amused, which doesn't surprise me. For some reason, she just loves conflict.

The back seat is eerily quiet. I fearfully glance back, and see Becca slowly, slowly moving her hand toward Jon's forearm. Danger! Danger! I have to do something . . . so I throw my Vege-tastic headpiece at her.

"Ow!" She yelps as a spike of plastic cauliflower pokes her in the shoulder. "Why did you do that?"

"Just slipped." I notice, though, that in her haste to defend herself against my clever assault, her hand has gone back to its rightful place.

The trip home is full of perilous almost-touches like that, and I have to try and deflect each one so a civil war doesn't erupt between the Queen Geeks. By the time we get to Becca's house, I've thrown everything at her except my boots. She jumps down from the van in frosty silence and huffs to the door, clearly angry.

"What's with her?" Fletcher asks as he steers back into traffic. "Who's next, by the way?"

Amber has moved to the seat next to Jon and they are much closer than he had been to Becca. Elisa puts her hand in the air. "I'll go next. This love fest is going to make me puke."

He drops her at her house, and that leaves us two couples in the car together. "So. What now?" Fletcher asks.

In the rearview mirror, I see Amber's hand is entwined in Jon's. "Maybe you guys could come over to my house. I'm sure Dad won't mind." Perhaps if I can keep an eye on them . . .

The two in the back don't even notice that my mouth is moving. Fletcher is humming some tune while he navigates onto the freeway. I'm just hoping we get to my house before they start face-hugging each other.

It's almost seven, and when we get to my house, Amber and Jon manage to get out of the car while still holding hands and I can feel the hormones pinging between them like radar signals. I try to get out of the car, but the handles of a plastic bag loop over the stick shift and stubbornly refuse to let go. Fletcher seems blissfully unaware that I'm stuck. He casually skips up the steps to my front door and opens it without knocking. "Hey," I call after him, tugging at the uncooperative bag. "Wait. Wait!"

Euphoria is programmed to be a nanny/domestic servant/policewoman. If someone breaks into our house (or opens the door without proper identification) she can take any measures necessary to insure the safety and stability of our home. This is bad at the moment; I know there are going to be some fireworks. And I'm right, of course.

Sirens scream from the porch; red lights undulate in waves across the swing. We all cover our ears, and as I stumble to the door (bag in tatters), Euphoria is there, tasering my boyfriend with an auxiliary claw she keeps hidden for special occasions.

With a yelp of pain Fletcher falls to the floor and crawls into the fetal position. "Are you all right?" I say as I crouch down beside him. "Do you know who I am?"

"You're the crazy woman who has a lethal droid for a pet." He rubs the part of his arm that was stunned by Euphoria's weapon. "Can we turn off the sirens, now that everyone in your neighborhood knows I'm a burglar or a rapist?"

"Euphoria, disengage." I key in a code on her back panel; the siren stops, the red light stops, and we're all left in traumatized silence. I help Fletcher to his feet. He flinches a little when we approach Euphoria.

"I'm terribly sorry," Euphoria says, sympathy in her voice. "I just didn't recognize you right away."

Jon brushes by us, carefully skirting the robot. "Geez. You don't believe in putting out the welcome mat, huh, Shelby?"

"Yeah," Amber says, scurrying after him. "Usually, if someone doesn't want you at their house, they just lock the door and hide behind the couch with the lights off. Could you guys do that next time?"

"You should probably let me go first anyway. That's just polite."

Euphoria is still reeling from her social blunder. "I just thought you were breaking into the house or something," she babbles. "I certainly don't make it a habit of injuring invited guests."

"So, as long as we're with you, she's cool, right?" Jon asks. He's still lurking behind Amber's tallness.

"Don't worry." I walk toward the TV room, and they all follow. "She wouldn't hurt anybody. That taser was only a mild shock."

"It was *not* mild," Fletcher says, wounded that I would downplay his injury.

"Where's Dad?" I ask as we plop on our sofas in front of the TV.

"He's out back." Euphoria trundles over to Fletcher. "Would you like something to drink, honey?"

"Sure. Whatever you have that's cold." He still leans away from her slightly.

"Diet cola okay?"

"Great."

Jon and Amber also are fine with diet cola, perhaps fearing a zap if they say they prefer lemon-lime. After Euphoria brings the drinks and two big bowls of popcorn, Fletcher says, "So? Now what?"

"What do you mean?" I ask. "Like, what should we do now? Watch a movie? Catch up on our reading?"

"No, no. I mean, now that the website thing is defunct, what are you going to do now? What's your new mission?"

Amber and I just look at each other. It's kind of weird not having Becca here. She always speaks for the Queen Geeks; in fact, when I think about it, no one ever asks me policy questions. So, I'm kind of at a loss. What *are* we going to do?

"It kind of seems like a shame to waste these great costumes and the website," Amber says, her comment trailing off into the land of unfinished lines designed to keep a prospective boyfriend nearby. "Maybe there's something we could do with them."

Jon shifts in his seat and casually puts his arm around Amber. Not good. As Becca's friend, I feel an obligation to try and thwart physical contact, at least when I'm in the room. I know Becca is going to grill me on what happened, and I cannot lie to her. I do a very juvenile thing: I throw popcorn at Amber's head. I have to really analyze this sometime; I seem to throw something at somebody whenever things get uncomfortable. Probably some deep, psychotic tendency there.

In this case, it sort of works, because she flinches and moves back to wipe salt and butter from her eye. "Why'd you do that?" she asks crossly. "I'm going to use your bathroom. I think that stuff's all over my eye makeup."

"I'll show you." I hop up, leaving the guys alone, and lead Amber down the hallway. "Listen, while we're alone, I wanted to ask you a favor." I stop at the bathroom door.

"What?" By the tone of her voice, I think she knows what I'm going to ask.

"Well . . . could you kind of cool it with Jon? I know it's not a fair request—"

"No, it's really not." She opens the bathroom door and turns toward me. "I know Becca still has a thing for him, but he is not into her. Doesn't she see that?"

She's right, of course. I don't know how to defend it. "She just wants what she wants. She's not used to being told 'no,' I guess."

"Well, maybe it's time she started to get used to it." Amber closes the door in my face. Yes, that went well.

"Okay, well, then I guess you can find your way back," I shout a bit too loudly as I shuffle back to the living room. The guys are engaged in a lively conversation about the Sith Lords (what is it with *Star Wars*?) and wondering if the face paint on some of the Sith Lords is actually a mutation brought about by evil or if it's just a genetic thing, like freckles. They really have too much time on their hands.

"So, back to my original question," Fletcher says, completely ditching the Dark Lord freckle discussion. "What is your club going to do now?"

"I don't know." I'm sick of talking about the club, honestly. Okay, to be more honest, I'm sick of talking about the club with Jon and Fletcher. I keep feeling like they're trying to insinuate themselves into our inner circle, like they're spies from the other side looking for organizing tips or fashion advice. But that's sort of stupid, huh? I mean, they're just interested because *we're* interested. Right?

"Anybody home?" Fletcher taps lightly on my skull.

"Sort of." The sliding glass door whooshes open in the front room; I hear Dad stumbling over something and uttering a mild curse. If there's something lying in his path, he will instinctually fall over it. "Hey, Dad!" I call, a bit too loudly.

He pops into the living room. "Hi, everybody. How was the Comic-Con?"

"Great." I watch as my friends look awkwardly at each other. Nobody likes to give too many details to dads. It seems like the larger the group, the more uncomfortable everybody is. Is this because nobody wants to look like a suck-up? I don't know. I'm just the observer. I can't explain the behavior. "We had a blast. Our costumes were a big hit."

"Yeah, it was all great until I got tasered," Fletcher adds. Dad arches an eyebrow and looks to me for explanation.

"Not at Comic-Con, Dad. It was Euphoria."

The look on his face goes from worried to freaked out. "Oh my God. She tasered *you*? She's only supposed to do that to people breaking into the house without authorized entry!"

"He actually just walked in ahead of me, that's all." I put a hand on my dad's forearm. "Nothing to worry about. Fletcher's not going to sue us. Are you, Fletcher?"

He tosses a handful of popcorn into his mouth. "Only if you break up with me."

"Break up?" Dad asks, then parks himself on the couch next to Fletcher. "That implies there's something *to* break up."

With my dad staring at him, Fletcher suddenly seems a bit less brave. "Uh, well, I just mean that we're dating. Nothing serious. Really, nothing serious at all."

"Gee, thanks." I pick up the TV remote. "Maybe I'll just call Euphoria in here and have her taser you again."

"No. No! That's okay." He turns to my dad and takes his hand, which looks really hilarious. "Mr. Chapelle, I want to come clean with you. Your daughter and I . . . well . . ." He looks over at me. I have no idea what he's going to say, but I hope it won't get me grounded, killed, or sent to a girl's boarding school. "Shelby and I have . . . eaten together."

Dad nods with that yeah-you-got-me face, and gets up. "Okay. I see I'm not wanted here." Turning to me, he says, "Can we talk later?"

There's that sinking feeling again. He's mentioned it twice, so it must be serious. I just nod and he walks out of the room, leaving me with the hormone twins, my boyfriend, and acute paranoia.

8

PLEASE, NOT THE TALK!

(or Some Bunny Loves Me)

We hang around for about an hour, talking about nothing. Fletcher doesn't bring up the club again, which is just as well. He and Amber and Jon take off eventually, leaving me with that yawning chasm of a conversation with my dad.

I try to sneak off to bed without him noticing, but he hovers in his den, just waiting for me to be alone, kind of like a parental stalker. "Hey, Shelby. Are all your friends gone?"

"Yep." I do that big fake yawn thing, hoping to avoid the conversation. "Boy, I'm tired. I think I'll just get to bed."

"Oh." He sounds so disappointed. Rats! Why does my dad have to do the puppy-dog eyes so well?

I say, "Why? Do you need something?" As soon as the words fly from my lips, my internal alarm system starts whining, revving up for a major panic attack.

Dad puts his arm around my shoulders and walks me toward the living room. "I just wanted to hear about your day."

Yeah, right. Just wants to hear about my day? Boy, that's lame. "Oh, it was okay. We had a good time. We didn't win the website competition, and my headpiece kept poking strangers in the neck and upper body, but otherwise, it was pretty fun. I got to see—"

We've reached the sofa, so he gently guides me to sit next to him. Bad news. "Sounds fun." He leans against the pillows and just stares at me.

"What is up with you, Dad?"

He bites the inside of his cheek, a bad habit that I do too when I'm nervous. "I want to talk about Fletcher." He looks like he just pulled off a really painful Band-Aid from a really scabby wound.

"Oh. Is that all?"

He leans forward suddenly and takes my hand. "Honey . . . I just want to be sure you're . . . safe."

Oh no. Please. Not this. Not my dad trying to talk to me about sex. Anything but that.

I feel myself blushing violently. "Oh, Dad. You don't have to worry about that—"

"Now, hear me out." He nods his head in what I guess he believes is a real paternal way, but he looks like one of those birds that dips its head into a cocktail and then flips back out. "You don't have to tell me anything. I just want to tell you some facts. Did you know that for every baby born to a mother under sixteen—"

"For God's sake, Dad!" I jump off the couch as if he put a bottle rocket under my butt. "I do not want to have this conversation!"

"Shelby. Sit down right now." He still has that dadlike tone that means I must obey him, so I sit. "You're just too young to have a child."

"Dad, I'd actually have to have sex to have a child, and I'm not having sex. End of story."

"But, honey, I was a teenage boy. I know how they think. Right now you say that you're not interested, but when you're in the heat of the moment—"

I cannot stand it another minute. I feel like my skin is blistering off my body, that hot oil has been poured in my ears and is draining to my kneecaps. I run screaming, literally, dash down the hall to my room, slam the door, and lock it from the inside. I stand against the door in the dark and listen for him; he doesn't follow me.

"Well, that went well." Euphoria is parked in her usual spot, recharging in my room. Her green lights blink on, off, on, off. "Why were you screaming?"

"You wouldn't understand." In the dark, I rummage through my drawer and pull out my oldest, least attractive nightgown to wear to bed. I feel sort of unclean, like I can never wear anything even remotely sexy again.

"Let me guess." She whirs confidently. "Your father wanted to talk to you about the birds and the bees."

"Do you even know what the birds and bees are?" Frustrated, I plop down on my bed and pull the covers up to my chin.

"I'm pretty well read. Plus, your father told me what he wanted to talk to you about. Why are you crying, Shelby?"

I am, indeed, crying. I really don't know why; sometimes I just do that. Euphoria, being a robot, doesn't really understand emotions that much, so it kind of confuses her. The closest thing in her experience is a fluid leak.

"Are you crying because your father was insensitive?" Her red lights now start to blink rapidly. "If he was, I'll give him a talking to. And maybe a taser."

I laugh in spite of myself. "No, no tasering necessary. He just wanted to talk about it."

"Why does that bother you?"

Why does it bother me? A good question. A very good question. I do not have a good answer. "I don't know. I want to go to sleep now."

"Hmmm." She turns on her music function and starts to play a sweet Irish lullaby with no words, no thoughts. Perfect for me at that moment. I lay on my bed and as I drift off to sleep, my pillow is wet and I'm exhausted.

I am awakened the next morning by the phone. Euphoria is nowhere in sight, so I have to answer it myself. How rude. "Hello?" I croak.

"You will never believe this." It's Becca. Of course.

"What will I never believe?" I stifle a yawn and notice the black streaks on my pillowcase. That's going to leave a stain. . . . Euphoria will be really pissed.

"I found a note on my front door this morning."

"Yeah?" The black streaks sort of form a pattern, kind of a Chinese I-Ching symbol or a rune or something. Maybe I should look it up—

"Are you listening to me?"

"Yes," I lie.

She sighs heavily. "You really need to get more sleep. Was Fletcher keeping you up all night?"

"Please. Let's talk about you." I know that's a favorite subject, so it shouldn't be that hard to get her to focus on that instead of me and my love life. "What was posted on your front door? A bloody handprint? A notice from the health department? What?"

"It was a letter." She pauses for dramatic effect. "From the bunny man."

I don't immediately remember the bunny man, I must admit. I search my brain database for references to bunnies, and all I come up with are Playboy bunnies, Easter bunnies, and Bugs Bunny. I can't imagine why any of these three would leave a note on Becca's front door.

She's impatient, though, so she explains: "The bunny man from the Comic-Con! He left me another poem."

Ah, yes. The rhyming rabbit. "And is it any more clear than the other one?"

"Not really." She clears her throat and I can tell by the in-flection (and yes, you can have an inflection when clearing your throat) that she wants me to invite myself over. But in-stead of doing that, I just hang silently on the phone. She says, "So . . . I guess I'll let you go."

My previous day has made me sort of cranky. In fact, it would probably be good if I talked with her about the whole

Dad/sex conversation and Fletcher and Jon and Amber. "Can Thea come and pick me up? I'll come over. Or you can come over here. But I'd rather come to your place. Dad and I had some weirdness last night."

"Let me check." She covers the receiver loosely with her hand, I know, because I can hear her screaming for her mom. "Thea! Thea! Where *are* you? Crap. She's never around when you need her." She uncovers the phone and says, "I can't find her at the moment. She's probably getting a green tea massage or something. I'll call you back." Click.

I grab the portable phone and wander into the kitchen, praying I won't run into Dad. If I have to talk about sex before I eat anything, I'll probably have the dry heaves. Luckily, only Euphoria is there, putting dishes away. "Good morning, Shelby."

"Hi, Euphoria." I grab a bowl and blindly pour some Golden Grahams into it, followed by skim milk. "Is there coffee?"

"You shouldn't drink coffee." She pours me half a cup anyway.

"Lots of stuff I shouldn't do, I suppose." I sip it; it is good. "Where's Dad?"

"He left early. Said he had to go into the office for something. But I can tell you, he seemed awfully worried about you. His blood pressure was high all night."

"I don't want to go into it." She whirs disappointedly. "Oh, don't be like that. I'm just tired, and I don't want to rehash the same discussion."

"You're going to Becca's house?"

"Have you been listening to my conversations again?" I pour more coffee, just to spite her.

"No. I just deduced it using good, old-fashioned logic." She finishes putting the dishes away, rolls over to me, and pats my hand.

Becca calls back and tells me that Thea is, indeed, coming over to pick me up. "But try to be ready when she gets there," she says, annoyed. "She's right in the middle of some mud sculpture, and if it dries too much, her work is ruined." She says the last part with a fake English accent.

"You're so mean about Thea's work." I pull on a pair of shorts while trying to balance the phone under my chin.

"I think her 'work' is a travesty against art. Remember last year's vegetable mosaic? That got trashed in the *L.A. Times*. They said it looked like a windshield repair truck crashed into the Farmer's Market."

"I still think you could be a little nicer. Anyway, I'll wash up and wait on the porch."

I grab my stuff (iPod, cell, bag, perfume) and take up my position on the swing. It's a warm morning, not too hot, with a breeze floating the smell of roses through the air. Mom used to love roses. She'd come outside and dig around their roots and cut off the dead parts so carefully. . . . What's strange is that when I sit down for a minute and think about her, I can't see her face in my memories. I see her hands. Her hands were always kind of red, from gardening or washing dishes (she did them by hand all the time, Dad says.) And she had a ring on one finger, a little gold ring that looked like a four-leaf clover with hollowed-out leaves, with a tiny diamond in the middle. I can see that ring whenever I think of her; Dad has it stowed in a safe place in anticipation of the magical day when I get old enough to "wear it responsibly."

I let my thoughts just kind of drift on the rose-scented air for a while, and close my eyes. I guess I fall asleep, because the next thing I know Thea is in my driveway in her Jeep, honking like the zombies are after her brain.

"Hurry, Shelby!" She waves frantically at me from the driver's seat. "I've got mud that's drying out!"

"I know, I know." I climb in and before I can even fasten my seat belt, she's peeling out down the driveway. That mud must be something special.

Once we get to Becca's, Thea bolts from the car, barely turning off the engine, and I get out a little more slowly. Becca comes running outside in her jammies waving what I presume to be the mystery poem.

She is so excited she's jumping a bit, sloshing coffee all over her well-tended lawn. "I need your help. I want to decode these things."

"Is it possible that it's just a prank? Somebody trying to get you all excited about nothing?"

She looks deflated. "Why would someone do that?"

"We've done it to other people, so why do *we* do it?" I say.

She cocks her head to one side like a puppy listening for a car, and thinks for a moment. "We've never done anything intentionally mean, though. Making me think that there's a mysterious man out there who likes me—"

"A mysterious *creature*. We cannot assume he's a man."

She snorts in annoyance. "Fine, a creature. A living, breathing something. Making me think that when there's no one really there is just mean. I just don't think that's what's going on. But let's go in the house. You probably want coffee."

"I do. Euphoria would only give me half a cup."

"Now *that's* mean."

Becca leads me to her kitchen, where a stack of books is piled on the glass-topped table and an intense reading light is focused on the note as if it's a criminal waiting to be interrogated.

"Wow. You are taking this seriously, aren't you?" I slide into a chair and pick up a few of the books, and check out the titles. "*The Annotated Alice. Wonderland Revealed. Poems of Lewis Carroll.* So, is this your summer project?"

She brings a bowl of Golden Grahams to the table, no milk, and digs into it with a spoon. "Want some?"

"Already had. Thanks. As I was saying, is this your summer project?"

She crunches loudly, making a face to tell me that she'd answer, but she has too much food in her mouth. Finally, she replies: "Not a summer project, really. Just kind of interesting."

"Well, you're spending an awful lot of time thinking about this guy. What happened to your undying love for Jon?"

She shakes her head sadly. "I'm afraid I have to admit defeat, Shelby. He is clearly into Amber."

"You're going to admit defeat." I cross my arms and give her my best I-don't-think-so stare.

"Sure, why not?" While munching her cereal, Becca squints at the letter. "Realistically, I don't have a shot at Jon. He couldn't care less about me."

"So why did you keep trying to touch him in the car yesterday?"

Her head snaps up, and her eyes are blazing. "What?"

"I was sitting in front. I saw you trying to touch his arm."

"I was not!"

"Okay, okay." I don't know why she's in such denial about this crush thing. It's sort of unlike her, really; she's usually brutally honest when it comes to self-evaluation. I make a mental note to keep a close eye on the Jon situation. "Let's have a look at the poem."

The handwriting is the same as what I remember on the other note, and the poem is written in basically the same style. Out loud, I read:

> 'Twas Brillig and the slithy toves,
> Were walking at the Comic-Con.
> All radiant wherever Becca goes,
> This bunny wants to be the one.

My evaluation? "That is some pretty crappy poetry."

Becca is biting her fingernails, and she wrinkles her nose at me. "Yeah, it is pretty bad, huh? Maybe the guy is just too in love to think straight."

"Well, it's obvious that it's got something to do with *Alice in Wonderland*, which I see you've already figured out," I say, pointing to the stack of books. "I guess I'd be wondering how this guy knows that you are an *Alice in Wonderland* fanatic. Doesn't that fact creep you out just a little bit?"

Becca clearly hasn't thought of that angle. She blinks a bit, bewildered.

We both stare at the stack of books, trying to puzzle out how some big lug in a rabbit suit would possibly know about this small detail, and I personally am a little big dismayed that he might have Google-stalked Becca.

Becca laughs, relieved. "Oh, I know! It's my MySpace. I have the whole thing done with Alice pictures and quotes. I totally forgot."

I'm secretly kind of relieved about that. At least the rabbit guy isn't some secret agent with super spying capabilities. I hope. "Well, good. Mystery solved. Beyond that, I don't think there's any secret message or anything. It's just kind of crappy poetry by a crush-struck guy in a rabbit suit."

"Right." Becca leans forward, eyes glowing with excitement. "But maybe there's a code hidden in there, some first-letter-of-each-word kind of code or something, to give me a hint about where to meet him."

This girl is desperate, I realize. I don't even know what to say. Becca has always been the one who just barely noticed guys, and she certainly never let them run her life. But here she is, obsessing over somebody she's never even met, and crushing over some guy who's dating her friend. It's kind of incomprehensible. "A code, huh?" I pick up a piece of paper and a pencil and begin writing down the first letter of each word.

"*T, b, a, t, s, t* is the first line. Unless he speaks Russian, I don't think it's relevant."

"No, no." She grabs the paper and pencil from me. "It could be scrambled ... *b, a, t, s,* that's bats ... and the double *t*s could be . . . for tee-tee. Tee-tee bats!" she whispers excitedly.

"Or titty bats!" I whisper back.

"You're not taking this seriously." She looks wounded.

"You just tried to make sense of titty bats. How seriously can I take it?"

She throws the pencil onto the table. "Why are you being so difficult about this? I just want to find out what the letter means!"

"It means some guy likes you, and he's too shy to tell you, and like many guys throughout the history of the world, he's written you a crappy poem to express his interest. End of story." I hear my own voice getting louder, more pointed. Why am I angry with her?

"It's all very well for you; you have a boyfriend."

"What does that have to do with anything?"

She stands, hands on hips, lips pursed tightly. We're at some impasse, I guess; it's been building up since summer started. She sighs and flops into a chair like a deflated balloon, throwing the letter to the floor as she sits. "Everybody is hooking up, and I'm just left here alone, living with Thea and her mud sculptures."

"You're jealous of me? And of Amber?"

"No, not jealous." She picks up one of the books from the table and thumbs through it as if she's looking for something very important. I think she's just distracting herself. "Last year, before Fletcher, you and I were together all the time. We did all kinds of stuff, and then we met Amber and Elisa, and the whole club thing happened . . . but now it's almost like we all walked through some big looking glass and we're on the other side, where everything isn't as it seems."

"I don't know what you mean."

"And that's the problem right there." She puts the book down forcefully on the table. "Last year, you would have understood. Now, it's all hormones all the time with you."

"All hormones! Who was the one telling me I wasn't giving Fletcher a fair chance, huh? Who was always telling me I was afraid of commitment and all that? And now that I am actually spending time with him, you're mad about it! How is that fair?"

She looks down at her knees, and I'm afraid she might actually cry. I don't think I've ever seen her cry. I can't believe I said those things to my best friend. I am the worst person in the history of bad people. She looks up at me, chin quivering, and says, "Titty bats."

We both laugh so hard tears run down our faces. Then we both start chanting, "titty bats, titty bats," until we get so loud that Thea comes storming in, covered in red clay mud up to her elbows.

"What is going on in here?" she yells. "I'm trying to create! I can hear you in my studio, for goddess' sake. Can you keep it down?"

Becca's reply is, of course, "Titty bats."

Thea throws her arms up in the air, growls in frustration, and stomps back, presumably to continue wallowing in high art.

The laughing dies down, and I feel much better, all in all. Becca comes over, puts an arm around my shoulders, and sways with me for a moment. "Sorry."

"For what?"

"For being stupid. You're right. I shouldn't be obsessing about guys, mine or yours, or ones we don't know yet. I don't know what's going on with me."

"We need a project," I say, hugging her as I let go.

"Definitely." She scoops the books off the table and picks up the discarded letter from the floor. "But I'm still curious about the bunny man."

9

BACK TO SCHOOL

(or August, the Cruelest Month of All)

It's August, and sitting on my bed one day, Becca screams and jumps up as if she's been scalded by hot oil. "Oh, God!"

"What?" I'm checking my room for deadly snakes or invisible animated voodoo dolls, but see nothing. "Why are you screaming?"

"Look at this!" She rips my Tolkien calendar (present from my dad for Christmas) from my wall. "We only have two weeks before school starts. Two weeks!"

"No." I check it and, sadly, verify that she's right. "How is that possible? We just started summer vacation!"

But it is true. The last two weeks slip like sand through our fingers. As hard as we try to stop it, the night before the first day of sophomore year arrives like a big, black storm cloud hovering over us, threatening to rain down pigeon poop on our beautiful sleek summer.

The four of us get together for supper at my house (pizza on the floor), and Dad wants in on the dismal depression so he hangs out with us.

"Will eating this much fat send me into a coma that will last til Thanksgiving?" Elisa asks as she stuffs yet another piece of veggie pizza into her mouth. I think she ate half the large pie all by herself.

Dad reaches over from the couch and snags a piece for himself. "I don't know why you girls are so upset about going back to school. I thought you liked school."

"Dad, it doesn't matter if you like school or not. Nobody wants to go back, even if they like it."

"Why not?" He squints at us, puzzled. How can you explain it to somebody who hasn't been in school for years?

Becca wipes sauce from her chin and gestures emphatically. "It's the freedom, Mr. Chapelle. It's not so much school, it's just anything."

"Exactly," Elisa adds. "I mean, if I *had* to go see a Johnny Depp movie every day, it wouldn't be fun." She considers this for a minute. "Okay, well, maybe that would be fun. But school? No."

Amber, who has been uncharacteristically quiet even for her, weighs in. "Actually, I'm sort of looking forward to school this year."

Elisa throws a dirty napkin at her. "That's only because of your *boyfriend*." She says it like it's a dirty word. "You probably scheduled all your electives together too." Amber blushes violently and concentrates extra hard on her pizza crust.

"Well," Dad says, yawning, "you girls had better mop up here, and then get going. You'll need your sleep for tomorrow."

"Oh, uh, Dad?"

"Hmm?"

"Can you give everybody a ride home?" I smile my brightest, cheeriest, perfect daughter smile at him. "Please?"

"And can we stop for ice cream, Dad? Huh?" Becca runs over to him and gives him a hug.

He smiles and shakes his head, defeated. "I'm a sucker for a pretty face. Or pretty faces, I should say. Sure, we can go get ice cream. And yes, I can take everybody home. It's the least I can do in preparation for tomorrow's impending doom, right?"

Euphoria rolls in to clean up the pizza remains. "Where are y'all going?" she asks as she vacuums crumbs silently off the floor.

"Ice cream!" Becca shoves her paper plate into Euphoria's trash compartment. "I wish you could taste it, Euphoria. It's one of the wonders of the world!"

"I'm sure it's fantastic, but food gives me repeating data strings." She hums a tune as we file out of the living room behind my dad like a bunch of hungry ducklings.

We pull into the Whippy Dip at seven, and the line is pretty long. It's a cool drive-through place all decorated with rainbow umbrellas over the tables. The nerve center is a little expanded shed that's painted to look like a red barn. The line of cars to go through the carryout part is about ten cars long, so Dad parks on the street and we all skip up to the walk-up line.

"Mmmm. What to choose?" Elisa licks her lips and studies the poster for the Caramel Turtle Explosion as if she's checking out a painting at the art museum.

We still have to wait for a while, but it's a nice evening, cool for a change. Dad puts an arm around my shoulders while the other girls babble about who they have for which classes, and how much they hate getting up in the morning. "So, you ready for tomorrow?"

"I don't know." I lean into him, and I enjoy the safe feeling of just hanging there for a minute. "I think maybe this year will be harder than last year."

"Well, if it's not harder, what's the point of going?" Elisa pipes up.

"Oh, I don't know. Less stress, more fun," Becca says, stretching lazily, arms reaching toward the wispy clouds.

"Aren't we going to try to change the world again this year?" Amber jokes. Becca abruptly shifts into high alert.

"We have a whole year this time," she says excitedly. "Think of the possibilities!"

I groan. "I don't want to think, period." It's our turn to order, so we all get buckets of ice cream topped with gooey fudge or caramel, and Dad even orders a cone. There's one table open, so Becca snags it and we all crowd under the rainbow umbrella to lick the drips from our ice cream and eat it before it melts altogether.

"So," Dad says between slurps of ice cream, "I assume your little club is still in existence?"

"Our 'little club,' Mr. Chapelle?" Becca says teasingly. "Queen Geeks is most certainly still going. And we will be doing even bigger and better stuff this year, right, ladies?"

"Like what?" Amber asks as she dangles a string of caramel from her spoon and wraps it around so she can get more into her mouth at once.

"We should keep the website up," Elisa says. "It was good, even if I didn't like the spandex."

"No more dances, that's all I ask," Amber says, shaking her head. "That was a lot of work, and I didn't get to get my groove on as much as I wanted."

"Get your groove on?" Becca throws her a disdainful look. "I didn't know you *had* a groove, Amber."

"Maybe you should get a barn and put on a show," Dad says innocently, not realizing how such a comment could fuel a frenzy of obsessive work for me. But it's too late. The genie is out of the bottle, so to speak, and I see by Becca's crazed expression that she's already started to calculate the exponential worth of a geek showcase.

"Yes!" she screams, gesturing with her spoon so violently that she flings whipped cream at Amber. "A geek show. Perfect. That would be a hoot! And we could charge admission, and use the money for . . . for . . ."

"Ice cream?" Elisa asks hopefully.

"Charity work?" Amber says.

"World domination?" I suggest.

"Well, something. But it could be a geek talent show, with all the geeky people bringing their weird talents to the stage. We could get the drama department to help too."

"They're already a bunch of geeks," Amber points out.

"True." Becca nods. "Maybe we could get a band too, somebody really popular but geeky."

"Are there any popular bands that are geeky?" I ask. Here's my thought on this big celebration of geekiness: I think we should just do something a little less big. Last year, we took over the spring dance, and that was a lot of fun, but a huge amount of work and stress. I thought maybe the website and Comic-Con would have purged Becca's system of the need to make an ostentatious spectacle of herself, but as usual, I am wrong. Ironically, I cannot tell her this, even though she's my best friend. Resistance is futile. So I'm stuck trying to keep my head down and minimize any damage to my ego, immune system, and grade point average.

Dad just laughs at us, which is his usual reaction to our wild schemes. "Well, if you need help with the lighting or robotics, let me know," he says casually, not comprehending the impact this statement will have on his life for the next few months. I understand the impact, because I know from experience that when somebody casually offers something to Becca, she takes it, and then some.

"Really, Mr. Chapelle?" she squeaks endearingly. It's one of her weapons. "You'd help us with lighting?"

"And robotics?" Elisa arches an eyebrow and nods. "Might work. With lights and robotics and geeky bands, we might be on to something. I don't think anyone would pay a dime to see me on stage, but Euphoria? That's another story."

"Oh, not Euphoria," I chime in. "That would be a bad idea."

"Why?" Becca grabs my arm. "It would be so cool. We could teach her to rap or something. Can you imagine?"

"But she's not really built to do that sort of thing," I say lamely, knowing it won't matter.

"Oh, I could make some adaptations to her programming," Dad says, leaning forward intently. "It wouldn't be that difficult."

"Our ice cream is all melted," I say. It is too. And with it, all my hopes of a normal school year, apparently.

My alarm goes off; it is still dark. Something is terribly, terribly wrong.

Oh, never mind. It's just the first day of school.

"Good morning, Shelby," Euphoria chirps. She starts playing the Beatles song of the same title, which is way too perky for me.

"Please." I groan, covering my head with my pillow. "Pretend I don't exist."

"Too late," she says, grabbing my covers with her claw and yanking them over my head. "Best to just hop out of bed and get going."

I do understand her logic, of course; it's best to just do something unpleasant as quickly as possible. After a shower and a cup of coffee (and a huge dollop of Euphoria's disapproval with the coffee), I navigate back to my room to be sure my clothes are okay. First-day-of-school clothes are always significant, even for geeks; it's your way of letting new people know what you're all about (as much as you can within the confines of preshrunk cotton and fake leather). For this first day of my sophomore year, I've chosen a red-and-black plaid mini (not too short), black nylon knee socks, my red-and-black tennies, a red cotton camisole, and a black gauzy overshirt, short-sleeved. Hair? Brushed, and that's as good as it gets on the first day. Luckily, I have great hair.

Dad bursts into my room without knocking. "Time to go, honey." He checks his watch, puts it to his ear, then bangs it against the wall. "I've got to work on this thing again. It didn't go off when I programmed it to beep."

"Maybe if you quit banging it against the wall . . ." I say as I contort my face and apply makeup.

"Shelby, do you really have to wear makeup to school? Does it matter what you look like?" He puts his hand on my shoulder and looks at my image in the mirror. "When you scrunch up your face like that, it really doesn't do much for you."

"Yeah, Dad, I'm going to go around school all day with my face like this." I turn around and give him a Bride of Frankenstein expression that would scare any ordinary person. My dad, of course, is not in any way ordinary.

"Yeah, that's attractive, keep doing that. All year, especially in front of boys."

I finish with a quick gloss of lipstick and turn. "Ta-da!" I do a quick spin for Dad. "I present to you, a high school sophomore!"

He groans and whacks himself in the forehead. "No! It's too soon!" We both laugh, and then the laugh kind of fades to smiles, and then Dad is hugging me a little too hard. "Hope you have a good first day of school."

"I will." He doesn't let go. "What's up, Dad? You're cutting off the circulation."

"Oh. Sorry." He releases me from his bear hug. "You just look so grown up. Last year you didn't look like that."

"Yeah, well, I'm older." I grab my backpack, which is blessedly empty, and give Dad an overly bright grin. "Okay, so, see you later! Will you be home?"

"I think so." He looks distracted, so I know something is up.

I kiss him on the cheek and pat his shoulder. "Okay, whatever it is, we'll talk when I get home."

He laughs again. "You sound like me!"

"Well," I say as I dash out the door, "I've learned interrogation techniques from the best!"

Walking to school sucks. Even with my iPod, it takes too long, and I know that when I do get to school, I'll be all sweaty, which is partly my fault because I'm wearing black in Southern California in August. It gives me time to think, though, which is good and bad. I think too much, really, so when I do have time with nothing else to do, thoughts jump around in my brain like popcorn in a hot pan, and sometimes they run into each other and cause an explosion that gives me a headache.

For example, I'm thinking about Fletcher as I walk to school. Images of him kissing me float in front of my eyes, and then his smile, and the feeling of his arm around me, and then those thoughts crash headlong into thoughts of Becca and the club, and about how I shouldn't be letting a guy dominate my thoughts. But when you think about something that you think you shouldn't be thinking about, you just think of it more intently. And that's why I'm always so confused.

One good thing: Time flies quickly when you tie yourself in mental knots, and so I'm at school before you know it. Green Pines has about 2,400 students, so on the first day the campus kind of resembles a rolling, green pasture full of blue-jeaned cattle grazing on Starbucks and cinnamon rolls. Everybody is waiting for their schedules, and the freshmen look especially bewildered. I wonder if I looked like that last year? Naw. I'm too cool for that, right?

We always meet at the Rock, a big boulder sitting in the middle of the lawn near the school's theater. Amber is already there, perched on top like nature's hood ornament, reading a book. "Hey," I call, waving to her.

"Hi, Shelby. What's up? Nice shoes." She closes the book, which looks suspiciously like a literature text.

"You're not doing homework already?"

"Yeah." She slides off the rock and tucks the book back into her pack. "Honors English. We had summer reading to do. At least it's Edgar Allan Poe. I love his stuff, all about death and crazy birds. Did you know he took opium?"

"I didn't know that." Amber, as it turns out, has taken a little too much Poe, and she's dressed in black (all black, as opposed to my outfit), including a long black trench coat with buckles from neck to knee. Her makeup is different too; it used to be pretty natural looking, but today she has wide black streaks across her eyes, and it makes her look a little like Cleopatra. If Cleopatra wore combat boots, I mean.

"Aren't you hot?" I touch the sleeve of the coat. She subtly moves away, just a step.

"No." She swings her long dark hair behind her. "It's actually not too bad."

"I've never seen that coat before."

"Oh," she says, smiling. "It's Jon's."

As if on cue, Becca runs up like a platinum-blond puppy just taken off the leash. "Hey, hey, hey, Queen Geeks!" She jumps up and down, the little spikes of her hair never moving. In honor of the first day of school, she has electric blue tips on the ends. It's one of our school colors. "I'm am so pumped about school this year. I have just been bursting with ideas! I was up all night thinking about GeekFest."

Amber and I shoot each other quizzical expressions. With her eye makeup, her quizzical expression looks like a caterpillar doing the hula. "GeekFest?" we say in unison.

Elisa pokes her face in between me and Amber. "Did someone say GeekFest? Is that like a Warped Tour for pencil pushers?"

"No." Becca waves her hands spastically. "It's just a fantastic idea I had. Actually, *we* had. Remember how we were talking about it last night, at the Whippy Dip?"

"I'm trying to forget." Elisa groans as she tries (and fails) to climb up on the boulder. "Anyway, the last thing I want to do is display my inherent geekiness to the world on a stage. It's one thing to do stuff behind the scenes, but we're talking potential full-scale humiliation here. I, for one, vote no."

Becca shoots her a withering look. "Fine. We can discuss it some more."

"Is that what I said?" Elisa looks at me, bewildered. "How does she mistranslate everything I say? Oh, and Amber, what's with the G.I. Joe trench coat? Are you plotting a takeover of the girls' bathroom or something?"

Amber just sniffs and looks the other way. "We'd better get our schedules." She starts walking toward the long line of tables staffed with harried counselors, and we follow.

"That was a great start to the year," Elisa mumbles to me as we follow in Becca's obviously pissed-off wake.

I go through my morning in sort of a fog. Period one, World History; period two, Tech Fundamentals; period three, English; period four, math. Honestly, I don't track anything anyone is saying because in each class it's just a course outline, class rules, and a seating chart. The first day, as I believe I said before, sucks. And Fletcher isn't in any of my classes, although Becca is in my period five P.E. class (right after lunch! Have they no mercy?!). Period six is Home Ec, or Home Ick, as I call it. Why do I need Home Ick if I have a robot to do my domestic bidding?

Lunchtime finally arrives after an agonizing morning of lectures and sleepiness. (And I *like* school, really; I can just imagine how utterly hideous it must be for the kids who really hate learning anything.) Last year our traditional lunch spot was under this little sapling tree near the English building, but it looks as if some seniors have confiscated it this year, so I just sort of hover around the general area waiting for somebody to show up.

Fletcher and I didn't really have lunch together much last year; we only started really being interested in each other right at the end. So I'm sort of surprised when he is the first to arrive.

"Hey," he says, pecking me on the cheek. "Did you bring lunch, or are you going to brave the line?"

I wave my blue nylon thermal bag at him. "I try not to eat the food here. I have a theory that they're trying to neutralize the brain cells we do have with trans fats and animal byproducts."

"You sound like one of those conspiracy theorists." He plops down under the sapling, totally ignoring the senior girls who are standing on the other side of it. They don't ignore him, though. They shoot him looks that would kill another girl, but since he's a guy, he ignores them. They look at me like I should be able to get him to move, but I decide to pretend I don't get it, and I plop down next to him. The girls drift away, sending nasty vibes washing back on us like a rancid outgoing tide.

Fletcher leans against the sapling and sighs contentedly. "Ah, it's good to be back, huh?"

"Are you high?" I unpack my peanut butter sandwich on sprouted whole wheat bread and take a chomp. I am starving. "It's so *not* good to be back."

"Aren't you thirsting for knowledge?"

"I'm thirsting for coffee, and if the barbarians that ran this place had any smidgen of human kindness, they'd provide it."

"Hey," Becca says cheerily as she joins us under the tree. She's dining on the famous Green Pines vegetarian jalapeno nachos today, guaranteed to rot even the strongest of stomachs. "Don't lecture me about my food, Shelby," she says, reading my mind. "I forgot to bring something, and this was the only thing hot that didn't involve mystery meat."

"I'm not sure mystery cheese is much better." I grab a chip and dip into the river of molten goo. "Mmmm. Tastes like Elmer's glue."

Amber and Elisa join us, and we have a nice little huddle of girls plus Fletcher noshing on various lunch items when Jon approaches. I can tell this because Amber suddenly sticks her boobs out and Becca's nostrils suddenly flare, and she scooches over closer to Amber so Jon can't sit between them. I'd hoped the whole Bermuda Triangle of love had been closed down for the year, but obviously that's only a wish, not a reality.

"Hi, Jon," Amber coos. She coos, I swear! It's getting more disgusting every time I see them together. I hope if I get like that, somebody throws a bucket of cold water over my head. He waves, smooths his flip of jet-black hair away from his eyes, and eases to the ground next to Amber.

"Hey, Jon, great to see you," Elisa says mockingly. "Isn't that black clothing kind of hot in the middle of August?"

"Ah, no," he answers, grinning. "I think it's better to wear black, because it absorbs the heat."

Elisa chokes on her uncooked Lean Pocket. "That's why you *don't* want to wear it, genius!"

"Actually, we wear it in protest of the heat," Amber says decidedly as she feeds Jon a piece of string cheese. "It's defiance. All the great writers wore black too. We can't really be truly great unless we wear black."

"You don't really believe that, do you?" Fletcher asks.

"No." Amber eats the rest of the cheese. "But it sounds semi-reasonable, huh? We just wear it because it looks good, to be honest. Right, Jon?"

He nods, fixing her with this look of utter devotion before he plants a big, wet kiss on her cheese-crumbed lips.

Elisa swats at him with the Lean Pocket wrapper. "Cut it out! Some of us are trying to eat here!"

Becca has been strangely silent through all of this. I watch her, and she is like a jungle cat figuring out a strategy to attack its prey. Kind of scary. I knew she wouldn't give up on Jon. It's going to be a long year.

"Hey," a deep voice booms from above. Is it God? Buddha? Superman? Upside down I see the white-blond eyebrows and hair of that giant guy I met at the movie theater.

"Hi, Carl." Fletcher waves at him. "Sit down. You guys, this is Carl Schwaiger." Everybody waves a wilty greeting as Carl the Giant lowers himself to the ground, which for him is not that easy. One of his legs is about as long as both of mine if they were lined up end to end.

"Well, this is turning into quite a party," Becca says frostily.

Carl scratches his freshly-shaved fuzzy blond hair. "Hot, huh?"

Becca examines him as if he's a bug under a microscope. "Yes, Carl. Yes, it's hot. Very good."

"Geez, no need to be nasty," I say. I'm the only one who can say it to her, and I feel it's my duty, even if Carl is a giant and seems to have the reasoning power of a Cheeto.

Carl just grins ear to ear, and looks pleased with himself for some reason.

We spend the rest of our too-short lunch talking about classes and general high school tragedies, and then the bell rings. Carl stands up and stretches, which dislodges a number of dead twigs that fall on Becca. "God! Look what you did!" she rages at him as she tries to brush the dead bits from her shirt.

"Oh, sorry," he blunders, trying to help her extract dried leaves from her blouse without coming anywhere near her boobs. He turns cherry red and she slaps his hand away. Fletcher is convulsing with laughter.

"Stop enjoying this," I hiss at him, giving him a slap on the forearm.

"Well, it's funny," he says, shrugging. "Walk you to class?"

"P.E." I give him the look of doom. "Becca and I both have it."

"Sounds like a dreaded disease. 'We both have it. Will we survive?' "

Elisa and Amber/Jon (I've started to think of them as one person) say their good-byes. Carl has shuffled away, and Becca is shaking her head as she joins us. "What is up with that guy, Fletcher? Is he developmentally challenged or something?"

"No, no," he says, stifling his snickers. "He's actually really smart."

"About what?" she asks as she picks up her backpack. We start our slow, unpleasant walk toward the gym.

"He's a science guy. Very into particle physics."

"How can you be 'into' particle physics?" Becca snorts. "He probably thinks particle physics is the science of sweeping up confetti after a football game."

"Bye," Fletcher says, giving me a real kiss that makes my socks roll up and my ears tingle. He runs toward the math building while we continue toward the doomnasium.

Becca lopes thoughtfully, but says nothing.

"Are you okay?" I ask.

"Not really." She keeps loping.

"Is it the Jon thing?"

She stops, gives me a lopsided grin, and puts an arm around me. "You know, I wish we were gay. Things would be so much easier."

"I doubt it." We walk in step with each other. "If you dated girls, they'd piss you off too."

"Yeah, but I could steal their clothes!"

10

RETURN OF THE QUEENS

(or A Festival of Geeks)

We get through the first week of school and Saturday I get to sleep in. There's nothing quite like it, that first Saturday after school starts; you wake up in the dark thinking you have to get up and get dressed, but then you have that beautiful realization that it's the weekend and you can go back to your summer slacker ways.

Except that my phone rings at about ten in the morning. "Doesn't everyone in the world know that teenagers aren't supposed to get up before noon on Saturday?" I groan as I blindly grope for the receiver. Euphoria isn't even there to help me, so I'm on my own. "Hello?" I croak.

"I've had a brainstorm!" Becca's voice explodes in my ear.

"Could you maybe freeze it and thaw it out later?"

"Come on, Shelby! Seriously. I'm coming over there."

"No—" But it's too late. The other line is dead, and judging from her tone of voice, she's probably flying to my house—behold, the power of coffee.

Dad is sitting at the table reading a newspaper, his glasses perched on the end of his nose. "You look like that Headless Horseman guy," I say, ruffling his hair.

"Ichabod Crane?" He peers at me over the top of the specs. "I think I'm much sexier than Ichabod Crane."

"No comment." I stumble into the kitchen and grab a box of cereal from the cupboard. "Where's Euphoria?"

Dad sighs heavily. "Ah. She's grieving over Fred."

"Why? What happened to Fred?"

"I was mowing the back and he ran over a huge piece of concrete."

"Not good. Internal injuries?"

Dad nods solemnly. "It's not a total loss, though. He's going to be an organ donor. I have three things on the drawing board—"

"Aw, that's just creepy." I sit across from him and dig a huge spoonful of cereal out of the bowl and hoist it to my mouth. "It's like parting out a member of the family."

"It's either that or take him to the dump. And that just seems undignified." Dad squints at my breakfast. "Corn flakes? Is that going to get you through the morning?"

"I have lots of sugar on them, so I'll be fine. Oh, Becca's on her way over. Just so you don't go parading around in your underwear."

"Well, that was my plan, but I guess I could fix the bathroom sink instead." He glances up at a wall clock. "Kind of early, huh?"

"Tell me about it. That girl never winds down." *Chomp, chomp.*

Dad gulps the last of his coffee, then looks at me contemplatively. "Honey, do you have any questions? About life? Boys? College? Anything?"

Every once in a while Dad gets this urge to parent me. Since my mom died, he's been sort of bad at it. It's not because he's a bad guy or anything, he just doesn't have that thing that most *moms* have: that sense of when to talk, what to do, how to comfort, when to butt out. He tries, though, which is more than I can say for some dads I know.

"I was kind of curious about particle physics."

I see him relax. Particle physics is much less dangerous than boys, in my dad's mind. "Oh. Well, that's a little hard to explain simply. It's the study of various parts of the atom and how they interact. Neutrons, electrons, protons, quarks—"

I don't really care that much about particle physics, to be honest. I just didn't want to talk about boys.

"And then when you get into some of the real quandaries, like string theory and the Grand Unified Theory, which is, by the way, sort of the Holy Grail of physics, then you really get into some passionate discussion." He's all flustered. Talking about science is for my dad what talking about *American Idol* is to other people. "Anyway," he continues without taking a breath, "how serious are you about Fletcher?"

I nearly choke on my corn flakes. "What?"

"I'd just like to know how you feel about him. You've been seeing a lot of him, and I just want to know where things are going."

It's weird. I love my dad, but I do *not* want to talk to him about my love life. There is just something fundamentally strange about telling your dad how you feel about a guy. I guess maybe this is because I've always been his girl, you know, his *little* girl. And when Mom died, it was kind of like he and I were a team by ourselves. I started dating a lot last year, but it was never serious at all. So now, I'm threatening to break up the team? And leave my poor, widowed dad alone? I suck. All I say is, "I don't know."

Dad coughs uncomfortably. "You don't know where things are going, or you don't know how you feel about him?"

"Dad, it's nothing to worry about. I know how to take care of myself." I concentrate really hard on my cereal, willing it to fly out of the bowl and hit the wall to distract my dad. It does not comply. So much for my super geektastic powers.

"I'm not worried, exactly." He leans over and covers my hand with his. "I just want to be part of the important things in your life. I feel like you were little, and now you're not . . . and since your mother . . . I just haven't been that involved, I guess."

I feel a knot building up in my throat. Must distract myself . . . "Hey, check this out!" I take some of the drier corn flakes from my bowl and try to stack them. I manage to stack five before they topple over. Dad just sighs again. He's starting to sound like a flat tire.

"Okay." He stands up, stretches, and strokes my hair. "Okay. Well, if you ever want to talk about it, I'm here. Want a ride to school, oh mighty corn-flake stacker?"

"It's Saturday, Dad, remember?" I scoop up the fallen flakes and return them to the bowl, then capture them on my spoon and cruelly eat them. There is no room for failure here, little flakes of corn. You must keep it together, not topple over sideways, or you get eaten.

When Becca arrives (Thea drops her off and then drives away in a cloud of artistically frustrated Jeep exhaust), we escape to my room. "What is she working on this time?" I ask.

Becca flops down onto my bed. "Oh, I think it was a piece commissioned by the La Jolla Snooty Art Society. They hired her to paint this hideous mural with racehorses and ladies in huge, expensive hats. It really pisses her off."

"Why did she agree to do it, then?"

"My dad is shorting her on the child support, so we kind of need the money. He has a serious case of P.I.T.A.S."

"P.I.T.A.S.?" It sounds kind of like "penis", but with a *t* in the middle.

"Oh, I never told you that one?" She sits up and laughs. "Pain in the Ass Syndrome. It's a not too rare disease affecting millions of divorced parents."

"Nice."

"Oh!" She jumps in place and digs into her pocket, producing a scrap of paper. "I got another poem! It was stuck in my math book. How did he do that without me knowing?"

"Maybe since you rarely crack open your math book . . ." I grab the paper and read.

Tweedledee and Tweedledum
Were twins both short of stature

The Cheshire Cat grinned all day long
Like I'd do if I had ya.

I look up at her. "That's incredibly bad."

"Sure, sure," she says, snatching her poem back. "But it's the thought that counts, right? I mean, this guy is seriously into pursuing me. How many guys do you know who would bother to write poems and sneak them into a book?"

"True." I play with a pencil, twirl it upside down, right side up. "You have no idea who it is?"

"Nope, but he must go to Green Pines." She turns over onto her belly and picks lint off my quilt. "It's kind of fun not knowing."

"Yeah. So, what do you want to do today?"

"Hmmm. Well, eating, for sure. Is your dad available for transport purposes?"

"No," I say without even checking. I don't want to deal with the potential boyfriend grilling in front of Becca. She'll probably tell him anything he wants to know, and everything I don't want him to know. I don't even know what that is, but I'm sure Becca will somehow figure it out and tell him. "Let's walk somewhere."

We decide on the park that's a block from my house. It has a swing set (which I still really love to play on) and tennis courts, so we take the cheap racquets and dirty, ratty tennis balls stowed in our garage. "Let's pack a lunch too," Becca suggests as she stuffs tennis balls into her pockets. We head for the kitchen.

Euphoria has resurfaced, and although it may be hard to believe, she looks depressed. Becca doesn't notice; she just randomly opens cupboards and drawers, finds a plastic grocery bag, and fills it with Oreos, a box of Cheez-Its, chewy granola bars, and a container of Chinese food she finds in the fridge.

"Uh . . . do we really need all that stuff?" I ask.

"We need to keep hydrated." She also throws in two cans of soda, a bottle of water, and two containers of chocolate pudding.

Euphoria sighs a deep, whiny sigh.

"Are you okay?" I ask.

"Oh, Shelby," she says sadly. "Don't fall in love."

Becca stops her savage hunt for junk food. "Euphoria? Are you *depressed*? Is that possible?"

How does one handle a depressed robot? The usual remedies don't work: chocolate, ice cream, mindless TV, sad music. "Can I do anything for you, Euphoria?" I ask.

"No, honey." She rolls slowly toward the sink. "With Fred gone, life just doesn't have the same glow that it did. Maybe I'll just put my claw down this garbage disposal."

"No!" we both yell in unison.

I grab her arm. "Don't you see how wrong it would be? Fred would want you to go on."

Becca turns Euphoria so she's staring right into her optical sensors. "Euphoria, Fred is in a better place—" She glances over at me to be sure that's right.

"He was parted out," I sort of whisper.

"—and I'm sure he'd want you to go on, to preserve his memory. There will be other lawn mowers, Euphoria. It may be too soon, but remember this: Once you've loved, you are more likely to love again. Isn't that right, Shelby?"

"Uh . . . I guess so." I'm not as up on the *Cosmo* psychology as Becca, but I assume she's correct.

"Now, we're going to the park. Why don't you go watch a movie? Maybe *Forbidden Planet*? I know how much you love Robby the Robot. Let him help you ease your suffering."

Euphoria bleeps forlornly. "Maybe I'll do that." She wheels around and says to me, "Shelby, when you come back, do you think you could give me an oil bath?"

"Sure." I give her a hug, and even a kiss on her shiny head. "Don't worry. It'll work out."

"I suppose," she says as she rolls toward the living room humming the theme song from *Titanic*.

"Wow," Becca says as we head out the front door. "Do they make robot antidepressants?"

It's a beautiful Saturday, not too hot, which is kind of unusual for August. Lots of little kids are orbiting around the play area, trying to get their summer fun in before the school year kicks into high gear. The only shady spot to sit is underneath a big, twisted oak tree. The swings are all occupied, unfortunately.

Becca stretches her long legs in front of her and reclines against the tree. "Ah. Weekends are like little summers."

"Except once we start getting massive amounts of homework, there won't be even little summers anymore."

"Don't be so negative." She takes off her sunglasses and sits up excitedly. "We have so much to do. I want our first meeting to be Friday, so we need to get organized."

The idea of doing another full-scale Queen Geek project makes me kind of queasy. I already feel overwhelmed by the sheer amount of sophomore schoolwork, and then there's

Fletcher to add to the mix. Plus, my robot is in need of serious therapy, and who knows about my dad? But I know I'll get dragged into it anyway, so I guess it's better to just face it. "What do you want to do?"

"I think on Friday we should first of all tell everyone about the website."

"The one Jon made?"

She nods. "Yeah. We can still use it. We can link to a MySpace page and build a whole network of Queen Geeks! And then"—she pauses for effect—"we have to work on GeekFest."

"Yeah, you said that before. What is that, exactly?"

"I've been thinking about it a lot."

"No. Really?"

She ignores my finely tuned sarcasm. "GeekFest will be a twisted talent show and film festival. We'll invite anyone to participate, with an audition, of course. We don't want anybody doing just any old act. And I think we should introduce the whole thing as the Geektastic Four! I was thinking of making a movie we could show at the show."

"A movie? When would we have time to make a movie?"

She looks a bit disappointed. She hates when I pull her helium balloon of hope to the ground and stick a pin in it. "Well, maybe that's too much. But I do like the idea of a show."

"Okay, so let's suppose we do a show. Where?"

"Well, duh," she replies, making a really dumb-looking face. "In the theater."

"Oh. You think the drama teacher is just going to let us borrow his theater?"

She hadn't thought of that, of course. She just assumes that whatever she wants to have happen, will happen. It's kind of an admirable quality unless you happen to be the person who gets the task of outlining why an outrageous plan won't work, or engineering the same outrageous plan so that it will. "Isn't Amber in drama?"

"She's taken a class, I think." I send an acorn skidding across the asphalt walkway. "But let's assume for the moment that we can get the theater. We sell tickets?"

"Sure. People don't like things that are free. If they don't pay for it, they think it must be lame."

"And what do we do with the money?"

She ponders this for a moment while scratching absently at her dragon tattoo. "We . . . spend it?"

"On what? We'll need to say what the money will be used for."

She squints at me and nods wisely. "You're right, Yoda. We do need to have a purpose. What should our cause be?"

"Let's bring it up at the meeting." I see a vacant swing and head over before a little kid snags it. They don't like to share. "Many brains are better than two."

She follows me, and when another kid occupying a swing sees her, he bolts off the seat and rushes to his mommy. Becca is, as I've said, pretty tall, and when she lets her tat show, it scares people sometimes. Especially little kids and old people, who I guess have an innate fear of dragons or tattoos or both.

I love swinging. It must be something to do with rocking as a baby, because there's no other logical reasons why I should like it so much. I love seeing the ground move and the sky shift, and the grass get blurry, and colors melt far away. There's a freedom in swinging that is hard to beat. It's not hard to do, you don't need expensive equipment, and even the athletically challenged can go as high as their weight and fear will allow them to go. Becca always swings higher than I do.

Her long legs slice through the air like stenciled scissors, and her pink tennies look like cotton candy against the sky. "I think it's going to be a great school year," she says resolutely, with just a hint of doubt in her voice.

We contact everyone and make all the necessary arrangements for the meeting to go forward on Friday. Elisa manages to convince Ms. McLachlan that we could use the room and leave it intact. (We had a bit of a mishap with some discarded Twinkies last year in the same room. Unfortunately, ants do not read the "no food allowed" sign posted near the trash can, so our smushed leftovers sent the little guys into an eating frenzy. Ms. McLachlan came in one morning and found a boatload of ant bodies exploded on her floor. Twinkies really aren't good for anyone.) Anyway, the week drags by and we finally get to Friday, and our all-important first meeting. Elisa, Amber, Becca, and I get there early so we can greet newcomers and such, and Ms. McLachlan stands looking puzzled as we put up our Geektastic Four posters and write the website address on the whiteboard.

A lot of the other girls from last year show up: Amitha Bargout, Claudette and Caroline (sisters), Sherrie Johnson, and tiny, mousy Cheryl Abbott, now a sophomore too. There are also a lot of new girls, some freshmen, a lot of sophomores like us, and even a junior or two. No seniors, which is to be expected. By that point they're usually getting off campus as soon as possible, and want nothing to do with clubs of any kind.

Becca beams with pride at the number of girls in the room, nearly thirty. "Hi, everyone," she says. "Welcome to this year's first meeting of the Queen Geek Social Club." She hands me a clipboard and gestures toward the left side of the room. "This is Shelby Chapelle, I'm Becca Gallagher, and we're passing around a clipboard so you can give us your name and e-mail." I guess I've been relegated to being the secretary for the club. Yawn. I sort of half-heartedly start passing the clipboard and curse my poopy attitude.

"Before we start, I'd like to introduce our four officers, myself, Shelby, and Elisa Crunch and Amber Fellerman, there in back."

Amber and Elisa wave sort of sheepishly. Becca continues. "So, our mission here is to be a safe haven for the geeks of Green Pines. Last year, many of you know, we became kind of famous for our Campaign for Calories, where we sent Twinkies to a modeling agency in L.A."

"You go, girl!" a very overweight girl in the front row pipes up. Everybody laughs.

"And we brought you movie hottie Brandon Keller last year, and the fantastic pirate-themed spring dance. So"—Becca is all smiles—"this year, we wanted to do something equally as great. Here's our idea: First, we gather more and more geeks to the fold, and we do this by getting the word out on our website. Get the word out to your friends, or anyone you think would be a likely candidate for the club, even if she doesn't live here. We want to start an online geek community too."

A sort of Emo-looking girl raises her hand. "Yeah. If you're just trying to get geeks, isn't that kind of discriminatory? I mean, aren't you asking people to put themselves into a kind of box?" I see other heads shaking a bit in agreement. "You're stereotyping people."

Becca pauses for a moment, and I see her strategizing an answer in her head. I know it will be the perfect answer, because that's how it always is. It would be a huge waste if she didn't become a politician, really. "Here's how I see it," she says finally. "Pretty much everybody who's a geek knows it, right?"

The Emo girl nods. "Sure, I guess."

"So, if you describe yourself as a geek, how am I stereotyping you? You chose to describe yourself that way for some reason."

A steady hum rises in the room. Another win for world domination!

"Here's the bottom line," Becca says, motioning for quiet. "You can call it whatever you want, but if you are a smart, funny, clever person who likes quirky stuff, sci-fi, horror, books, whatever isn't mainstream America, then I guess you could qualify as a geek. Does that mean we're all alike? No. But we do have things in common. And isn't that why people make clubs in the first place?"

I expect one of those scenes from movies where one person stands and starts to clap very slowly, then others rise and join in until there's a standing ovation. Instead, everyone just sort of shrugs or makes a kind of resigned-looking face, and the meeting goes forward. Reality is never as exciting as a movie. That's a serious design flaw, if you ask me.

"Could you guys help me pass these out?" Becca asks, waving a stack of lemon-colored fliers.

"What's this?" I whisper as I grab a small batch and begin passing.

"GeekFest," she whispers back. "We need to get the momentum going soon if we want to make it by Christmas."

"Christm—" I begin to shriek, but she interrupts.

"If you look at the flier, you'll see that one of the activities we want to do is called GeekFest. Now, this is not your run-of-the-mill talent show. This is a multimedia, integrated, state-of-the-art festival to showcase our campus' most talented geeks. We envision film screenings, live acts, music, comedy, anything. It just needs to be good, no goofs or people just doing it to look stupid. So, that's the basic idea, but of course, we want your input."

She waits patiently while no one says anything. I think the new kids are kind of overwhelmed by her intense enthusiasm. As her best friend, it is my job to bail her out, so I raise my hand. "So, what kind of things might you guys want to do in the GeekFest? Oh, and did I mention that all the money we make will be going toward a goal that you decide?"

"Can we just split it up thirty ways and go buy a pack of gum?" Somebody from the back says.

"No, no," Becca says. "We want to use the money for something good for all of us. We can talk about that later, I guess. But right now, we need to know if this is something you all want to do. If it isn't, then we should think of something else."

Amber stands in back. "Here's why I think it's a good idea." She walks slowly toward the front of the room. "The jocks get pep vallies. The band kids get parades. Student government gets pretty much anything they want. What do we get? We get a badly read bulletin announcement once a week if we're lucky. Don't we deserve to be seen?"

"Yeah," Elisa joins in. "Last year, when we did the dance, everybody knew who we were. We were even on TV. Well, you know how it is in high school, it's all like 'what have you done lately?' So I say, if it will get us attention and some money to toss around, let's go for it. I for one already have my act all planned."

"You do?" Becca arches an eyebrow.

"Sure." Elisa does a really awkward hip-hop move. "I plan to mosh to my own rap song."

Caroline, one of the sisters, says, "You don't mosh with hip hop, Elisa. Anyways, you can't do it on your own. You need a pit full of people to mosh."

"Oh." Elisa looks kind of disappointed. "Maybe I can bust a move, then."

Caroline rolls her eyes and shakes her head. "Listen, I think this is a good idea and all, but aren't you afraid people will just come to make fun of us?"

"Not if it's good." Becca points to Claudette, Caroline's sister. "Don't you have a singing duo or something?"

They look at each other as if a family secret has been outed. "Uh . . . we rap," Caroline says hesitantly. "Kind of. But we usually don't rap in front of other people."

"Then what's the point?" Becca says, firing up her world domination guns. "I mean, if nobody hears you, you aren't really communicating anything, so what's the point?"

"We entertain each other," Claudette says, crossing her arms in front of her. "That's good enough for me."

"Well, hang on," Caroline replies, a bit softer. Her sister gives her the wide-eyed stare of death so common in high school. "Or not." She looks down at her shoes.

"Okay, well, think about it." Becca passes out little stickers with the website address on them. "For now, just go to the website, check it out, get on the blog, tell other people about it. We'll meet again next week. Thanks for coming."

The room erupts into idle chatter and the chomping of potato chips and apples as Becca slumps dejectedly onto Ms. McLachlan's rotating stool. "What's wrong?" I ask, knowing what's wrong. But sometimes you just have to ask anyway, just to be polite.

"They don't seem to care at all!" She moans, putting her spiky blond head on the podium in front of her.

Amber and Elisa have gathered for moral support. "Hey, don't be discouraged," Amber says. "Look how many people came! I mean, that was better than last year when we started. Look on the bright side."

Becca turns her head sideways and grimaces, squinting with one skeptical eye. "When the Emo girl tries to make me feel better, I know it's bad."

"I am not Emo, dammit!" Amber yells loudly enough for everybody in the room to stop talking at once, resulting in that awkward silence that make everyone uncomfortable. "I . . . it's not like *Finding Nemo*. Dammit," she says half-heartedly, hoping her true Emo nature has not been revealed. Maybe she should have been the Amazing Miss Moody instead of Art-tastic. All the other girls resume their discussions, and soon enough the bell rings signaling the end of lunch. Cruel, cruel bell.

We follow the stream of girls out of the room, and Becca grabs my arm. "Listen, Shelby," she says urgently, "plan to spend this weekend with me figuring out what to do. Okay? I really need your help."

As we cross campus toward the doomnasium, Fletcher trots up beside me. Becca sighs heavily and runs the other way. "Do I smell bad or something?" he asks, gesturing toward the departing Becca.

"No." He slips his hand in mine. "We just had a not-so-stellar meeting. She talked about GeekFest and people weren't wild."

"GeekFest, huh?" He thinks for a moment, then stops me in midstride, turns me toward him, and plants a big wet kiss on my lips. It lasts awhile too, enough so that other kids start making smoochy noises and tell us to get a room. I break away, feeling flushed, embarrassed, and tingly. "What were we talking about?"

"Uh . . ." is all I can say. See, this is why I don't like love. It reduces all your language skills to single syllables. If I could just find a way to reconfigure the hormones in—he kisses me again, and all I can think of is yum, yum, yum, yes.

"So, see you later?" he asks, unaware that he has somehow sucked all my brain cells out through my lips.

"Uh . . ." He stands there, waiting for an answer that does not come.

"Shel, see you later? Yes? I have to talk to you about this weekend." He gives me a quick peck and ruffles my hair. "Meet me after school at the Rock."

"Yeah." He waves, and I watch his dash of reddish hair disappear in the sea of teenaged bodies. I float to P.E., unaware that my feet are actually moving. I really wish he wouldn't do that. Kind of.

I get to the Rock after school, and as I sit there watching the streams of kids go by, I see Fletcher approaching from my left and Becca approaching from my right, and my immediate thought is "there is going to be a horrendous collision." They reach me at the same time, and each starts talking.

"We need to spend the entire weekend working on Geek-Fest," Becca says decisively, while Fletcher says, "There's a party on Saturday. It's an all-day thing, and my friend's counting on us to help set up." Each seems surprised by the other's presence. They frown at each other, then both look at me.

"Uh . . ." Again with the monosyllabic response. It's becoming a habit. Maybe I have permanent hormone-induced brain damage.

"Well?" Becca stands with hands on hips, daring me to defy the edict of the Queen Geek.

"Shelby?" Fletcher crosses his arms, shifts his weight to one foot and fixes me with a quizzical stare.

I shift my focus from one to the other, unable to respond. As seconds tick by, I can tell they're both getting really frustrated. So, I do what any sensible girl would do: I run like hell in the other direction.

11

BOYFRIENDS AND GIRLFRIENDS

(or When in Doubt, Run)

I actually run all the way home. Isn't that insane? I realize two things: One, I am in terrible shape. And two, I have an issue with conflict.

After falling up the porch stairs, I scramble through the front door, slam it behind me, and lean against it, as if I will be able to single-handedly stop the onslaught of disappointment that will be washing up any minute. Both my best friend and my boyfriend now think I am an unfaithful, untrustworthy, unreliable chicken, and they are right.

Euphoria rolls in, claws poised in a fighting stance, red lights flashing. "Oh," she says, relaxing her arms. "It's you. I thought someone was breaking down the front door."

"Just me." I'm still panting, trying to catch my breath.

"Why were you running? Was something chasing you?" She scans my vital signs. "Your respiration rate is very high, and your adrenaline levels would give a gorilla a heart attack! My goodness, come sit down! I'll get you some water."

She rolls toward the kitchen as I collapse onto the living room sofa. What was I thinking? Running away isn't going to solve anything, and I know it. They're probably both going to come to the house, arguing, and then they'll break into my room at night, and they'll try to kidnap me, but it will all just result in a tragic rubber band fight that leaves one or more of us minus an eye. "Lock the door!" I yell to Euphoria.

As Euphoria fetches me a glass of water (after locking the door), Dad comes in from his workshop. "Hey, Shelby," he says, waving absently in my direction.

"Mr. Chapelle, your daughter is having an episode."

"Hmmm?" He stops in midstep, reroutes himself, and comes over to the couch. "What episode?"

"I think it's the one where the girl pisses off everybody she knows and dies a hopeless, lonely old maid with no friends," I say, covering my face with my hands.

Dad arches an eyebrow and sits next to me. "Euphoria, could you give us a few moments alone?"

Euphoria snorts indignantly (which sounds like a coffee grinder grinding rusty bolts), and exits toward the kitchen.

"Now," Dad says, turning to me. "What is going on? You're all red."

"I ran home from school." I gulp the water to buy some time.

"Why?"

Before I can answer, I hear scuffling on the porch, and the rise and fall of argument, and then a loud, forceful pounding. I say, "Let's pretend we've moved."

More pounding. "Shelby! C'mon! Open the door!"

"Is that Fletcher?" Dad asks. I nod.

"Seriously! We just want to talk to you!"

"And Becca?" Dad crosses his arms in front of him. "Sounds interesting. I think I saw this once on a soap opera."

"You've never watched a soap opera in your life." I stand up, finish the water, and take a deep breath. "This is going to be tough, but I have to face it."

"Did the three of you have a fight?" Dad stands too, ready to intervene if things get ugly. Or uglier, I guess I should say.

"Kind of." Continued banging on the door, yelling, and a sound like somebody trying to pick the lock come through the wall. "Better let them in before they break something."

Dad slowly unlocks and opens the door. Fletcher and Becca are still arguing, unaware that the door is open. "She doesn't belong to you," Becca snaps.

"And you don't just get to order her around like she's your maid or something either!" Fletcher snaps back. They both seem to sense that they are being watched, and turn toward us. "Oh, hey, Mr. Chapelle," they say in unison.

"Hi, kids. What's up?" He leans against the jamb and crosses his arms. "Anything I can do for you?"

Becca spots me over Dad's shoulder. "We just need to talk to Shelby. Nothing important."

"Nothing important!" Fletcher sputters. "What do you mean? It's absolutely important."

Becca starts chattering at him and he chatters back, and finally Dad has to do his coach whistle to get them to shut up. "Hold on!" He does the time-out hand gesture. "Why don't you both come in so the neighbors don't think you're a pair of rabid magazine salespeople?" They just keep chattering away. "Stop it!" Dad finally yells, in that way that only dads can do. It automatically silences all chattering teenagers and puts fear into the heart of anyone within earshot. "Let's all sit down like rational people and discuss whatever the problem is."

Dad marches us into the living room. Euphoria rolls in silently, claws clicking in idle frustration. She really hates conflict.

I am careful to sit in an armchair by myself, so nobody thinks I'm taking sides. Fletcher notices this, and since he can't sit with me, he leans over and gives me a kiss on the cheek. Becca sees it, growls, and drags him to the couch. Dad sits on an overstuffed footstool, staying as far away from us as possible while still remaining in the room. I get this weird mental image of him in a lion tamer's costume with a shiny whip and a waxed moustache.

"Now," he says reasonably. "Let's figure out what the problem is. You three don't want to spend your time fighting, right?" As everyone starts to argue, he yells, "Okay, okay. One at a time! Becca, go first."

She smiles at Fletcher in a snotty, superior way. "Well, I've just been trying to get some time with Shelby so we can plan our club events for the year. This weekend is critical. We had plans, Fletcher decided to lay this big heavy guilt trip on her so she wouldn't be able to do anything this weekend, and—"

"Hang on," Fletcher interrupts. "I never said anything about guilt."

Dad shakes his head. "No interruptions. Go on, Becca."

She leans back into the couch and stares at the ceiling. "I guess I'm just a little hurt that I'm not more important than some guy."

"I'm not 'some guy,' Becca!" Fletcher actually sounds hurt. "I've supported your club, and I've done a lot to help, with the dance last year, with the website, all of that. That makes me just some guy?"

Becca doesn't answer. She just sits with her arms crossed, staring at the ceiling.

Dad turns to Fletcher. "Okay, so what's the issue, in your opinion?"

He glances at me, and I can see that he's actually hurt by this whole thing. "I . . . I just want to spend some quality time alone with Shelby, without all her friends hanging out. I don't think that's weird, and I don't think it means that she can't have friends. Like I said, I've done a lot of stuff *with* her friends. This weekend was the first time I've ever asked her to do anything with some of *my* friends, and it becomes World War Three."

Becca snorts, and glares at a patch of ceiling that's as far from Fletcher as possible.

Dad sighs, and finally comes to me, which I have been dreading since we all sat down. "So, Shelby. What do you think?"

Becca stops her ceiling gazing and looks toward me. Fletcher turns and also waits for my amazing comment. Nothing comes out of my mouth.

"Shelby?" Dad waves at me. "You've heard what they said. What do you think?"

In my mind, it's like I'm on some crazy game show. The clock is ticking, and that annoying game show music is *tink-tink*ing behind my brain, getting louder and louder. Whatever I say will be the wrong answer. There is no way to win the washer and dryer; I probably won't even get a can of dog food as a consolation prize. In fact, it's very possible that I'll be taken out, tied to a tree, and covered in fire ants instead.

"Uh" is all I manage to say. Everyone seems very frustrated and disgusted with me. Even Euphoria seems to bleep disapprovingly.

"We need a little more than that," Becca snaps. She bounces up off the couch. "Look, if you'd rather spend time with your boyfriend than with your friends, I understand. But we have to go on without you, you know." She points at Fletcher. "He wants to keep you for himself, but we want to use your talents to help make the world a better place. Which is more important?"

"Oh, come on!" Fletcher jumps up too, and because the two of them are both pretty tall, it looks even scarier from my safe little armchair. "You act like this is about the club, but it's about you. You just like to control everything and everybody you come in contact with. All I want is a normal relationship with her. I don't want to control every minute of her life, and I don't make her feel bad if she wants to just have fun instead of wanting to change the world and all that crap."

"Great." Becca smirks at him. "Yeah, I can see how going to a party with *your* friends is so much better than changing the world, Fletcher."

Dad has kind of given up on this, I guess; he's just sitting there, his head bobbing back and forth like he's watching a tennis match. Fletcher finally turns to me and says, "Okay. Do you want a relationship, or not? If you do, we have to spend time together alone."

Becca turns to me and says, "Or are your real friends more important than your hormones?"

Which leaves me back where I started. Except that it's very hard to run away from your own living room.

"Couldn't I spend most of Saturday with Becca and then go to the party Saturday night with Fletcher?" I ask hesitantly.

They both look at each other, and at Dad, and then finally at me. "Uh . . . yeah, I guess that would work," Becca says, the wind out of her sails.

"That's it?" Dad says, annoyed. "That's all it took? Couldn't you all have done that without the drama?"

"Mr. Chapelle," Euphoria pipes up, "they *are* teenagers. Drama is what they do."

Fletcher turns to me and gives me a lopsided grin. "So? Spend your day with Becca and the girls, and then I'll come get you at seven. Does that work?"

I nod, disbelieving that it could be that easy. Why do we always blow everything out of proportion and make it seem like the end of the world if a hangnail sticks out? Geez. Maybe Euphoria is right. Maybe we're just programmed to make it difficult for ourselves.

There's an awkward moment when we all go to the front door, and it seems like another battle is about to brew over who leaves first. Since they both walked to my house, the question now is whether they'll both walk back to school. Dad figures this out and offers to give them both a ride. As he grabs his keys from the hall table, he kisses me on the forehead, and whispers in my ear, "Now you can be alone for a while before your social calendar starts to rev up again."

So, with all this opportunity for reflective time, what do I do? I turn on the TV and watch *Outer Limits* all night, pausing only to thank Dad in a monotone voice for being my mediator, and to eat a quart of ice cream before passing out on my bed.

Saturday I keep waking up, ever though I'm exhausted. After a call from Becca, I eat and wait for the other Queen Geeks to show up for a marathon planning session. Euphoria once again criticizes my choice of cereal, chides me for drinking coffee, and mentions that I don't seem to have slept very well. Big shock.

We crash in my living room for the planning session. Amber has somehow grown more goth over the last day, and is wearing the long, black trench coat, black leggings, and a T-shirt that tells the world, "My Prozac Fits in My Pez Dispenser!"

"Yeah, nice shirt, Amber," Elisa says, downing a Diet Pepsi. "Are you trying to depress people by your mere presence? Isn't your poetry depressing enough?"

Amber swishes her long, dark hair from her face, revealing some seriously thick black eyeliner and electric-blue eye shadow that make her look like a drugstore geisha. "It's really not supposed to be depressing." She reaches for her ice water with a twist of lemon. She's on a cleansing diet too. "It's kind of a humorous comment on the random use of antidepressants in our consumer culture. We treat them like candy."

"Yeah, I guess if you cram them into your Satan Pez dispenser, people might think that you're not taking your mental illness seriously." Elisa rolls her eyes and reaches for a handful of cheese crackers from a bowl Euphoria has set out for us.

Becca frowns at a clipboard full of notes and says, "Geek-Fest. When? Where? What do we need?"

"Well, we need talented geeks," Amber offers. "And people to watch them."

Elisa whips out Wembley and starts to punch buttons. "We also need to decide if we sell tickets, how much they'll cost. And if we want to outlay cost for refreshments and such."

Becca scribbles furiously. "All right. It's September. If we plan for right before Thanksgiving, we could pull that off, and we could have money for next year. So, Friday we start getting people to commit to developing acts for the show. Amber, you know the drama director?"

She nods. "He's really sweet. I'm sure he'll let us use the space, as long as we promise not to mess anything up. We might be able to get some of the tech guys to work the lights and stuff too."

"Hmmm," Elisa says, stroking her chin, "who do we know who's a tech guy in drama?"

"Okay, okay, Jon's in it," Amber confesses, smiling slightly. "That's not a bad thing. He can help us."

Becca stops scribbling for a moment and folds her hands on the clipboard. "Okay. First of all, we need to be clear on something: We have to be careful about getting guys involved in the club. This is Queen Geeks, and guys might mess things up. Just think about the dance last year! That had the potential to be a disaster, but we pulled it off. I don't want another near miss."

Amber shrugs her shoulders noncommitally. "Anyway, I'd be happy to read some of my poetry. I've been working on a multimedia interactive video thing to go with it."

"Does it involve Pez or Prozac?" Elisa asks, eyes twinkling.

Before you know it, it's five and it's time for me to get ready for the party with Fletcher. Thea comes over to pick everyone up, and as they leave, Becca gives me a big hug. "Sorry for all the issues," she says, smiling slightly. "Have fun tonight."

Two hours to get ready, and I feel like I'm barely awake! But I somehow manage to throw together a decent outfit, brush my hair, do my makeup, and I'm sitting on the sofa when Fletcher arrives at seven. Dad is on hand to grill him.

"Make sure you're back by midnight, no later," he says, wagging his finger. Like that ever has any effect.

"No problem," Fletcher replies, slipping an arm around my shoulders. "It's not even very far away."

Dad kind of shifts from one foot to the other and acts like he has something else to say. "Okay, then. Have fun." He doesn't move.

"Dad," I ask, "is there something else?"

"Hmm?"

"You seem kind of preoccupied. Is there something else?"

"Oh." He makes a funny face, sucking his upper lip into his nostrils so he looks like a mutated duck. "Just wanted to remind you not to drink or anything."

Drinking! Ah. We actually haven't talked much about that one. In fact, we haven't had too many actual direct conversations about any of the established teenaged evils: smoking, alcohol, and sex (except for that one awkward birds and bees thing). Drugs kind of fit into those categories too, I guess, but those are the biggest three, probably because parents figure that if you don't smoke or drink, you're probably not going to skip straight to narcotics. If only they heard what I hear in the girls' bathroom at break. Probably better my dad doesn't hear it, actually.

Fletcher smiles and shakes Dad's hand. "You don't need to worry about that. This is not that kind of party, and Carl's parents will be there too."

"Carl?" I just now realize that we're attending a celebration at the house of the giant. "We're going to a party at Carl's house?"

"Yeah." Fletcher waves to my dad, grabs my arm, and hustles me out the front door.

I stop on the porch. "I wish you'd told me it was his party. I don't even know him!"

"This is a great way to fix that." He's already opened the car door and looks like a doorman waiting for a tip.

"I don't know if I *want* to fix that."

He marches back to me, all patience and understanding. "Hey, I know he's not your friend, but you're doing this for me, remember? Just be a good sport. He's actually a really cool guy if you take the time to get to know him."

I reluctantly get into the car (the old beater again) and wonder if I will be able to get some time alone at the giant's house so I can hunt for the magic beans.

We drive in silence for a while, during which time I get to reflect on why exactly Fletcher is absolutely wrong for me. Anyone who would force me to go to some dumb party is really not someone who has my best interests at heart, right? I mean, if he really cared, he would have just said, "Oh, never

mind about the party then. We can go to the movies or something. I wouldn't want to put you in an awkward situation."
But no. Instead, it's "hey, you're supposed to do this for me,
remember?" It's all about him.

"So?" He butts into my private thoughts. "Did everything go okay this afternoon? Did you all decide how to save
the world?"

I grunt sullenly and count hedges as we drive. Not too
many people have them anymore, I discover.

"Are you going to do this all night?" he asks.

I grunt sullenly and change to counting fake lawn ani-
mals. I find two deer, one rabbit, and something that's either
a dead, stuffed dog or a really ratty statue.

"Fine." Now he sounds angry. See? It's all about him. No
sensitivity.

He parks the car and gets out without offering to open
my door for me. Even though I hate it when he opens the
door for me, it bugs me that he doesn't at least offer. He
walks up a cobblestone path to the open front door of an
old house. I scramble to catch up. I don't want to walk in by
myself, of course.

Inside, semi-loud punk music is playing, and wall-to-wall
kids line each room. I see Fletcher's hair through the crowd,
but can't get to him. I am absolutely furious that he has
ditched me, and I consider calling my dad for a ride, but
then I see Amber and Jon.

"Hey," Amber says, waving a hand with a bunch of
silver-spiked jewelry on it. "What's up? I didn't know you
were friends with Carl."

"I'm not." I glance around again and see no sign of my supposed boyfriend. "Fletcher knows him. He dragged me along even though I'd rather be knitting or something."

"Carl's cool." Jon takes a long sip from a can of soda. "He's not just a football player."

"Right." I ignore that comment and spot what seems to be the kitchen. "I'm going to get something to drink. You guys need anything?"

They both shake their heads, then go back to focusing on each other as if nothing else exists. The kitchen is the most packed room in the house, of course; everyone at a party always seems to hang in the kitchen. Out in back, there's a patio lit with tiki torches, and I spot a big red cooler full of drinks, so I head there.

Dunking my hand into the icy water to fish out a diet soda (which is at the absolute bottom, of course), I sense that Fletcher is standing behind me. "Yes?"

"Why are you being such a . . ." He grabs the soda from me and pops the top. "Being so difficult?" He licks the foam off the can and hands it to me.

"Thanks. I'll get another. I don't want your germs." I fish into the cooler again, but he grabs my hand and pulls me up. "Hey."

"What did I do to make you so mad?"

"If you don't know, then I don't see why I should tell you." I pop the top off the soda, take a good, long drink, and belch loudly.

"Nice." He grabs the can. "Do you think you could try to be less obnoxious? These are my friends."

"Sorry if I'm embarrassing you." I grab the soda back. "If you cared at all about how I feel, you wouldn't have dragged me to this stupid party anyway. I mean, I don't know anyone, and I don't see why it matters if I meet your friends, really. Why is that such a big deal?"

Fletcher examines me critically as if I'm a lab experiment gone horribly green and fuzzy. "You can't tell me that you don't get why I want you to meet my friends. Didn't you want me to meet yours?"

"I wouldn't have cared." Having drained the soda, I crush the can. It kind of hurts, but I won't let him know that. "As far as I'm concerned, our dating life is totally separate from everything else."

"Then it's not a real part of your life, is it?"

I don't want to make him mad, but it seems like I just can't help myself. There's a part of me that wants to just smile and apologize, but most of me wants to just run away and forget I ever met him. Instead of letting him know any of this, I just belch again. Really loudly, and for all to hear.

"I don't want you to treat me this way." He comes closer to me, breathing in my face, a firm hand on my arm. "I haven't done anything to you except want you to meet my friends. Most girls would be happy about that. I realize you are not most girls, but I do expect you to act like a decent person and not a jerk."

"Only guys are jerks," I reply, yanking my arm away.

"I don't want to use any of the words I'd *really* choose. Jerk was about as close as I could get. But I agree—it doesn't do you justice."

He walks away. I mean, he actually just walks away.

I watch him, puzzled. Does this mean we're breaking up? Have I been rejected? Relationships need referees.

Inside, there's a chair in a corner, so I put myself in it. The music and the noise swirl around me, but all I feel is a black hole in the middle of my stomach. As I carefully study the pattern of laces on my tennies, a deep voice rumbles above me. "Hi, Shelby. Is everything okay?"

It's Carl. Standing above me, he looks like he could easily dent his own ceiling. "Hi, Carl. No, I'm fine."

"Hmm." He squats down next to me. "Did you and Fletch have a fight?"

"No, Fletch and I did not have a fight," I say in an ultra-snotty tone that I would hate if I heard it coming from some-one else. "He's basically just ditched me, left me here with no one to talk to."

"*I'm* talking to you," he points out. Poor, simple Carl.

"Yes, you are." I stand up and smile a big, fake smile at him. "Nice party. If you see Fletch again, can you tell him I hope he chokes on a pita chip?"

"You're not leaving, are you?" He gives me a look that is at once disbelieving and hopeful, I think.

"Yeah, I have to call my dad and get back home. My robot is suicidal. I'm afraid to leave her alone." I whip out my cell and quick key my dad, hoping he answers.

"Hmm. Too bad. We were just about to do karaoke." He shrugs and walks away.

The phone rings and rings, and finally Dad picks up. "Hello?" He sounds annoyed.

"Can you come pick me up?"

"What?" I hear some banging and metallic clangs in the background. "Say again."

"Dad, can you come and get me?" I practically yell. Between the music at Carl's and my dad's science project, I'm surprised he can tell it's me.

"Shelby, it's not a good time. I'm right in the middle of something." Another deafening crash followed by a loud humming causes me to hold the phone away from my ear.

"Umm. Dad? They're drinking here," I lie.

"Be right there. What's the address?" I give it to him, smugly aware that I am a horrible person who deserves karaoke. "Be there in about twenty minutes. Wait outside." The line goes dead.

While I'm waiting, I sort of detach from the rest of the party. A big group is moshed together in the living room, where Carl's parents are presiding over a rousing sing-a-long to "My Sharona." I believe we need legislation to stop such things. Anyway, I figure I can at least get a little free entertainment out of it before I blow out of here, so I prop myself against the door frame to watch the hideous singing.

After the group choral butchering, Carl gets up. He grabs the mic and starts to sing "It's a Small World After All" to a hip-hop beat. It's possible that this, too, should be illegal. I check my phone and realize I still have eighteen minutes left. At least. I wish I did drink.

Amber pops up next to me, minus Jon. "Hey. Where's your boyfriend?"

"Oh, him?" I smile that fake smile again. I'm getting very good at it. "I think we broke up."

"What?" Her Cleopatra eyes open wide, making her look like a living anime cartoon. "Why? You guys are perfect together!"

"Not really. He just wants me to conform, to be his little girly girlfriend. Like, he dragged me to this stupid party when I didn't want to come, and then he tried to make friends with my dad. He says we need to have 'alone time' if we want to be a couple, which of course means time away from *my* friends. Can you believe that?"

She just blinks. "Well, don't you *want* to be alone with him?"

I dimly hear the karaoke machine start a new tune. It's something I know from somewhere; it's one of those little itches in the back of your mind, when you know something but can't quite retrieve the information. "Ah! What's that song?" I try to see into the living room, but there are too many people in the way.

Amber cranes her neck to see over the heads of the crowd. "Sounds like something from the eighties."

Jon has resurfaced; he puts his arm around Amber as if it belongs there. "Oh, yeah," he says, offering Amber a swig from his blue-plastic cup. "That's an old Thompson Twins song." All that thumpy bass and echoing drum machine sound floods from the room as bunches of kids start to clap and sing along to the chorus: "Hold me now, warm my heart/Stay with me . . ." A male voice, slightly out of tune, starts to sing the verse, which ends with something about asking for forgiveness even if you don't know what you're asking it for.

And then everybody sings "Hold me now!" and on and on. And of course by this time, I've figured out who's singing. I feel myself go all red, and Amber pokes me in the ribs with her spiky jewelry. Jon is just grinning from ear to ear, and then Carl walks over and gives my upper arm a jockish squeeze. "Hey, c'mon," he rumbles in my ear, "I think that song's for you."

Carl, who is taller than anyone else at his party, muscles his way through the thick carpet of kids with me in tow. I would kick and scream if I had room, but the place is packed, so I just coast behind him like a ragdoll criminal being dragged to a public hanging.

For there, standing on a coffee table in the middle of Carl's packed living room, is my boyfriend, Fletcher, pumping his fists in the air and singing his lungs out about how he wants to hold me now and warm my heart and all that. Carl sort of dumps me in the middle of the living room, front and center, so I'm surrounded by a bunch of strangers who now know that I'm the object of this karaoke nightmare love letter. Fletcher grins and, still singing, offers his free hand to me. I stand there, stunned, like a deer hypnotized by the light of a disco ball.

The Thompson Twins continue their bass-thumpery and the song winds down. The kids in the living room clap, whistle, whoop, and cheer. I feel like I'm in the middle of a stupid teen movie where the heroine has that defining moment where her boyfriend makes it all okay and they embrace and then kiss, and then the credits roll. Except that I am frozen to that spot with embarrassment and a little bit of anger. How dare Fletcher bring our problems out in the open, and trivialize them by boiling them down to a stupid eighties song?

People are now pushing me toward him, and I'm resisting, but it's like being in a mosh pit: You just sort of go where the crowd shoves you. I end up in front of Fletcher's knees as the next song starts on the karaoke machine. "Hey," he calls down to me. "Did you like your song?"

I can sense that people are just watching us. Everybody loves a happy ending, I guess, and they all want me to smile and do the girlish thing and just run up to him and kiss him. I know this is what he wants too, and I guess maybe a part of me wants to do it. But instead, I just stand there with a feeling of intense shock and embarrassment welling up from my belly button to my eyes, which are starting to get annoyingly wet.

I look up and focus on his eyes. I can tell that he thinks we're all good, that everything is fixed with this one song. But I don't feel that way. I feel like I've been thrown into the back of a truck and abducted by the love fairy, sprinkled with pixie dust, and hooked up to electrodes while sitting in a Jacuzzi. It might sound nice, but it's not a pleasant feeling.

And like any sane pixie-dusted person hooked up to electrodes in a Jacuzzi would do, I fight my way out and escape.

BREAKING FREE

(or One-Way Ticket to Solitude)

I don't even know how I get outside, but I notice a change in light and heat, so I know I've made it. The darkness is cool and comforting; I run down the path away from Carl's house, then past his gate, then down the street into nothing. I don't even care where I go.

I keep running until I run out of breath and feel like my sides will split. Then I sit on the edge of a curb and start crying like a dumb baby.

After about ten years of this, I remember that I am lost and need to get home eventually. I pull out my cell phone and call my dad.

"Hello?"

"Dad?"

"Are you okay, honey? Where are you?" He sounds very worried. I guess I would too, if my daughter called sounding all freaked out. I make an effort to tone it down.

"Where are you? Are you almost here?"

I can feel a wave of panic coming from the phone. "What did he do?"

"Oh, no, Dad, it's not like that. He just sang karaoke."

Dad coughs, and from the long pause I can tell he's confused. Who wouldn't be? "I'm already on my way. So, are you still at the party?"

"No," I say, wiping the tears from my face. "I ran out. I'm somewhere outside."

"Shelby! You just ran out of the house, and you don't even know where you are? Are you wearing your watch?"

My watch. After my mom died, Dad made me this wristwatch that has a GPS chip in it, so he can always find me if I get lost. I always felt it was a bit paranoid. Of course, on the one occasion where it would come in handy, it's sitting on my dresser at home. "Uh . . . no."

"How far are you from the party?"

"Um . . . I think it's in Golden Hill. I'm kind of near the golf course, I think. Let me look at the street signs." I check them, and tell Dad.

"You don't know how to get back to the party?"

"Not really. I just sort of ran."

"Hmm. From karaoke, huh? We really need to talk about what's dangerous and what's not, I guess. Okay, stay put. I'll be there as soon as I can be." The phone goes dead.

With no roaring in my ears from my own crying, and no phone, the neighborhood is suddenly incredibly quiet. A few porch lights twinkle here and there in front of the old houses, but there's a blanket of silence around all of it. I just stretch my legs out over the curb, lean against a light post, and soak up the nothing.

When my phone buzzes, I nearly jump high enough to hit my head on the light fixture. "Hello?"

"It's Amber. Where are you?"

"I . . . kind of ran away."

"You run away from home, not from a party."

I switch the phone to my other ear. "Oh, sorry. I didn't get that memo."

"Ha-ha. Fletcher is worried about you."

"Well, *he* didn't call." Did I want him to? I don't even know.

Amber sighs heavily and in the background I hear the karaoke machine start up again, this time with "Harden My Heart", a perfect eighties song for me. "What is the deal? Why are you giving him such a hard time? Don't you like him?"

I pause for a long time. I do not know the answer to this pop quiz, and there is no way to cheat. "I really don't know how I feel." There, that's my answer! Brief and entirely useless!

"He's a really great guy. . . ." Amber says, waiting for me to fill in the blank.

"Yeah, I know. Maybe you should go out with him." Nice evasive action, if I do say so myself.

"Well, what are you doing?" she asks impatiently.

A great question. What am I doing? Why am I being such an idiot? Again, I have no answers. "I'm waiting for my dad to pick me up."

"Oh." She sounds kind of frosty. "Would you like me to tell Fletcher that you're not dead or mutilated or anything?"

"I guess."

"Great. Well, have fun." She hangs up.

Silence again. This gives me a great opportunity to listen to the ten thousand voices in my head that are all fighting with each other. One group thinks I should just give up on guys altogether because I am so obviously not ready for a relationship, and the other voices think I'm an idiot for letting him go, and then there is a tiny, tiny group of voices that say they are hungry and want Little Debbie snack cakes. I'm inclined to go with the snacking and ignore the other stuff.

Luckily, my dad shows up before my voices can have a full-on rumble, and I climb into the safe front seat of the Volvo feeling extremely relieved. "Thanks for the ride," I mumble.

He navigates down the calm street, and says, "Let's talk about this. Why did you run out?"

"I told you. Karaoke." I rummage around in the glove compartment of the car. "Do you have any food in here?"

"Shelby." He sighs heavily. There's a lot of that going on around me. I hope I'm not causing dangerous levels of greenhouse gases. "We really need to talk about this."

"Why?" The only food he has is stupid breath mints.

"Because I see you doing some things that are not good for you." We get onto the freeway and I start counting pretty lights. "I think you're afraid."

"Dad, you know, I could be out drinking or having sex or any number of other really bad things. Most dads would be really glad that I don't want to date or go to parties."

"Well, yeah, I see your point." He shakes his head, unable to argue with my flawless logic. "And of course I'm glad that you're not into any of that other stuff. But dating is kind of a normal thing to do when you're in high school. I expect you to go out with boys. But you seem kind of afraid of really getting involved."

"Oh, you want me to be a child bride or something?"

"Come on, honey. That is not what I said."

"Maybe I should just go back and start a naked swimming orgy in the pool and then get myself pregnant. Would that make you happy?"

"Shelby!" Dad is nearing panic too; I can hear it in his voice. "Just stop it."

We both retreat to our various mental corners; I stare out the window and rerun the conversation in my head, wondering how I would handle it if a daughter of mine talked like that. I'd probably flip out and send her to a convent or something. Maybe I should consider that, actually. . . .

We drive home the rest of the way in silence. Once we get home, I drift over to the couch and turn on the TV. Dad drops his keys on the hall table and follows me, turning off the TV before he sits next to me.

"What?" I yawn.

"I want to talk about why you're avoiding Fletcher when you so obviously like him."

I turn toward him and study his black-and-gray crazy hair, and his brown eyes, now with wrinkles scrunched around the edges. "I don't like him."

"I know you do!" I start to look for the remote, but Dad grabs my chin and makes me focus on him. "We're going to talk about this, Shelby. I don't want you to start making mistakes that you'll regret."

"Dad, you sound like I'm doing some really horrible thing. All I want is to make my life simpler. Fletcher doesn't make it simple."

"Is this because of your friends?" He lets go of my chin and I sink back into the velvet couch cushions. "Are you feeling torn between being a friend and being a girlfriend?"

"No."

He just stares at me for a minute, and then throws his hands up in surrender. "Okay. You're right. Maybe you're just not ready to date anybody seriously. Maybe you just need to be by yourself for a while." He stands up, puts a hand on my shoulder, and says, "But I don't want you to do it forever. Being alone is kind of . . . painful."

Of course, he's talking about Mom, which I knew he would. Whenever we talk about anything serious, Mom comes up. "I'm not going to be alone forever." I concentrate very hard on my shoes. "Neither are you, I bet."

He makes a weird noise in his throat and walks out of the room. I dive into the comfort of *Forbidden Planet,* and then watch three episodes of *Lost in Space.* My phone keeps buzzing. I ignore it.

The next morning, I wake up on the couch drooling on the velvet cushions. Euphoria is gently shaking my shoulder, and it feels like a herd of dirty camels spit in my mouth. "Wake up, honey."

"It's Sunday." This statement should be sufficient to make anyone go away, but it doesn't work with Euphoria, because days of the week are irrelevant to her.

"Becca is at the front door." She leans a little closer. "She seems a tad upset. I'd rather not deal with her, if it's all the same to you."

When someone intimidates a robot, that's something. I pull myself up, using the cushions for support, and manage to achieve some sense of upright. "What time is it?" I ask, squinting at the wall clock that remains obstinately blurry.

"It's ten. Please get up, Shelby. I'll make you some coffee."

Can't argue with that. I roll off the couch and scratch indelicately, then head for the front door. Becca is sitting on the porch swing, her legs kicking the banister with unfocused fury.

"Hi," I say tentatively.

She whips her head around and smiles a big, fake smile. "Hey." She stops the perpetual motion, scoots over, and pats the seat next to her. "Sit."

"Do I have to?"

"Uh . . . yeah."

I drag myself to the swing, plop down, and go ragdoll, trying to pull off a I'm-goth-my-life-sucks attitude. It never works for me; my skin's too good. "I don't know why you're all upset. I'd think you'd be glad."

She doesn't answer right away. "What conversation are we having, exactly?"

"Aren't you here to chew me out about last night?"

She laughs her donkey honk gut-buster laugh. "Last night? You mean your big party date with Fletcher? Please." She starts to swing again, more gently this time. "He called me when you wouldn't answer. He told me what happened."

"What did he say?"

Euphoria rolls out onto the porch with two steaming mugs of coffee in claw. "Here, girls, coffee with just the right amount of cream." She hands one to Becca, one to me, and then crosses her skinny metal arms, waiting.

"Thanks, Euphoria." We both sort of stare at her, hoping she'll take the hint. However, it's really difficult to hint at someone who really can't make use of body language. "Okay, so, thanks again."

"You're welcome." She just stands there.

Becca clears her throat. "So, Euphoria, we kind of wanted to be alone."

"Oh." I sense her disappointment. "I thought maybe I could help."

"I don't think anything will help." I groan, then taste the first delicious, wonderful sip of brew. "This might, though. It's really good. Ethiopian Fancy, huh?"

Euphoria lights up, pleased. "You noticed! See? I'm sensitive. Let me listen."

"Fine," Becca says impatiently. She turns to me. "Fletcher called and told me that you won't talk to him. Is that true?"

"Kind of," I mumble, diving in for another gulp.

"And that he sang karaoke to try and get you to forgive him for whatever he did that pissed you off?"

"Thompson Twins. 'Hold Me Now'. I had to leave."

"Totally understandable." She contemplates her coffee mug, swirls the ripple of cream around with her finger. "But, I guess what I want to know is . . . do you want to break up with him or what?"

Euphoria's lights blink expectantly, which kind of irritates me. "I don't know." I pull my legs up under me and cradle the hot cup of coffee, peering into it as if it were a Magic 8-Ball that might tell me what to do. There's nothing in there but coffee and a gnat that is really, really hyper. "He didn't do anything, that's what's crazy. I just keep feeling like I want to pick a fight with him. I want to just run away whenever he wants to talk about anything important."

Becca nods knowingly. "It's just too much right now, isn't it?"

"I guess."

Euphoria pipes up. "But when you first started going out with him, your heart rate and respiration were very high, and I noticed a lot of endorphins circulating, which seems to indicate—"

"Thanks, Euphoria," Becca says, jumping off the swing and hooking her cup onto Euphoria's claw. "Could you warm that up for me?"

Euphoria's lights blink. "I suppose. It's still pretty hot, though. . . ."

"Thanks." Becca helps rotate Euphoria and points her toward the front door. Euphoria might not be intuitive, but she doesn't need a brick wall to fall on her. She takes off.

"Now." Becca sits, a little too gleefully, next to me. "You're just not ready for a big commitment. What's wrong with that? You two are just in different places. Right? And that's not to say that you can't date again later. Maybe just take a break."

"Yeah. That's true. I could just take a break." The more I repeat it in my head, the better it sounds. We won't break up, we'll just take a break. A vacation. An all-expense paid trip to solitude. "Why is this so important to you?"

Becca's eyes get wide, and she sighs heavily, then drops the cheery cheerleader face. "Okay. To be honest, I have self-ish motives."

"Really?" I sip my coffee, trying to avoid the cranked-up gnat. "I would never have guessed."

"Yeah, okay. Be sarcastic. But I hate feeling like I'm los-ing you to a boyfriend, not after all the stuff we did last year. And, Shelby, I can't do any of it without you. That's the truth." She looks down at her shoes, the bright pink tennies, and licks her lips. "I know you like Fletcher, maybe even love him. But you haven't been happy, and I doubt that he's been happy either. So, why don't you just take a break and go back to how it was before?"

What she says makes sense, and I feel this tremendous sense of relief. Just going back to nothing would kind of be better, really. I know it will be tough for Fletcher, but for me, I think it will be a lot easier. "Yeah," I say to her, smiling. "I think a break is in order. Not a breakup. Just a break."

She smiles gently and pats my shoulder. For the first time since the summer, it feels like the old Queen Geeks are back in action. "Oh, and I forgot to tell you! I got another poem."

"From Wonder Rabbit?"

"Yeah." She sighs contentedly. "See, that's the perfect boyfriend. Somebody you don't know who worships you from afar."

We spend most of the rest of Sunday talking about GeekFest and about our upcoming meeting. My phone keeps buzzing, and Euphoria comes in about every two hours and says

Fletcher's on the phone, and every time I get this little kick in my stomach. But Becca puts a hand on my shoulder, smiles knowingly, and I just tell Euphoria to take another message.

At school the next week, Becca and I implement our new plan, Operation Disappear. Of course, we tell Amber and Elisa, and swear Amber to absolute secrecy since she's still overtaken by the hormones of the dark side. We change all of our meeting places, we bring our own lunches so we can avoid the cafeteria, we even wear our hair in different ways (and, in Elisa's case, inside a Sherlock Holmes hunting hat) to escape notice. Since Fletcher and I have no classes in common, it's relatively easy to avoid him; I just dodge into the girl's bathroom until right before the bell rings, and then dash to class. There are a couple of close calls, but he hardly even gets near me.

I feel a little bad about being so immature about it, but I also have a blast because it's just me and the girls again. We giggle like we're ten and sneaking into the movies when we hide in the bathroom in between classes. On Friday morning before school, Elisa brings in funky hats for all of us; we meet in the girl's P.E. bathroom to go undercover.

"Amber, you get to wear the fairy princess hat with the skull-and-crossbones stars," Elisa says, fixing the shimmery headpiece into Amber's long, dark hair. "And, Becca, to accommodate all your little spikes, I'm giving you this hair net, complete with fat rollers dangling off the ends." She snugs the cap over Becca's head, and we all have fun trying to force her little hair spikes to poke out through the mesh. "And finally, for Shelby, I have the ultimate in boy-dodging apparel: a rasta hat with long dreadlocks." She pulls out a red, yellow, and green knit cap that's attached to realistic-looking polyester dreads. She pulls it down over my ears, and with the help of a makeup compact, I can see that I truly look like Ziggy Marley from the back, especially if I wear some baggy clothes. "He'll never know it's you!"

"Won't people be talking about this, and then won't Fletcher find out what she looks like?" Amber asks, yanking the fairy crown from her head. "This is so silly, you guys. Why don't you just talk to him?"

Becca answers. "Shelby wants a break, and she doesn't want to make a scene. I'm sure she'll talk to him. Later." Amber purses her lips disapprovingly at our lack of maturity. "What are you wearing, Elisa?"

Elisa grins, and pulls out a waist-length black wig and Hollywood sunglasses. "Probably as close as I'll ever get to being Cher. Thank God."

Friday is meeting day, of course, and I go through the morning feeling giddy about what we're going to do. We have great plans about GeekFest, and we started a MySpace page for the club, and things just seem to be all sorted out again. I practically skip to Ms. McLachlan's room, my rasta dreadlocks swinging along behind me. Never mind that Fletcher's voice keeps echoing in the back of mind.

The room is packed full of girls, and they are all chatting excitedly. Becca and her glorious hair net are already there, Elisa stands sort of primping near the door in her movie star getup, and Amber is in the back of the room, minus her fairy hat. Becca claps her hands and welcomes the thirty or so girls as Elisa closes the classroom door. "Welcome to meeting two of the Queen Geek Social Club," she says. "It's such a rush to see all you guys here to help with our projects. First of all, I want to welcome any newcomers. We do have a website, and if you could talk to Elisa, our resident movie star over there, she'll get your name on our mailing list. Now—" The door opens slowly, and Becca says, "Come on in, we just got started."

I'm reading a flier about GeekFest, so I don't notice why everyone suddenly shuts up. I look up, and Fletcher is standing in the doorway, with Jon in tow. "Hi." He waves to everyone, very chipper. I feel like someone has punched me in the gut.

Becca cocks her head at him. "Hi. We're having a meeting, so if you don't mind . . ."

"Nope. I don't mind." He plops down on the floor and tucks his legs up under him. Jon does the same.

"Uh . . . okay. Let me be more direct. Could you please leave?" A low hum of whispers starts to fill the room. Most of the girls don't know what's going on, but of course, they will know within about three seconds. Gossip travels fast.

"Why should we leave?" Fletcher asks nonchalantly.

"This is a meeting of the Queen Geek Social Club," Becca says evenly. "Members only."

"Well, Jon and I want to join." Fletcher smiles maddeningly.

Becca looks as if her head will explode. "Dammit, you can't join. You're not girls!"

Amitha Bargout taps Fletcher on the shoulder. "Maybe you should start your own club."

"I really want to join," he says. "I want to be part of this amazing undertaking. I hear you're going to change the world."

Now the chatter is full blown, and I feel my face turning an unpleasant shade of red. I rip off the rasta hat and throw it at Fletcher. "Why are you doing this?"

"Because you won't talk to me," he answers defiantly.

"If I don't want to talk to you, I don't have to."

"No, but you also can't keep me out of your club. Check out your club charter."

Becca, who seems poised to let loose a stream of nastiness on the boys, stops before she even utters a word. "What . . . did . . . you . . . say?" she whispers venomously.

Fletcher stands up and dusts off his pants. "I said, your school wide club charter states that a school club cannot discriminate against any potential members. Jon and I want to join."

The place goes nuts. Girls stand up, faces contorted in various degrees of anger or amusement or puzzlement. "Fine, fine," Becca says through clenched teeth. "Sit down, everybody."

The boys return to their spots on the floor.

Glaring at them, Becca continues. "Obviously, we will get to the bottom of this, and we won't let them derail what we want to do." But I can tell that she's a bit less excited, a bit less enthusiastic than she had been, and a bit less sure of herself. "So, let's talk about committees. We'll need someone to be in charge of lighting. Anyone in theater?"

Jon raises his hand, and so does Amber. Becca looks like she might spit on Jon, but instead, she nods toward the back of the room. "Amber. Thanks." She jots the name on her clipboard so furiously that she breaks the lead in her mechanical pencil. "And next we need someone who can work on programs."

"I can program!" Jon shouts.

"Programs for the show," Elisa says harshly. "Geez, and you call yourself a genius?"

Claudette and Caroline raise their hands and volunteer for program duty. Other girls volunteer for stuff. This goes on for about ten minutes until all the committees are formed, and each time Becca announces a new one, Fletcher or Jon or both of them raise their hands and make a general nuisance of themselves. I want to punch them out. What did I ever seen in him? Other than his wit, charm, good looks, and sexiness?

The bell rings, ending lunch. "That's all. See you next week," Becca says as cheerfully as she can while in the midst of a murderous rage. As girls file out of the room, Fletcher and Jon stand up and start to leave too. Becca blocks their path. "Where are you going?"

"I thought you'd be thrilled for us to leave," Fletcher says. He turns to me. "I know you aren't speaking to me for some reason, but I care about you so much that I'll come in here where I know I'll get spit on and abused, and I'll sit on that cold floor just to be near you!"

"The floor is carpeted," Elisa notes.

Fletcher ignores her. "When you decide you'd like to have a real conversation, let me know." Inside, I'm screaming, "Yes! I want to!" but all I do is stare at my shoes.

Becca gets in his face. "She doesn't want to talk to you or she would. Maybe you should leave her alone. Or should I report you for stalking?"

"Good one. Are you her personal bodyguard?"

"I could be."

Amber has rushed to the front of the room and nervously inserts herself between Becca and Fletcher. "Now, listen. If you guys get in a fight, the club will fold, and you'll both get suspended. That's stupid." She glances at me. "Shelby, could you tell them?"

In my head, I have lots of great, snippy comments as well as a bunch of sappy apologies and even a few panicky crying jags, all waiting to emerge. So, to keep all of them corralled, I say, "Just go."

Fletcher looks at me, gives me a little crooked half-smile, and his eyes soften as he says, "Okay. But we do need to talk. When you're ready." He turns to go.

"So, you're not going to press this club thing?" Becca asks.

"Oh, no, I'm still joining your club," he answers. "I don't walk away from anything this good." He waves at me, then he and Jon dodge into the churning sea of teenagers.

"Let's go to class," Amber suggests, tugging at my arm as an English class files in. Elisa and Becca follow behind, silent.

When we get to the place where we all part ways and Becca and I go to our hellish P.E. class, it's an unspoken agreement that we will get together after school. "My house?" I ask. Everyone nods.

"Meet at the theater instead of the Rock," Amber says as she turns toward the math building. "We can go the back way."

Becca seems as stunned as I am. Her eyes are round saucers, and she walks like someone in shock. I expect I look the same. As we change in the girl's locker room, she turns to me and says, "You know this is war, right?"

"Why?"

"Why?" She slams the door a little too hard, and a few other girls glance over to see if there's a catfight imminent. "Because he's going to go to the student senate or the principal and complain if we try to keep him out of the club. And they *will* shut us down."

"How can they do that?" I close my locker too, a bit more gently.

"Because of those stupid civil rights laws that say you can't discriminate based on gender or race."

"Yeah, those have really gotten in the way." Sometimes Becca can be a little self-absorbed. I guess we all can be. "But I still don't see how he can shut down the club."

We walk toward the field where our teacher, Mr. Cruces, is patiently counting heads as if we are a bunch of cows going to the old slaughterhouse. That's about what I feel like, as a matter of fact. Becca says, "He'll say we're discriminating! It's a public school. They won't let us exclude anyone who really wants to join."

"Can't we tell them that he's only doing it out of spite?"

"Sure, we can tell them that." Mr. Cruces checks to be sure we're dressed properly and then we jog at a snail's pace along the edge of the huge baseball field. "But Fletcher will say he's just doing it because he wants to be part of our activities. He'll find a way around it, believe me. No, what we really need to do is persuade him that he doesn't *want* to join."

"How can we do that?"

"You can start going out with him again, and then he'll forget about it."

"Not an option at this point." I jog even more slowly than I had been at the thought of dating Fletcher at all. And then I think about his eyes, and him kissing me, and then the damned thumping-bass karaoke—

"Well, then, we just have to make his life a living hell, I guess." She grins demonically and runs ahead a few paces, leaving me at the end of the line with Mr. Cruces blowing his whistle in my ear.

13

THE CULT OF THE EXPIRED SOUP

(or You Say Tomato, I Say Too Tired)

After school, we meet like spies at the theater. Elisa is still wearing her wig and glasses. Becca and I start laughing.

"What?" she says. "I thought we were going under-cover."

"Yes," Becca says. "No one would ever know that you're in disguise."

"Where's Amber?" I ask, checking around for signs of Fletcher. "We need to get going."

As if on cue, Amber scampers up, out of breath. "I just talked to Mr. Willfield. He said we can schedule a performance for our show right before Thanksgiving. Isn't that great?"

"Is Mr. Willfield an imaginary friend?" Elisa asks as we walk. She strips off the wig and glasses and stuffs them into her backpack.

"No, he's the drama teacher." Amber shrugs out of her long black coat and folds it over her arm. "He says the drama department will be finished with the fall show at the end of October, and after that, it's all ours!"

"You're not wearing your goth coat?" Elisa says, wheezing slightly in her attempt to make her short legs keep up with Becca's long strides.

"Too hot." Amber wipes her foreheard with her no-fingered glove. "I don't think I'm going to be able to maintain my gothness. It's too uncomfortable, and I'm not suffering enough to carry it off."

"You'd suffer more if you keep the coat on," Elisa suggests.

We get to the corner, the place where we'd be most likely to see our newly sworn enemies; instead, we just see the regular parade of traffic. Minivans, pickup trucks, and beater cars with mismatched doors are ready to bolt forward as soon as the light changes. I scan the traffic for Fletcher's car and immediately hate myself for doing it.

Once we get to my house, we camp out in the living room. Euphoria is delighted to have houseguests. "What can I bring you? Coffee? Water? Tea? Soda? Assorted fruit juices?" She lights up with glee. "I just made a fresh batch of lemonade."

We all opt for lemonade; since Euphoria can make anything with the chemically perfect mix of ingredients, anything homemade always beats the store-bought stuff. When she rolls in with the pitcher, she also has a tray full of weird-looking brown things in the shape of, I swear, Fred the former lawnmower.

"Euphoria," Becca asks, holding one of the food items up to the light, "is this edible? What is it?"

"I'm so glad you asked." Euphoria whirs and hums, and a piece of paper scrolls from her printer compartment. She picks it up gently and hands it to Becca. "This is a picture of Fred. I used it to construct the baked goods. They are the image of Fred. If we eat him, he lives within us."

"Creepy," Elisa mutters as she grabs one, examines it, then bites what would be Fred's head off. "Hmm. It's not really sweet. What's in it?"

"It's all of Fred's favorites. Tofu, baker's yeast, kibble, and maraschino cherries."

"'Scuse me," Elisa says as she turns green and runs for the bathroom.

The rest of us politely decline the Fred cookies, but pour glass after glass of lemonade. Just thinking about the ingredients makes me kind of queasy and thirsty and kind of like I want to bark. Or bake something.

"What do we do?" Becca asks after things settle down and Euphoria rolls back to the kitchen. "What's our strategy for getting rid of this obnoxious pest?"

"You make it sound like he's a cockroach."

"If the feelers fit . . ."

"Fine," I say, feeling truly less than fine. "Can we just drop it? I'd really like to talk about something else."

"Okay," Becca says, nodding. "Let's talk about GeekFest. Amber, you said Mr. Wills-his-name—"

"Willfield."

"—Willfield said we could use the theater after October. Elisa, get out your calendar."

Elisa pulls her Palm Pilot from its holster. "Please don't refer to Wembley as my 'calendar'. It's demeaning."

"We *so* need to get you a date," Amber mutters, shaking her head.

"How many weeks between Halloween and Thanksgiving?" Becca peers over her shoulder.

"Looks like four." She does some quick calculations. "We'd need to audition acts, have rehearsals and do the show in that time."

Amber swings her legs over the edge of the couch. "What about if we had auditions before that, but used that time to actually run the show, with the tech stuff? That would give us more time to really get it right."

"So . . ." Becca squints at the ceiling, calculating in her head. "Let's say we put in announcements next week. What's the date today, anyway?"

"September fifteen," I pipe in. "Too soon for any auditions.

Becca pours more lemonade. "Of course it's too soon for auditions. But we can get people to start thinking about it. And then auditions . . . When? Where?"

"I think in two weeks." Elisa scribbles on Wembley with her stylus. "That's the end of September, and that gives us time in October to get things together and to advertise it and get whatever we need. And rehearse the acts on a split schedule, correlating dates with sports, band, and choir practices as well as significant grading dates."

"With that calculating mind, it's too bad you're not a guy," Becca snips. "You could date Euphoria."

"Enough about my love life!" Elisa slams the cover on Wembley. "Sorry, sweetie," she mutters, stroking its case. As Amber said, we really *do* need to get her a date.

I drain the last of the lemonade from my glass. "I absolutely can't work without some baked goods that are kibble-free. Let's raid the kitchen."

No one ever disagrees with the idea of a kitchen raid. We find a box of organic oatmeal-chocolate-chip granola snacks, some ice cream bars with freezer burn, and Halloween candy left over from last year. Euphoria is all in a snit about us messing up her kitchen, so we tromp back to the pantry room, where archaeological foods wait to be excavated.

A naked light bulb shines on the stacks of boxes and bags of food. The pantry is large enough for the four of us to walk into, but there's not much room to move around; therefore, we keep elbowing each other and stepping on each others' shoelaces. Squatting on the floor, Becca peers into a dingy cupboard. "Is anything in here actually edible?"

"Wow." Amber reaches up onto a top shelf and pulls out a four pack of those heat-and-eat soup cans. "Check it out. I used to eat these all the time for lunch."

"Tomato soup. That sounds kind of good." Elisa grabs the cans and turns them over. "Does soup expire?"

"Everything goes bad eventually." I grab the cans from her and locate the expiration date. "Uh, yeah. These expired a year ago. My dad never cleans this stuff up, and he never tells Euphoria to do it either, so it just sits here expiring."

Becca has picked up the cans and is squinting at the side panel. "Check it out. You can call a hotline number if you want to know anything about soup." She looks up, a sparkle in her eye. "Shall we?"

"What are we going to ask them?" I'm almost afraid of the answer.

"Well, we ask them what we do with expired soup, I guess. Is it safe to eat? Can it be used for evil purposes? That sort of thing."

"Ah. Evil purposes. I figured that's where you were going with it."

"So? Shelby's a spoilsport, but what about you two?" She grins maniacally at Elisa and Amber.

"I couldn't do it," Amber says. "I'd just crack up."

"I don't have any minutes left on my cell phone," Elisa says firmly.

Becca sighs in exaggerated frustration and grabs the soup cans. "Fine, I'll do it. Come on."

We all follow her into the living room, where she takes out her cell phone and keys in the 1–888 number for the company's soup hotline. I watch her in amazement. She just isn't concerned about anything she does! She'll talk to anyone, do anything that sounds interesting. I wish I had that kind of . . . whatever it is that she has.

"Okay, it's ringing!" she whispers excitedly. Even though this is a totally immature and stupid thing to do, I sort of feel into it, and I want to hear what she says, and I can tell the other girls do too, because we're all staring intently at Becca and the phone. "Electronic menu of options . . . No, I don't want any holiday recipes. . . . No, I don't need help reading the directions. . . . No, I'm not interested in your soup-of-the-month club. . . . Oh, hi!" She puts it on speaker phone so we can all be part of the magic.

"Hello, this is Pat, I'll be your soup specialist this evening. How can I help you?"

"Soup Specialist?" Becca says seriously while making a goofy face. "Is that really your job?"

"Yes, it is. How can I help you?" Pat doesn't sound like the type who likes her soup to be mocked.

"Well, Pat," Becca says as if it's a matter of great importance, "I have these cans of tomato soup here, and it says they're expired, but I wanted to know: Is it safe to eat them anyway?"

"We don't recommend that you consume any product that is expired," Pat explains patiently, as if we are all too stupid to really understand that. "We cannot guarantee the safety of any expired product."

"Hmmm." Becca turns the can over in her hand. "So, is there anything I *can* do with this soup? I mean, could I stack this soup up and make it into a little altar, and start my own cult? The Cult of the Expired Soup?"

Pat kind of chuckles. She's not all business, after all. "Well, yes, I guess you could do that."

"And could I charge admission to see the almighty expired cans that started it all? I mean, can I put up a shrine in my yard or something, and then create a whole line of Expired Soup–related products that could be purchased by my worshippers?"

"I'd advise against anything that violates copyright," Pat cautions. "But if you think you can persuade people to listen to you, I say go for it."

By this point, we're all strangling with restrained laughter, and even Becca is fighting very hard to keep a straight face. "Well, Pat, thanks for your help. I have a new mission in life now, thanks to you."

"You're welcome," Pat answers. "Have a great day."

"Have a soup-er day!" Becca yells and hangs up the phone. We all just explode in gut-busting laughter to the point where I can't even catch my breath. It feels really good to just roll on the floor laughing so hard my belly hurts. I haven't laughed much lately.

"Oh my God, Becca, you are insane!" Amber says, her voice shaky. "I cannot believe you did that."

"And you didn't laugh!' Elisa adds, wiping her eyes. "I don't know how you did *that*."

Becca is staring intently at the cans. I can tell by the gleam in her eyes that we're way past the joke. "Uh . . . you don't really want to start a religious cult, do you?" I ask. With Becca, you never rule anything out.

"No, no," she says, waving a hand at me impatiently. "But I think Pat may have inspired me to think of a suitable torture for our cockroach."

"You're going to make him eat the soup?" Elisa grimaces. "I don't think that's a good idea, Becca. I mean, what if he pukes all over your shoes or goes to the hospital or—"

"No, no, I'm not going to make him eat the soup!" Becca jumps up and down excitedly. "What we do is this: We collect empty cans of soup, as many as we can get. We go to his house and we stack them up in front of his door, so when he comes out in the morning, he knocks them all over and it's a huge mess. And then we can put them in his locker, in his car, everywhere! He might get the concept that trying to be part of our group isn't such a great idea. I mean, we don't want to hurt him, but we do want to get the point across: He's not welcome."

"I don't know," Amber says, squinting at the guilty-looking soup cans. "Isn't that sort of like harassment?"

"What harassment?" Becca snorts. "Leaving a few cans here and there?"

"What if he trips, cuts himself, gets tetanus, and dies?" Elisa asks, folding her arms in front of her with determination. "We could be liable, you know."

"I've changed my mind." Becca twirls a can by its flip top. "Elisa should be a lawyer, not an accountant."

"Wow, I've been promoted," Elisa says sarcastically.

Euphoria calls from the kitchen, "Are you all going to want supper?"

I look from girl to girl. Elisa finally says, "Well, as long as there's no kibble involved, I'm up for it."

"Let's order a pizza," Becca suggests.

"Ah, let me cook!" Euphoria bleeps from the kitchen. "I never get to cook for more than two people. And Mr. Chapelle hardly counts; he never eats anything but Pringles potato chips and soup!"

At the mere mention of soup, we all bust out laughing again. And then I realize how much Fletcher would love this joke, and suddenly soup makes me sad.

After the Friday night feast from Euphoria, everyone goes home stuffed, even Becca. I'm forced to face my archenemy, homework. This, of course, makes the weekend about as much fun as kibble cookies.

My phone has been buzzing less and less. I put it on my desk so I can see it if it goes off, and see who's calling. Although I should be glad Fletcher has taken the hint and is leaving me alone, I can't help but feel disappointed. I mean, if he really did like me, or even love me, how can he just give up like that? Honestly, it really shows what someone is made of, down deep.

Monday it's raining, so Dad drives me to school, which means an interrogation. "So, what's going on between you and Fletcher?"

I fake a huge yawn that keeps me from answering, then slowly sip coffee from my travel mug.

"Hello?" He reaches over and taps me on the head. "Did you hear me?"

"Yes, I heard you." I slap at his hand as if it's an annoying mosquito, nearly dumping my coffee onto my jeans. "I've just been really busy."

"Hmmm." He maneuvers through the rainy side streets before getting onto the freeway. Even though school's only one exit away, Dad gets frustrated with surface streets and all those "poky old ladies" clogging up the road. "Euphoria mentioned that you've got a school project involving soup cans."

I nearly choke. "Uh . . . wow. I think she was just hearing weird stuff. We were watching a movie." I realize as I babble that none of what I'm saying really answers his question, but I'm sort of hoping he won't notice that. Of course, that's stupid, because my dad is literally a rocket scientist, so not a whole lot gets past him. However, I do have a secret weapon that, if used sparingly, will deflect all questions. "I've got terrible cramps." I open the glove box. "Do you have any tampons in here?"

Dad frowns and grips the steering wheel even more tightly. He's just kind of bewildered by female function, and I know he dreads talking about anything involving the word "menstrual." I've used this strategy before, but you have to be careful; if you overuse it, then they get suspicious and start keeping track, and suddenly they calculate that you have a period every two weeks instead of every four, or every first and third week, and then it's either confess or go to the doctor for a thorough checkup. As I said, you have to play it just right. I'm kind of desperate, because I really don't want to talk about Fletcher.

But he won't let it go. "So? Are you two still seeing each other or not?"

We've arrived at school, and traffic is totally clogged because of the rain. It's like nobody has ever seen water on asphalt before. Because of this, we sit in front of the parking lot, stuck. "I think I'll just get out here," I say, reaching for the door handle.

Dad locks the door with the flick of a button and gives me a lopsided smile, so I say "Oh, very clever. You can make me sit here, but you can't make me talk."

"What did he do, exactly?" We inch forward, raindrops splattering the glass, first in intense sheets, then in trickles. "I really want to know."

"As I said, I'd think you'd be glad. Most dads don't want their daughters to date, period. I'm voluntarily swearing off guys, and you don't even have to get involved! How lucky are you?"

He chuckles, which, to me, is the exactly wrong response.

"Why are you laughing at me?" I hear myself, and I sound pretty shrill and girlish. I'm guessing if I saw the expression on my face, I wouldn't like that either.

"I'm not laughing at you, Shelby. I just want you to tell me what's going on. I—" Just as I've run out of excuses, somebody bangs furiously on the wet window. Through the hazy streaks of water, I see Becca's spiky hair under a leopard-print umbrella.

"Gotta go, Dad." I lean over, kiss him on the cheek, and flip the lock before he can shut it again. "Love you." I slam the car door before he can even respond. I don't even look back as I follow Becca through the downpour and we run toward the drama building.

We get to the alcove before Becca says anything. "You will never even believe what I have in my pocket!" She drops the umbrella, flinging water droplets all over the floor, and reaches into her backpack. "I've got it all on tape!" she says, producing a compact DV recorder.

"You've got what on tape?"

"Just watch." She flips open the view screen and presses "play." At first, all I see is a dark, murky picture, but soon it switches to nightshot and I see a house with a porch light shining, and a small yard with a redwood fence. "What am I looking at? Your Barbie Dream House?"

"Wait for it." Two figures run into the frame and approach the front door of the house. They're all dressed in black and carry bulky sacks. The two figures crouch next to a line of hedges, then carefully put the sacks on the ground. They begin pulling something out of the bags, and then seem to bundle several objects into the makeshift aprons of their bulky hoodie sweatshirts. Then they approach the front door, and kneel. "Okay, it's some weird religious thing, right?"

"No, no." Becca giggles, and that's about the first time I've heard her do *that*. "Watch."

The figures hover over the doorstep, and they obscure the view. Whoever is holding the camera (and it sounds like Elisa) whispers urgently, "Hurry up! I see a light on up-stairs!" The two marauders see it too, and jump up silently, grabbing their bags and running toward the camera, which focuses for one more moment to reveal a four-foot-tall stack of soup cans built in a sloppy pyramid.

Becca presses the forward button on the camera. "Okay, so we took off, but we left Elisa's camera in the tree to capture the moment of supreme surprise. Check it out." The scene gets lighter and lighter as the sun comes up, and finally the front door opens. Fletcher isn't paying any attention; he's zipping up his backpack, juggling his car keys, and yelling something over his shoulder to someone in the house. He careens full on into the soup-can pyramid. One second he's upright, the next, he's flat on his back, surrounded by cans in various states of destruction. It looks like he had some pretty heavy stuff in his backpack; some of the little soldiers seem dented beyond repair.

Becca guffaws with her donkey honk laugh, and rewinds the tape again. "Look at it in slow motion. It's priceless!" She shows me Fletcher coming out of his house, more slowly this time, but still looking depressed, flustered, unorganized. The moment his foot connects with the bottom line of cans, he loses his footing, looks down, and an expression of disbe-lief and confusion fills his face. Then he crashes down (in slow motion), falling like a war hero taking a bullet on the field of battle.

"Is that awesome?" Becca checks the alcove, which is now pretty full of people since we're only ten minutes away from the first bell. "I have *got* to find a way to get that on Panther TV!"

I feel sort of sick. I guess watching Fletcher get punked like that should have been great for me; after all, I'm mad at him, right? But instead, all I feel is the aforementioned nausea. Becca's frowning at me as she tucks the DV recorder into her backpack. "Are you okay? You look a little green."

"Yeah," I mumble. "Fine."

"Wasn't it awesome?" She stares at me, and finally punches me in the arm. Kind of hard. "Wake up!"

"To be honest, I thought it was kind of stupid." I walk toward the double doors, knowing that this comment will cost me some serious lecturing. Becca can be quite righteous when she thinks she's done the noble work of the Queen Geeks.

She cuts in front of me, blocks the door with her tremendous limbs, and laughs. Laughs!

"I don't see why you think it's funny." I try to get around her, but she's too big and too fast. "Can I go to class, please?"

"Wait." She motions toward the stairway leading up to the second floor, and Elisa and Amber dash out. "Shelby, I give you the Queen Geeks of the Round Can."

"That's kind of a personal comment." Elisa snorts at her own dumb joke. No one else does. "Okay, sorry. Anyway, Shelby, how did you feel about seeing Fletcher take a nosedive into dozens of cans of tomato soup?"

Amber stands next to her. "Did it make you feel good or not?"

Actually, I feel like crying. I try to dart away, in any direction, but one of them is blocking me no matter which way I go. It's like a game of human keep-away, and I'm the ball. I am definitely going to blow at any moment, and a Mount Vesuvius of tears will flow down my cheeks, flooding the alcove and sending us all to our doom—

Becca, Amber, and Elisa grab each others' hands and form a ring-around-the-rosies circle. "Admit it," Becca hisses, "you love him."

"You didn't want to see him hurt," says Elisa.

"Or humiliated," says Amber.

"Or cut on rusty metal," Elisa adds. By the looks she gets from the others, I figure that wasn't part of the script. The first bell rings.

"Here's the point," Becca says, her voice getting louder so it carries over the din of kids going to class. "You do really care about him. Pretending that you don't is a lie, and we all know what happens to liars!"

"They get cut on rusty metal," Elisa said knowingly.

"No, they live unhappy lives and their souls are blackened forever," Amber says matter-of-factly. "And they pay retail for everything."

Becca puts an arm around my shoulder as we walk out into the misty drizzle flanked by Amber and Elisa. "Our eloquent point is this: You must get back together with him. We can't stand to see you miserable, and even though we'd like to have you all to ourselves, it's not fair to make you choose between him and us. We want you to be happy, and you won't be happy without Fletcher. So, Fletcher stays."

"What about the soup cans?" I ask, pretending that I have something in my eye.

"It took us a freakin' weekend just to get *that* many," Elisa mutters. "It was way worse than the Twinkies from last year, and you can't eat them."

I stop and turn to Becca, then hug her in front of everybody. I don't care what anybody thinks. Whatever. I hug Amber and Elisa too, and I feel this great sense of relief, like a two-ton soup can has been lifted from my shoulders.

And I have a real burning desire to see Fletcher.

14

PARTY OF ONE

(or Halloween Blues)

At lunch, I pull out my cell phone and key in Fletcher's number. It rings and rings. I try it again. No answer.

I'm parked at the entrance to the cafeteria, which on rainy days smells like wet dogs rubbed with Pine-Sol. It's a great appetite suppressant. Although the weather has gone from downpour to spitty drizzle, it's currently dry except for drips from the building overhangs. I see Becca striding across the senior lawn toward me, getting some pretty nasty looks from the seniors brave (or stupid) enough to claim their territory outside despite the weather.

"So," she says, shaking droplets from her blond spikes, "did you call him?"

"I tried." I fold the phone and put it back in my pocket. "He's not answering."

"Probably the weather." She scopes the food lines and finds the shortest one. "I'm starving. C'mon."

I actually don't have much of an appetite. We get in line behind a group of football players (you can tell by the massive backs and the fact that they tote five-gallon jugs of water around), and I happen to catch the end of a conversation: "Yeah, so I think that's over. Now he can go back to being normal again," a black kid says to a tall, skinny blond guy.

"She's pretty out there," the blond agrees, punching a shorter kid with mousy brown dreadlocks and a wannabe mustache. "Scott, you gonna go for it?"

"I don't go for no sloppy seconds," Scott replies, which makes all the guys laugh. We're almost to the serving line when the first kid says, "He said she's all talk anyhow, and she's got that huge freaky friend with the tattoo—" And then the guy speaking glances back, sees us, and immediately has a coughing fit as he grabs his tray.

Becca's face has clouded over and I am afraid for the safety of the football squad. "Hey," I say softly, touching her arm. "Don't worry about it." But on the inside, I feel like throwing myself into a vat of French fry grease and ending it all.

We get our food as the football players, who've now all noticed that we're standing there, slink to the farthest corner of the room. I walk, zombielike, to a small table and drop my tray with a clatter, jostling my nutritious lunch of cherry Jell-O, pretzels, and chocolate milk, which were the only things I could see to grab with tears blurring my eyes.

Becca covers one of my hands with her silver-ringed fingers. "Listen," she says gently. "They don't know anything. Let's just go talk to him."

"I finally decide to let him in again, and this is what happens?" I say, sadness catching at my voice. "It's like the universe is trying to tell me I'm an idiot for even thinking something might work out."

"You want me to talk to him?" she asks, stabbing a huge forkful of Caesar salad and stuffing it into her mouth.

"I don't know. This is so screwed up. I shouldn't even be allowed to think about having relationships." We both eat our lunches in silence, me slurping little spoonfuls of red goo while Becca munches. I don't even like Jell-O. But really, it's all I deserve.

After a while, Becca glances at her phone, and then gathers our trash onto one tray. "Bell's going to ring. I'll try to catch him after P.E. Ready to go?"

We trudge across the campus, and I feel like I'm dragging rusty chains behind me. How is it possible for one person to poison a perfectly nice little relationship with someone before it even really gets off the ground? I mean, we didn't even spend all that much time together! I guess I just have a talent for losing people.

P.E. sucks, as usual, but because it's been raining, we have to stay inside the doomnasium. Mr. Cruces keeps trotting around us like a sheepdog nosing at stray mutton, and I keep dragging my feet as the other sheep trot around the track. "Chapelle, let's pick it up, okay?"

I don't answer. I sense I am bordering on insubordination, but like a kamikaze pilot circling over a sushi factory, I am resigned to the fact that I am going to cause a big stink. "Chapelle, did you hear me?" Cruces's Marine voice starts oozing out of his crew cut when he gets mad. My lack of response infuriates him. I usually smile politely and apologize for being human, but today, I just don't care. "Chapelle, out of the line," he yells at me. I'm supposed to pull out of traffic and go to the designated chew-out spot under the basketball hoop, but I just keep trudging around the circle like a pony at a carnival.

Becca slows down (she always outruns me, of course) and pulls up next to me. "Shelby, you'd better stop," she hisses. "He'll give you a referral!"

I don't even care. I just keep trudging. I'm going so slow now that other girls are bumping into me like I'm a piece of rotten driftwood clogging up the stream. Row, row, row your driftwood, gently down the drain. . . . As I'm singing to myself, I feel a strong hand on my shoulder. It's a campus supervisor, the guy we all nicknamed the Termin-Asian because he's a Japanese cage fighter outside of school, and he's so big he could probably create his own weather system if he sweated or cried enough. "Shelby Chapelle?"

The Termin-Asian grabs my arm firmly but gently, and pulls me out of the group and toward the double doors. "Where are we going?" I ask.

He snorts. "Tahiti."

"Cool."

Where we really go is the vice principal's office. I've never been there, actually; usually, the only kids who see the inside of the V.P. offices are the ones who get dress coded, do drugs, have fights, or destroy or steal stuff.

They park me on a chair in the hallway, and I stare at the wall ahead of me. It's full of artwork done by students in sketch class, and these are all pictures of containers being opened with things popping out of them. There's a Christmas present with a big red bow, and a doll with a skull waves from the open box; a wooden treasure chest with a skull hand crawling out, clutching an iPod; a pink candy box with a white satin ribbon containing tiny chocolates with the faces of real babies peering out. Maybe they're dropping acid in art class.

"Shelby?" A tan, blond woman holding some paperwork stands at the end of the hallway. "I'm Mrs. Boyed. Come on in."

I follow her into a nice office with a classy carpet, trophies on shelves, and pictures of students on a corkboard next to the desk. "Sit," she says, indicating a chair opposite her desk. "So, you had some trouble in P.E.? What's going on?"

"Nothing," I mumble, staring down at my shoes.

She studies me. "Mr. Cruces told the supervisor you refuse to participate."

"I was moving."

She laughs a bit. "Yeah, he says you never stopped moving, but you were going so slowly that you were causing traffic jams, and you weren't listening to anything he said. You can see how that would be a problem, right?" I nod. She taps some keys on her computer. "You've never had any discipline problems, Shelby. What's going on with you?"

I can't tell her what's going on with me. Nobody cares about stupid boyfriend stuff. "I just don't feel very well today. It's probably my period." Maybe that will work?

"Yeah, I don't think so." Nope. Not on a woman, I guess. "Something is bothering you. Did somebody say something to you? Anybody threaten you?" I shake my head. "Girlfriend?

Boyfriend?" Aw. Stupid hormones. I start crying. I think I should have my tear ducts removed. "Boyfriend. Ah."

She pushes a box of blue tissues over to me, and I yank out a big handful, then blow my nose with no thought to how loud it would be or how embarrassed I would be. I just can't care. "It's really nothing," I hear myself say. But I don't sound like myself. I sound like somebody with a real problem. My voice is all shaky and weird, and my throat feels tight, like I can't breathe.

"So, it's a boyfriend thing," Mrs. Boyed says, nodding as I cry like a stupid baby. "All I can tell you is that it goes away eventually. It seems like the biggest thing in the world right now, but when you get to be twenty-one, or maybe even next year, you won't even remember it was a problem. And I also know that none of that helps at all." She shuffles the paperwork, and sighs. "As to the thing in Mr. Cruces's class, I'll give you a warning, and ask that in the future if you feel like you're just not capable of doing P.E., you take a nonsuit day, just don't get dressed. You'll get points docked from your grade, but you won't have a confrontation." She signs the form, then pushes it across the desk to me. "Sign there, and expect your dad to talk to you about it when you get home."

"My dad?"

"Sure. If you get a referral, we call home. But as I said, you're not in major trouble. Just explain what we talked about, and I'm sure it will all work out." Yeah. She doesn't know my dad.

I leave the office feeling worse than when I got there, if that's possible. P.E. is almost over, though, so thankfully I don't have to go back there. All I have is period six, and instead of going, I start walking off campus. This is not something I usually do; in fact, I've only skipped high school once, and I faked sick that time. This is the first time I've ever just ditched and walked off. There's a feeling of danger to it, but mostly, I just feel tired.

I can't go home, of course. So, instead, I head to the park near the high school. I find a bank of vacant swings, throw my backpack on the ground, hop on, and just start to pump my legs as hard as I can, driving the swing upward in a pleasant arc toward the hot blue sky. I don't know how long I do this, but I get tired, so I find a patch under a tree and lie down for a nap.

The next thing I know, Becca is shaking me awake. "Hey, what are you doing?" She looks sweaty and hot, and not in the best mood. "We've all been walking all over the world looking for you. Hang on." She pulls out her cell and calls someone. "I found her. She's at the park, by the swings."

My head feels buggy, like ants have been crawling on it, and my mouth is dry. "What time is it?"

"Four." She drops down to the ground and sits across from me. "What happened after P.E.?"

"I saw Mrs. Boyed. She gave me a warning. I ditched."

Becca studies me, frowning. "This is really not like you, Shelby. Since when have you let a guy ruin your life? I mean, I really like Fletcher and all, but you have us, you have the club, you have yourself. Why do you need *any* guy?"

"Oh, yeah, like when you were all nuts over Jon, huh?" I hear the sharp edge in my voice. "But I guess that's different, because it's you."

"I didn't ditch school." She glances over toward the baseball field behind the trees, and then stands up. "Okay, well, I'm heading out. Call me later."

"Where are you going?"

"I'll talk to you tonight. I'll plan to come over too. Thea can stop whatever dumb project she's working on to give me a ride. I'll be there around five or six unless I hear from you." When she stands up, her dragon tattoo is parallel to my face, and I stare into the slanted green eyes of the lizard, who seems to be sticking his forked tongue out at me. "Love you, Shelby."

As I watch her leave, I hear footsteps behind me. "Hey," Fletcher says gently. "Didn't want to scare you. I'm not a mad stalker or anything." He sits down next to me, crosses his legs and gives me a hug. A brotherly hug. "I hear you had a bad day, huh?"

I just lean into his shoulder and start crying again. He strokes my hair and we sit there for what seems like hours. When I finally come up for air, I've left a little black puddle on the sleeve of his T-shirt. He's smiling sweetly at me; he kisses my forehead. "Whatever is going on with you, I get it. You need time and some room, and I don't need that, so we're having problems. I'll always be your friend, Shelby, so don't forget that."

"You'll always be my friend?" A knife stabs at my heart. That's what guys always say when they never intend on actually speaking to you again. "Look, I know I've been kind of a jerk, but I really care about you, you know that, right?"

He looks down at his shoes. "I know you do, as much as you can. But you're just not in a place where you can be with me. I don't think it's about me. And honestly"—he gives me a crooked smile—"I could probably love you. But I can't do all this drama, and I need somebody who isn't afraid of what we could have together." He cups my face gently in his hands and kisses my lips tenderly, sending electricity shooting through every nerve in my body. "But like I said, I'll always be your friend."

"Wait—" I try to clutch at his pant leg as he stands up. "I can try harder."

He squats down, shaking his head. "See, that's it. You can't *try* to love somebody. You just do it. I'm sorry if I hurt you, and I hope you know I didn't mean to. I'll talk to you soon." He pats my head as he leaves, and I watch him fade into the trees; I follow his silhouette, a dark wavy figure drifting through the heat across the brown-green baseball field.

I get home somehow. Dad is on the porch waiting, as I knew he would be. "Hey," he calls, sounding overly casual. He's pretending to read the paper. "How was school?"

"Fantastic." I try to escape into the house, but no such luck.

"Come sit down." He moves over to make room for me on the swing. "School called."

I don't say anything. We start swinging slowly, rhythmically, and he puts an arm around my shoulders. I lean into him like I used to do when I was little, and we just sit there, swinging, for a long time. Finally, he says, "You're only fifteen. Things change."

"Too many things have already changed." For some reason, I'm thinking about Mom, which I always tend to do whenever I feel really depressed. Dad knows it too; I think he must do the same thing.

"You've had more to deal with in your life than people who are three times your age," he whispers in my ear. "It doesn't just go away."

"Why not?"

He chuckles a little, but I can tell he's sad too, thinking about her. "It just doesn't. I don't want it to, really. I want to remember her. Even if it hurts."

"What does that have to do with this whole mess?"

Dad doesn't answer. I don't know if it's because he doesn't know, or because he doesn't want to say, but the question just hangs there like a cloud full of rain waiting to let loose on a dusty field, making everything a muddy mess.

As promised, Becca comes over, with Amber and Elisa crammed into the back of Thea's Jeep. "Get in!" she yells over the din of the motor. I look at Dad, and he nods. "Go ahead. Just be back in a couple of hours, okay?"

I know I look like absolute and utter hammer-beaten crap, but I get in anyway, wedging between Amber and Elisa. Not enough seat belts, but we've never worried about that; wedged that tightly, I doubt I could even move if the Jeep rolled. "Where are we going?" I yell.

"Surprise!" everybody screams. Despite the day-long cry fest, I feel just a teeny bit better.

Thea drives for about fifteen minutes (and that's kind of like being on the scariest thrill ride ever, except you can never get off or push the emergency stop button), and then steers the car into the parking lot of a strip mall. "Okay," Becca calls from the front seat. "Guess what we're doing?"

"We're going to bust the ninety-nine cent store for selling stuff for a dollar?"

"Wrong. Guess again." Amber giggles and Elisa spits into a tissue and rubs mascara off my cheek.

"I don't know." I swat at Elisa. "Stop spitting on me!"

"Just don't want you to look like a raccoon. Somebody will think you already bought your costume."

"Elisa!" Everyone, including Thea, yelps in horror. Momentarily, I see why. We pull up and park in front of the most enormous Halloween store I've ever seen.

Becca unsnaps her seat belt, then turns around fully, beaming at me. "We knew you were sad, so we thought, what can we do that will really take your mind off of this whole thing? I mean, besides club stuff? And we thought—"

"A Halloween party!" Amber shrieks, jumping up and down in her seat like she's two. "At your house!"

"My house?"

Thea turns too. "We already talked to your dad about it. When the girls told me what happened, I did what I always do when I'm depressed: I try to create. And Halloween's only a few weeks away. We are going to create the best party ever, and find you the most amazing costume you've ever seen!"

Even though I still feel like my heart is made of chunks of concrete, I admit that I feel ever-so-slightly better. We pile out of the Jeep and enter the temple of Halloween known as Masquerade. This is a store that only shows up before Halloween, but it has every possible decoration and costume piece ever made in Taiwan or China.

Some sweaty-looking guy in a Frankenstein suit greets us at the door. "Boo," he says, without much enthusiasm. "Welcome to Masquerade, where prices are so low, it's scary!" He scratches indelicately at his neck bolts and yawns as we walk through.

"So lifelike," Elisa mutters, poking his chest with her finger as she walks by.

Thea gathers us in a knot in front of the steaming plastic cauldrons. "Okay. So, Shelby, do you have any Halloween decorations at your house?"

"Euphoria," Amber says. I throw her a disapproving look. "Well, she could be a decoration. If you pimped her out."

"I'm not pimping out my robot." I turn to Thea and say, "We have some stuff, but it's in storage, and from what I remember, it's pretty crappy. Cardboard skeletons, that kind of stuff."

"Hmmm." Thea rubs at her nose ring as she thinks. This is a habit she always has had since I've known her, but it still throws me; I always expect her to yank the thing out of her nose and begin to bleed profusely. "What kind of theme do we want?"

"Besides 'terrifying yet fun'?" Becca asks sarcastically. "God, Mom, it's just a party, not the second coming of Picasso!"

Thea ignores her. "I mean, we should have some idea of the general theme before we start looking. It'll save us time, Becca. Now. I'd propose you go for a Haunted Mansion kind of thing. Cobwebs, moving portraits, haunted mirrors, stuff like that."

"That sounds kind of expensive," I say. My dad has enough money, but he's not rich or anything. I don't think he'd approve of me spending his hard-earned cash on cobwebs, especially when we have our own and they're free.

"Money is no object," Thea chirps. "I'm paying. I'm actually going to use some of these things in a photographic montage I'm doing for the Bowling Green State University pop culture museum. So, it's all write-off-able!"

With our mission firmly in mind (that is, to make my house as haunted as possible using resin and batteries), we split up and wander through the store. I check out the haunted portraits, because I've always thought they looked cool. You've probably seen them; they look like old photographs of real people, but they shift and turn into skeletons or some other ghoulish version of the same person when you move. As I walk through the gallery of shifting zombie-people, I realize that I don't feel quite as bad as I did. Maybe it's because, in perspective, my life and problems don't seem too bad, really. At least I'm not the living dead.

"Friend of yours?" Becca asks as she points to a particularly creepy Victorian lady in a bride's gown who shifts into a skeleton corpse.

"That's probably going to be me," I joke. Kind of.

Becca smiles and puts an arm around me. "Quit talking like that. This is a temporary dating setback. In the meantime, you will throw yourself into this party, into the Queen Geeks, into GeekFest, and into your amazing friendships. You want to buy the corpse bride?"

"Might as well, if we're going for a Haunted Mansion theme." I grab one from the stack, and put it into the cart

Becca is pushing. "We should probably get a groom, just to be fair. What about this one?" It's a young, geeky guy who turns into the devil, complete with cute little horns, glowing red eyes, and a spiky tail.

"Hmmm. What would your psychiatrist say?" She grabs one anyway.

After an hour of cruising around the store, we all meet up near the despondent Frankenstein greeter, who sits on a stool made of resin bones reading a BMX magazine. Thea flits from cart to cart, checking out our haul. "Oh, I love those portraits," she exclaims over our wedded couple. "And Amber found a haunted mirror."

"Check it out." Amber holds it up, and when I look into it, my face looks like it's melting all over itself. "Real attractive, huh?"

"Guess my sunscreen didn't work," I say, moving my face from side to side to see the goopy, waxy clumps of skin seem to drip down my cheeks.

Elisa produces fake cobwebs, three ancient-looking tombstones, assorted stuffed ravens and rubber snakes, and a weird disembodied bald man's head in a crystal ball. "I got a date," she says, kissing the globe.

"What's it do?" Becca asks, grabbing the bowling-ball-sized crystal sphere.

"Check it out." Elisa sets it on a shelf, flips a switch, and the eyes open. The mouth moves, kind of like a fish without water, and then, from a cheesy speaker, the voice says, "Your fate will be decided by a woman in red."

"It's a fortune-telling thing!" Amber nudges everyone aside and waves at the ball. "Is it motion sensitive?"

In answer, the head belches.

"That's classy." Becca turns it over and switches it off. "It would probably be pretty fun, though."

We get all our stuff to the checkout and Thea foots the bill, which is a lot higher than I would ever expect for a pile of plastic and stuff you use once a year. As we try to find a way to wedge all the stuff into the Jeep while still leaving room for us, Becca starts talking about GeekFest. For a second, a ghostly tinge of sadness over Fletcher pops up, but then it kind of gets buried under her unrelenting enthusiasm.

"We're doing auditions a week from Wednesday," Becca says. "We need to figure out what we want to say to advertise it."

"We need to make it sound cool," Amber suggests.

"It's GeekFest. How can it be cool?" Elisa snorts as she climbs awkwardly into the Jeep. "I think we should ask the club members to participate, and we need a reason that everybody else would care about it. What if it's a fund-raiser for something really important to everyone?"

We all just think about it for a minute, and then all thoughts are blown away by the thunderous revving of the Jeep. Since it's so tough to have a conversation over the roar, we all just sit with our thoughts until Thea pulls into my driveway and the noise finally cuts out.

Dad is sitting on the porch again, something he's been doing entirely too much, in my opinion. "Hey," he calls. "Did you stock up on scary stuff?"

"Yep," Elisa says, charging up the steps. "We even got a fortune-teller who works for free."

Thea and the rest of us grab bags and boxes to carry into the house. Dad jumps up, trots down the steps, and grabs the mirror from Thea. "Here, let me help."

She frowns at him, puzzled. "It's not all that heavy, you know."

He frowns back, equally puzzled. "Yeah, but . . . I just felt like I should help."

Satisfied, she shrugs and grabs another box, then follows Dad up the steps. I don't think she's used to having a man around who actually does something useful. Anyway, we follow them into the house, where Euphoria is already clucking over where she's going to put everything. "Til Halloween!" she shrieks metallically. "That's more than a month away! Where can I put all of this until then?"

Thea has never seen Euphoria, which is kind of amazing; I realize she's actually never set foot in my house. She usually just zips up the driveway, drops off or picks up, and flits away again. She stands, holding a box of cobwebs, staring openmouthed at my robot. Gingerly, she creeps a little closer, and pokes Euphoria gently, to which Euphoria replies, "Hands off, miss. I practice all the martial arts."

Dad puts down the mirror and intervenes. "This is Euphoria. Don't let her intimidate you. It takes her a while to get comfortable with new people."

"Get comfortable—" Thea repeats vaguely.

Dad can see she's freaked out, and freaking Thea out is pretty hard to do. "Well," he stammers, "I made her. She's sort of a domestic and personal assistant."

Euphoria emits an ear-splitting bleep. "I'll have you know that I am neither a domestic nor a personal servant. I—"

"I never said servant. Did I say servant?" Dad looks to us for confirmation. We all shake our heads and murmur protests.

"Oh." Her bleeps get a little less intense, and she finally amps down. "Sorry. I'm just a little sensitive. People have prejudices against the A.I. community, you know."

"A.I.?" Thea murmurs, then looks at Dad.

"Artificial intelligence," he says, patting Euphoria's upper claw. "She's programmed to make decisions and react in real time to all kinds of situations."

"And you made this?"

Euphoria bleeps again, offended. "I'm not a 'this'!" she cries indignantly, then rolls off to the kitchen, I assume. That's usually where she goes when she's upset.

Thea licks her lips, and shakes her head as if trying to clear away a particularly bothersome hallucination. "Well, that *is* interesting." She refocuses on Dad. "I assume you have a name besides Dad?"

"Uh . . ." Dad stutters, and starts to turn red. Kind of weird. It's not like his name is strange or anything. "It's Richard. Rich for short." He extends his hand to shake on it, and Thea smiles shyly and stares at her feet.

Becca makes the crazy sign around her ear, and puts an arm around Thea. "Come on, Mom. Time to go bye-bye."

"Oh." Thea clears her throat nervously. "Sure, honey. I do need to get back. I left some clay drying in the studio."

"Are you an artist?" Dad asks.

"Oh, kind of," Thea answers again with that shy girl voice. It's kind of creeping me out.

"Yeah, yeah, she's fantastic," Becca says, scooting in between them and practically shoving her mom out the door. "Seriously, we've got to go."

Dad watches from the front door as everyone heads for the Jeep. As he closes the door, I hear him murmur, "Artist, hmm?"

"What?"

"Oh, nothing." He locks the door, and turns to me, putting both hands on my shoulders. "Feeling better?"

"I guess." His face looks a little different, kind of sweaty and a little bit younger. "Do you feel okay?"

"Oh, sure." He swipes at his salt-and-pepper hair, which always curls in odd ways, and rubs his forehead. "Just sort of tired. I've been thinking a lot about a new project at work. And I've been worried about you."

I put an arm around his shoulders. "Don't worry about me. I'm just going to keep really busy."

"Hmm." We walk arm in arm toward the kitchen, where Euphoria is chopping something at a furious rate. "Well, that works for a while. But eventually, whatever you feel comes out anyway."

I grab another knife from the butcher's block and help Euphoria hack some vegetables.

15

FRESH-SQUEEZED FESTIVAL

(or Come for the Humiliation, Stay for the Juice)

The rest of the week supremely sucks, to be honest. It's hot as a pancake griddle in Hell, and even though we have air-conditioning, every time you walk outside it's a blast furnace. Teachers start piling on homework, and out of nowhere we have tests on stuff that I don't even know exists. (To be fair, that's probably my fault. I haven't really been paying attention very much. Okay, not at all.) We Queen Geeks try having a study session, but geometry always dissolves into discussion of GeekFest, and English seems to morph into plans for the Halloween party, so we don't get much done.

Friday morning, I feel especially nervous as I walk to school, already sweating because of the heat. It's our first meeting after Fletcher and Jon invaded, and I wonder if they'll be back. Somehow I've managed to avoid Fletcher all week and haven't heard word one from him, so I kind of think not. I secretly wish he would call. We are supposed to be "friends" now, right?

Girls chatter and laugh as Becca beams at them like a goddess bestowing light on the humble worshippers. "Let's get started," she sings. "We have to tell you all about Geek-Fest." She explains the concept, and then opens it up to a discussion of what the fund-raising focus might be.

Amitha Bargout raises her hand. "What if we raised money for a charity?"

"Would a lot of kids care about that?" Becca asks. Most of the girls shake their heads no, which is kind of a sad commentary on high school, but what are you going to do? It's probably true.

Caroline stands up. "I think a worthy cause is a great idea. We just have to make it sexy."

"It's hard to make world hunger and diseases very sexy," Elisa points out.

"True." Caroline turns to face the rest of the girls. "But it's all how you spin it, right?"

"You have an idea, huh?" Becca asks, eyes twinkling. "Okay, go ahead. What is it?"

Caroline smiles, and points to her sister, Claudette. "We did something at our church a few years ago that was great, and it made lots of money and got a lot of people to participate. We did a ticket raffle, so that when you paid admission, you got a ticket stub. Whatever amount of money was collected for that night, you got some percentage of it—forty, fifty, whatever—and the rest went to the church. Or, in this case, whatever cause we decide to adopt."

The chatter starts again immediately, visions of dollar signs dancing in girls' heads. Becca tries to calm them down, but finally has to wolf whistle to get them to shut up. "Okay, that sounds like a good idea. So, where will the money go? Any worthy causes you all want to discuss?"

"Us?" Elisa shouts. "Pizza?"

"Very unselfish," Amber replies. "I think we should do something to support the arts."

While this whole very worthwhile discussion goes forward, I keep watching the door. This is how shallow of a person I am: Instead of thinking about poor, starving orphans with no shoes, I am thinking about whether or not Fletcher Berkowitz will walk through the door. That is really pathetic. I try to refocus my mind on worthwhile charities—Salvation Army, Habitat for Humanity, Mothers Against Drunk Driving—but then everything keeps getting all mixed up with Fletcher again, so my ideas come out Salivation Army, Habit-Forming Hunk-manity, stuff like that. I told you it was pathetic.

When I rejoin the actual conversation already in progress, Amitha is talking about the environment. "If the planet tanks, then so does everything else. That's why I think we should raise money for recycling bins on campus. It's sad that we don't have any way for the whole school to recycle!"

"I agree about the planet and stuff," a mousy blonde in the front row says. "But I think we should be raising money to redecorate the campus. Our campus environment is so bland. I mean, even if we could just paint everything purple—"

The room erupts in a noisy shouting down of purple paint. "Hang on!" Becca yells. "We have to do something that we're actually allowed to do! I don't think they'll let us just repaint the school, even if we want to."

Lunchtime always goes so fast when we have a meeting, and today is no exception. Elisa gives Becca the sign that time is running out. "Okay, well, think of what cause you want to work for and we'll talk next week. Until then . . ." She passes out bright orange fliers. "We need these put up all over campus. We're holding auditions next Friday after school in the theater, and we need a lot of people to be there to audition their acts. Please talk about it to your classes. Tell them about the raffle prize, even if we don't know what the charity will be. See you next Friday. And please plan to do something in the show. The more outrageous, the better!"

We walk toward P.E., which will be especially awful with the temperature hovering around hellish. "Why don't you come over after school and we'll go swimming?" Becca suggests. "Thea is picking me up. She says the extreme heat is bad for my adolescent chi."

"Whatever that means."

"Exactly. But if it gets me a ride home, I'm all over it."

We get to her house (after being lectured by Thea about our ying and yang and chi), and strip off our clothes as quickly as possible. There is no comfortable clothing in Southern California during a September heat wave.

"Race you!" Becca yells from her room as I'm still struggling into one of her spare suits in the bathroom. It looks bad, of course; she's a lot taller than I am, and it kind of hangs on me, but since it's just us, it doesn't matter. That's the beauty of best friends; you can look like you're wearing an ill-fitting spandex baggy and they just don't care.

The plunge into the water is heavenly, shocking, numbing, invigorating. Exactly the prescription for my first full week without even the hope of love and affection. As I rise to the surface, I feel Becca's stupid shark grabber toy poking at my head. "Cut it out!"

She makes the shark talk to me. "Are you feeling depressed, baby?" she asks in her best gravelly shark-from-Jersey voice. "C'mere, let ol' Jaws show you what a real French kiss feels like!" The plastic fish's mouth is opening and closing spastically while Becca makes disgusting smoochy noises.

I slap it away, but can't help laughing. "Probably the best date I'll have this year." I pull myself out of the pool, grab a sun-warmed towel, and take a moment to enjoy the fuzzy loveliness of being wrapped in fluff.

"Seriously, though, you've got to snap out of it." Becca rubs sunscreen on her shoulders. "You can't let it ruin your life!"

"Easy for you to say," I mutter, the words slipping out before I can even think about them.

Frosty silence. "What?"

"Nothing. Sorry." I try to grab the sunscreen from her, but she snatches the bottle away and stares at me over the tops of her groovy movie-star sunglasses.

"Easy for me to say? Why? Because I'm a big loser and I've never *had* a boyfriend?"

"You know I didn't mean it that way."

She eases up a bit. "Sure." She stands at the edge of the pool, body straight and perfect, and she slices into the surface of the blue-green water with barely a splash. It's a miracle she *hasn't* had a boyfriend. If she had, she probably wouldn't have anything to do with me. Most guys are too afraid of her to bother, though, but if one ever gets past that . . . well . . . I don't want to think about what it would be like without Becca now that I've had life *with* her. I realize that sounds kind of stalker-obsessive Selena-fan-club-lady-ish, but she seriously changed my life, and now that this thing with Fletcher has twisted toward dysfunction, she's probably the only thing that will keep me sane.

She cleanly undulates through the water, touches the other side of the pool, and comes back, barely coming up for air. When she does emerge, her blond spikes come first, and she looks like a punk Statue of Liberty being dredged from the New York harbor.

"What are you going to do for the show?" She towels off and plops down next to me on a green lounge chair.

"Hmmm?"

"What is your act going to be?"

I stare at her, dumbfounded. "Act? I'm not doing an act!"

Her jaw drops in exaggerated surprise. "What? You're not going to get up in front of a bunch of people and bare your soul? You? The princess of intimacy?"

I concentrate on rubbing lotion on my legs. "I don't think that has much to do with the show. The fact is, I have no talent."

"You do. I've seen you dance."

"Right. I'm going to get up in front of the school and pull a Napoleon Dynamite? I don't think so."

She stretches her arms behind her luxuriously. "Anyway, I was thinking karaoke would be more the thing."

Karaoke. Just the word makes me nauseous. I think of that stupid party, and the song. . . . "I'm going to the bathroom."

"Flushing the toilet won't make it go away!" she calls after me. I think she means my discomfort.

When I get home on Saturday (after spending the night at Becca's), I find that Euphoria and my dad have a new hobby—they're trying to build a mate for her. They're in the garage pounding and welding and riveting something.

"So, Euphoria's consulting on this, huh?" I ask. She's hovering over my dad, holding one of those snake-necked car mechanic lights in one of her claws.

"I want to be sure he gets the hardware wired correctly," Euphoria drawls. "With Fred, things just never were right."

Dad pauses, looks up and says, "He had a screw loose!" He laughs as if he's the Last Comic Standing, while Euphoria and I both just stare at him. "Well, fine. I thought it was funny. He'd think it's funny too, if he were functional." He taps on what I suppose is the head (made from aluminum hubcaps and a silver stereo speaker) and says, "We guys have to stick together, right, Eugene?"

"Eugene?" I pick up a bundle of fiber-optic cable lying on the worktable. "You couldn't think of a better robot name than Eugene?"

"Suggestions?" Dad asks, as he focuses on the inner workings of Eugene's processors with a soddering iron and a pair of tweezers.

"I don't know . . . something more scientific or mechanical. Albert, maybe. Einstein, Galileo, Kawasaki."

Euphoria beeps loudly. "I like Eugene. It makes him seem more approachable and open."

"More human?"

"Exactly."

"Considering he has car parts for ears, that's kind of ironic." I pick up a rag and wipe a stray spot of grease from Euphoria's neck plate.

Dad squints at Eugene's rivets and says, "Thea called me about the Halloween party, and she's offered to help get it organized, and decorate the house, and help get some of the food together." He snaps some part into place on Eugene's hubcap head. "There. Now all we need is some programming and a battery."

"Thea is going to help you cook?" I can't help laughing. "I don't think Thea has ever actually made anything herself. That should be interesting. I bet her idea of helping is to make Meredith come over and help you."

"We don't need help, anyway," Euphoria says, sounding kind of hurt. "We've managed just fine for this long."

"Still," Dad says, grunting with the exertion of standing Eugene upright, "I think it would be a good idea to have another parent involved. These girls are pretty wild. I don't think the two of us could possibly keep them contained, Euphoria."

I spend the weekend in something of a daze. Becca calls to talk about our upcoming GeekFest auditions. I do homework. I lie on my bed and stare at the phosphorescent stars glued to my ceiling. I count them. Every time I count them the number is different, which makes me wonder if it's me or if some weird warp in the space/time continuum is messing with my mind. Probably I just can't count.

Monday begins an endless week of trying not to think about what a mess I've made of my life. All I do is go to class, sort of pay attention, eat lunch with my friends (and I barely talk), and go home every single day. I spend a lot of time swinging on the porch swing, playing a game with myself about whether or not I can get my leg to go between the banisters without getting it jammed and broken. Dad hovers around me, maybe sensing the deep emotional pit I've thrown myself into. "Want to go to a movie?" he asks.

"No." Movies remind me of Fletcher.

"How about ice cream?"

"No." Ice cream reminds me of Fletcher.

"Maybe we could take a road trip over the weekend to Lake Tahoe."

"No." Four of the letters in Fletcher's name are also in the name Lake Tahoe. It's a good thing I'm totally over him or it might really start to get in the way of my life.

Friday finally comes, and it's time for auditions after school. We've plastered the campus with Day-Glo orange posters advertising our fantastic raffle and the GeekFest, and I hear some kids talking about it. Mr. Willfield meets us at the door to the theater.

"So, just be careful that you don't let anyone touch any of the set pieces," he is telling Amber as I walk up. "Especially the barn and the shoe. People like to climb in the shoe, and it's only made of chicken wire and paper, so they could put a foot right through it."

"Put a foot right through a shoe!" I quip, laughing uproariously at my own stupid joke. Somebody's got to do it. Obviously, I'm turning into my dad and will have a long, painful life full of puns, and my only friends will eventually be people who laugh at those *Jackass* movies. Okay, probably not even the

Jackass people. They prefer physical humor, especially it if involves the mutilation of body parts or the disbursement of embarrassing fluids. I'm doomed to a pun-filled life of loneliness.

Amber knocks on my head as if I am a wooden door. "Hello? Did you hear what he said?"

"Huh?"

"Mr. Willfield said that we have to be careful with the set pieces for their show, and that we should just leave the lights the way they are," Amber says, all business. "Did you make the audition forms, by the way?"

Oops. Fortunately for me, Becca rolls up at just that moment. "I made them." She produces a very optimistic stack of paper.

Mr. Willfield looks a bit nervous about leaving his theater for us to ruin. "Just be careful," he says, waggling a finger at me specifically. "I'm leaving, and I've arranged for someone else to lock up the theater when you're finished. Just leave it the way you found it, that's all I ask. Oh, and no food or drink in there."

He waves with one hand as he heaves a heavy leather bag onto one shoulder and marches off toward the teacher's parking lot. Elisa, who's just navigated through the swarms of sweaty teenagers stampeding to get home, watches him speed off. "For a short guy, he walks really fast," she comments.

"It's the art," Amber says airily. "It just makes you live life more deeply."

As we follow her into the dimly lit theater, Elisa mumbles, "So, what are the rest of us doing? Paddling in the shallow end?"

Within a few minutes, Amitha, Caroline, and Claudette appear, and Becca assigns them to door duty, where they are to give out audition forms to the willing victims who show up. The rest of us take seats in the front row, and wait.

After about fifteen minutes, the small talk has sort of gotten tired, and Becca cranes her neck toward the back of the theater, frowning. "Where is everybody?"

After another fifteen minutes, she charges into the lobby. Then, followed by Amitha and the sisters, she trudges back into the theater looking forlorn and dejected. "Nobody came. Not one person," she says.

"Yeah, I wonder why people would stay away from something named GeekFest?" Elisa says.

"Shut up." Becca plops back into her seat and the other girls join us. "Now what?"

"Well," Caroline says, "why don't we just do it ourselves?"

"Who's gonna pay to see us do anything?" Elisa snorts.

"It's all how you package it," Claudette says, thumping her chair arm for emphasis. "If we make it look good, it will *be* good."

Becca jumps up, somewhat revived. "That's right. So, do we have a theme or something?"

"Art coffeehouse. Bohemian." Amber closes her Cleopatra eyes and envisions some beatnik paradise. "But that would be hard to do in here. We need a smaller place, with tables and candles and espresso . . ."

"We have to do it in here so we have enough seats to sell enough tickets to get enough people interested!"

"Why exactly *are* we doing this?" I hear my voice as if it's outside my body. "Isn't this a lot of effort for nothing?"

Becca drops her chin and stares at me with the bird-of-prey stare she gets when she's really pissed. "Excuse me?"

"Just listen." I get up from my chair, walk to the front of the scuffed black stage, and hoist myself up so I'm sitting on the edge. "We need a reason to do this, a reason to care about it. That's probably why no one auditioned. There's no purpose, no focus."

"Or they just prefer to play video games and watch TV," Elisa offers.

I ignore her. "If you really want this to work, we have to have a real reason that we want to do it, other than perpetuating our own little club."

Everyone just sits there, staring into space. I hear dust bunnies kicking each other. I understand their frustration.

"Let's raise money for a juice bar," Elisa says.

We all stop and stare at her genius. A juice bar! Who wouldn't want that? Smoothies every day, whenever. That would be an amazing thing. "And once the smoothie bar is up and running, the money made could help keep it going." Elisa whips out Wembley and does some calculations. "If we sold about twenty per day at four dollars each, I think we could do it. That is, if we have enough money to start, to get equipment and stuff."

"Somebody will have to ask permission from the office," Amitha cautions.

"You're the designated geek," Becca says. "They love you up there. You get perfect grades, and you're in Key Club."

So, after a few more minutes of pointless chatter and excitement, we leave since no one is auditioning. Everyone whips out cell phones and calls for rides, but I slip away and head for the street on foot. Why? Even though we're about to embark on this big juice bar adventure of embarrassment, all I can think of is how much it won't matter because nobody loves me. I know this sounds ridiculously pathetic, but once again I start to wallow in the swamp of self-imposed rejection. I decide to walk home. As I get to the street, I hear monster footsteps pounding on the pavement behind me. Becca catches up, barely panting at all. "Hey," she says, putting an arm around my neck. "Trying to run away?"

"Just wanted to be alone." I keep walking, leaving her a few steps behind, amazed.

"Alone?" She scurries to me and matches my pace. "Why?"

I kick at a stone on the sidewalk. "I don't know. I'm just not good company."

"Is this about Fletcher?" She sounds annoyed.

"No," I answer. "It's about me, I think."

"Listen, Shelby, you have got to snap out of this." She hustles in front of me and blocks my path. "You've become this totally different person. Why don't you just call him, or just let it go?"

"He's made it pretty clear he doesn't want to have anything to do with me." I think about all the phone messages he left, all the times my phone was vibrating and I ignored it. Maybe it's me who doesn't want to have anything to do with him. But it sure doesn't feel like that.

"You know that's not true." She strides silently beside me, waiting for an answer. Do I know it's not true? I think back to our date at the restaurant, the movies, just hanging out. . . . I don't know. She says, "I have a great idea."

"That's one of those phrases that makes the skin on the back of my neck crawl."

"No, seriously. I have a plan for you to get him back."

I stop, and she continues on for a couple of steps (because someone her size just doesn't brake quickly), and I just stare at her in disbelief. "You want to do another project that is about me getting my boyfriend back?"

"You sound so surprised." She folds her arms across her chest and bites the inside of her cheek as if she's concentrating very hard. "It's like I never do anything nice for anyone."

I kindly don't respond, but keep walking past her.

"What? What are you saying, that I don't ever do anything nice for anyone?"

"It's just that most of what you do revolves around the most important person in your life: you." I turn and face her and she plows into me, knocking both of us butt-first onto the sidewalk. I land in a dusty pile of dead weeds that passes for landscaping and she gets a scrape on one knee.

"I bleed for you," she whines, faking a major injury. "See? How much more can I do, Shelby? Please tell me!" She uses her most exaggerated drama voice, puts a hand over her eyes and wails, "Oh, God, please help me set things right with Shelby, and let her forgive me for my horrible self-absorbedness."

"Self-absorbedness?"

She comes out of the drama pose. "I'm trying to make an impact. Don't correct my grammar."

"That's actually not grammar, it's—"

"Shut up!" She stands, grabs my hand and yanks me off the sidewalk. "I'm not the selfish ass you think I am."

"You're some other selfish ass?" I can't help but smile at her as she grits her teeth, links arms with me, and forces me forward.

"You think that because I didn't want to share you with Fletcher that I'm glad you two have broken up?" I say nothing, and she takes it as a yes, which it is. "Well, that's great. That makes me sounds like the worst friend ever. I didn't like sharing you, but if it made you happy . . . well . . . I was okay with it."

"It didn't feel like that. But it wasn't your fault we broke up. It was me." It's the first time I've said it out loud, and it stings. It was pretty much *all* my fault, and the part that was Fletcher's happened because I treated him like an undesirable old shoe.

"It doesn't matter whose fault it was anyway." She lets go of my arm and, grabs my hand, swings my arm rhythmically as we walk. "The point is, if I did anything to make it worse, I'm sorry."

It catches me by surprise. I've never heard her say those words, not to anyone. It causes me to stop walking. "What did you say?"

She stops too, and seems puzzled by my amazement. "I said I was sorry. You want me to prick my finger and mingle my blood with yours and swear on the ghost of my dead aunt Tillie—"

"You have an aunt Tillie?"

"No." We both giggle, a little at first, but then the giggles become big booming laughs that echo across the stone retaining wall near the freeway and fill the sky, scaring birds and stray clouds.

"Can you stay over tonight?" I ask after we've calmed down and the guy selling flowers on the corner has gone to hide behind his green umbrella. She says yes, and it feels like last year, when it was just us, and all we had to do was hang out and plan our global domination. Good times.

Dad and Euphoria are once again in the garage tinkering with Eugene when we get home. "He's kind of sexy, Euphoria," Becca teases.

"He's well shaped, and his circuits are quite powerful," Euphoria says evenly, but her red lights are flashing more brightly than usual. "I can't wait until he talks!"

"And then you won't be able to wait til he stops talking," Dad jokes.

"Becca's staying over, Dad." I pick up a magazine lying open to a picture of a creepy, cobwebby Victorian living room. "Thinking of redecorating?"

"Hmmm?" He's tightening something in Eugene's midsection, so he has to crane his neck to look up at the magazine. "Oh. Thea and I were looking for ideas for the party."

Becca's eyes get wide, and I hear a little gasp. "Thea . . . as in, my mom?"

"Yeah." Dad is so distracted with Eugene that he doesn't see the panic in Becca's eyes. I guess he must feel it, though, because he frowns and stands up straight, rubbing his oil-coated hands on his jeans. "Is something wrong?"

"You're letting my mom help you plan the Halloween party?" She sounds almost frightened, which is extremely unusual. "Excuse me a minute." She whips her cell phone out of her pocket and charges off toward the house.

Dad chuckles and glances over at me to see if some joke is being played on him. I just shrug, because honestly, I can't figure out why she'd be so freaked out about her mom helping. "So, how's it going with Eugene?"

"He's almost ready. What's going on with Becca, anyway?" I can hear her voice rising, getting louder, and she sounds pretty upset.

"I don't know." I stretch out past the garage door to see if I can get a glimpse of the argument. All I see are Becca's blond spikes bobbing above the Mexican fan palm at the front door. Dad pantomimes for me to go and listen in on the conversation, making an exaggerated face that says either, "Go find out what they're saying" or "My facial muscles are spastic and I look like a monkey." Intuitively, I know he wants me to eavesdrop, so I drop to a squat, inch forward and huddle next to the palm.

"You have no right to get involved," Becca is saying angrily. "I don't want you helping with the party. I don't want you involved in my life at all, if you want to know the truth. If it weren't for my friends, I'd go live with Melvin, even though I hate him."

I don't hear the other side of the conversation, but I can tell it can't be good. Finally, Becca says, "Only if you promise not to mess it up. It's not going to turn into a showcase for your artwork, Mother, do you understand? And there better not be any *other* reason you want to help." I hear the phone slap shut, and I skitter back to Dad, trying to look as natural as a person can when they've been spying on their best friend. I only have time to shoot him a bewildered look before she marches back to us. "So," she says, overly cheerful. "Where were we?"

"Everything okay?" I ask.

"Sure. Just had to touch base with good ol' Mom. You know how she worries. Let's go get something to eat." She turns on her heel and heads for the front door. I just shrug at my dad and follow her.

When I catch up (remember, she has those long legs and can outrun pretty much anyone, especially if food's involved), she's already pulling a chocolate torte out of the fridge. "Wow, didn't take you long to find that."

Grabbing a fork from the drawer, she plops the cake on the counter and digs in. She chews angrily, barely stopping to breathe in between bites. Finally, she says, "My mom is trying to ruin my life."

It's hard for me to respond to this; since my mom is dead, I can't exactly say, "Yeah, I know what you mean," because honestly, I'd give pretty much anything to have her back. When Becca starts the predictable gripe about her mom, I usually tune out, but this seems worse than usual. What I say is: "Sorry."

"Well, she wants to help with the party." She says it as if her mom offered to bake a cake full of poison or something. She stares at me, anticipating that I'll get the point, but of course, I don't. She sighs, frustrated at my obvious slowness. "She wants to stick her nose into everything. Why do you think she's so excited to help, huh? She doesn't do anything unless it's good for her in some way."

"Maybe she just wants to be part of your life." I get a fork and start eating too.

As quickly as she got angry, Becca's mood changes, and she's all enthusiasm and sunshine again. Maybe it's the chocolate. "I got another letter from the rabbit."

"You're kidding." I stab at the cake again. "Another poem?"

She nods as she chews another massive chocolate mouthful. "Same stuff. Here." She digs into her jeans pocket and produces a grubby note that's been read and reread a bunch of times. "Here we go:

> *Oh, Becca, sweet, when will you see*
> *This rabbit longs for your company?*
> *We all do play so many parts*
> *But I want you as my Queen of Hearts.*

Isn't that amazing?" Her face glows with excitement, and with the hotness of guys in rabbit suits.

"But what good is it if you don't know him?" She deflates a bit, and frowns. "It's cute, but that's what, three notes, and he's never talked to you? Seems like it's a yank."

She hasn't thought of that, obviously, and I don't think she appreciates me suggesting it, but in true Becca fashion, she just skewers more cake and changes the subject. "Let's talk about the plan to save your marriage."

"What?"

"Well, your future marriage to Fletcher. Now, what are you going to do at GeekFest that will get him back?"

"Ah, I don't think I want to—"

"Well, luckily for you, I've already thought of the perfect thing. Picture this: You do a karaoke song that expresses your undying love for him and admits to the confusion that made you a total moron."

"I haven't heard that on the radio." I take another bite of chocolate and picture myself on a stage in front of tens of people (I mean, face it, are we really going to get *hundreds* of people? Probably not). The idea of me doing karaoke in my room alone terrifies me, so I don't see any way that I could do it in front of anyone else. "Not a good idea, anyway."

"Yes, it is! Think of the irony, the symmetry, the . . . the . . ."

"Stupidity," I offer.

"Don't be so negative. It's very unattractive." She covers the cake with plastic wrap and puts it back in the fridge before I can protest. "Let's go on the web and look for your song."

"I'm not doing it."

"Yes, you are. But I know you're scared, so I have another great idea: We'll all sing with you!"

"We?"

"Amber, Elisa, me. Maybe even Euphoria! Why not? That would totally be a ticket seller! 'Come See Shelby Chapelle and Her Dancing Robot!' Don't you think people would pay to see that?"

I don't answer because my head is spinning. "Let's do something else for a while. Let's work on the Halloween party."

We go to my room and plan to spend most of the afternoon writing and recording fortunes to be used with the bald-headed guy in the crystal ball that we bought at the Masquerade store. He tells fortunes, but we decide they are too lame and cheesy, so we want to record our own. "How about this one?" Becca squints at her paper. "'In times like these, it is advisable to bribe the hostess with all the money in your pocket to guard against food poisoning.'" She grins at me. "Funny?"

"Not so much." I tap my pen on the notebook on which I'm writing, and my fortunes are equally as lame. "'Never walk your duck without a paddle.' *I* don't even know what that means."

Euphoria rolls in bleeping sadly. "Eugene is just giving your father fits," she says. "He can't get the processor and the voice command module to synch up. I'm afraid he may never be whole again."

"He wasn't whole to begin with, Euphoria," Becca reminds her. "He's hubcaps and staplers, right?"

Euphoria sighs heavily.

"We're writing fortunes. Want to help?" I ask her.

"I suppose." She notices the bald-headed guy gazing vacantly from the crystal ball. "He's kind of cute."

"Again, not really a whole person," Becca points out. "Don't keep dating the same kind of guy. It's really a pointless pattern."

Euphoria snorts. "So, how does writing a fortune work?"

"It's usually just a one-line thing, sort of mysterious, maybe funny. Here, listen to the bald guy do one." Becca switches him on, and the head lights up and seems to blink. His fishy mouth opens and some bubbles float out. He says, "In the land of the blind, the one-eyed man is king."

Becca arches her eyebrows. "Hey, that's pretty deep for a disembodied head."

Euphoria turns the head over, and scans the electronics inside. "Oh, this is simple. He just has a loop of phrases here, and it's motion activated."

Becca jumps up and acts as if she's been shot. "Oh my God! I just got the most amazing idea!"

She puts her hands on what passes for Euphoria's shoulders. "Listen. You can be our fortune-teller. You can actually respond to each individual person. . . . It wouldn't be totally random! They could ask you questions and you could answer!"

"I don't know. . . ." Euphoria says, but I can tell by her lights that she's somewhat intrigued.

"And we could dress you up like a gypsy!" Becca whirls around, caught up in her own idea. "This is so amazing. Oh, and we could have you do it at the GeekFest too! Before the show even starts! And we could charge extra!"

"Hang on," I say. "Dad might not even let us take her out."

"Your father can't just tell me what to do," Euphoria says, mildly annoyed.

I wonder if Dad knows she feels like that, but I don't bring it up. "But you don't really want to subject yourself to that, do you, Euphoria? All those kids pawing you, asking you stupid questions. . . . Wouldn't that be boring?"

"I never get to leave the house," she whines. "I'd love to do something outside!"

"And at the Halloween party," Becca reminds her. "This could introduce you to a whole new class of people!"

I have a feeling in the pit of my stomach that tells me this is a bad idea, but as usual, I say nothing. Once Becca decides on something, that's pretty much it. "I'll be back. I'm going to the bathroom," I mumble, feeling nauseous.

I look in the mirror at myself, something I haven't done much lately. I look different than I did last year, I think. More worried, less confident. And the corners of my mouth seem like they're turning downward. I wonder if that's how people start to be old: Maybe it starts with one little sad thing that puts a tiny wrinkle at the edge of your lips, and then more small, sad things happen, leaving you with bunches of wrinkles and lines, all tying back to some tiny tragedy. I bet thinking about this will give me a wrinkle.

When I get back to the kitchen, Euphoria is trying out various gypsy fortune-teller voices. "Good evening," she drones, sounding like a cross between Cruella De Vil and Shaquille O'Neal. "May I tell your fortune?"

"That's pretty good," Becca says as she wraps a tea towel around Euphoria's head. "Try it with an accent. Like Dracula."

She does try it, and it's kind of incomprehensible, like she's saying, "Goo deepening, meow dahlia four tune."

Becca frowns and says, "Yeah, we'll practice that."

16

SILLY RABBIT, TRICKS ARE FOR GIRLS

(or Scary, Scary Night)

At our next meeting, we tell all the girls about our idea for the juice bar, and everyone is excited. Amitha tells us that the principal has given the okay, and so we can start advertising for the show, which will be right before Thanksgiving. We sign up about seven other girls for GeekFest acts (one of which involves flame-eating guinea pigs), which makes the show about an hour, which is perfect. The rest all agree to make sure nobody at school is unaware of the fact that we might get a juice and smoothie bar.

Rehearsing for the GeekFest is kind of annoying. We get together most weekends, mostly at my house, and mostly talk about nothing and sprinkle in occasional rehearsing. Amber is totally ready with her Office Supply Poetry act;

Elisa has decided to do a dramatic reading of the song "She Blinded Me With Science" and Becca is going to do some piece of performance art. Even though I have no idea what it is, I'm sure it will probably be embarrassing and may get us thrown out of school.

"We still need a song for you to do," Becca whines at me one Saturday as we sit around eating Cheez-Its and Diet Pepsi. If you mix the two things, they sort of start to feel like cheddar-flavored plaster in your stomach.

"I don't want to do a song," I insist, reaching for more crackers. Addictive snack foods should be illegal.

Amitha, Caroline, Claudette, and two other girls have shown up for this Saturday rehearsal and Cheez-It orgy. Caroline and Claudette can actually sing, so as far as I'm concerned they don't get to criticize me. But Amitha says, "Shelby, if you're frightened, maybe we could all stand with you. As backup singers."

Becca practically does a back flip off the couch. "Beautiful! That's just what I said she needed, backup singers! We can be the Supremes to her Diana Ross! The Black Eyes to her Peas! The—"

"Hold on." Sometimes I wish I had a rope or something that I could use to tie Becca to a piece of furniture so she wouldn't hop around like a bunny rabbit on crack. But that's just who she is, I guess. "I can't sing, and it won't matter how many people are on stage with me, I still won't be able to sing. Why are you so stuck on this?"

"You want—no, you *need*—to patch this up with Fletcher. You guys are so right for each other, it's almost like you ordered him off the Internet."

"Well, then I should get my money back," I mumble.

Amitha gestures to get our attention. "I have an idea," she says meekly. "What about that song 'Always Something There to Remind Me'? Almost everyone knows that. And it's so perfect for what you're going through with Fletcher. And . . ." She scurries into the hallway and comes back carrying a strangely shaped case. "I have a special twist that will make it even more . . . well . . . special."

She pulls out a thing that looks kind of like a guitar, but with a long, skinny neck and a rounded body. "What's that?"

"It's a sitar," she says proudly. "My dad taught me how to play. He brought it all the way from India, and it belonged to my grandfather. And this," she says, producing a CD, "is the karaoke version of your song. So, ladies, shall we make musical history?"

"You're going to play the sitar to a rock song?" Elisa asks, her face wrinkled as if she'd smelled something bad.

"Don't judge it til you've heard it." Amitha strums a chord on the sitar, and it does sound beautiful. "I've already learned the chords."

"Euphoria!" Becca yells. Euphoria rolls in and bleeps expectantly. The other girls have already met her by this time; their first sight of her made them kind of nervous, but now they're used to her. "Can you play this CD?"

Euphoria takes it delicately in her claw and pops it into an audio bay. "Track?"

"Eight," Amitha answers. "That's the track with the singers so you can hear how it goes."

Euphoria finds the track and music starts pouring out of her ears. Amitha plucks the strings of the sitar and strums on it too, producing oddly beautiful chords that mesh with the song being played. The lyrics to the song keep repeating in my head:

> I *was born to love [you], and I will never be free.*
> *You'll always be a part of me.*

It's exactly how I feel, how no matter where I go or what I do, I keep seeing his face and feeling as if he's right behind me, even when no one is there.

The other girls are all watching for my reaction. I can feel their eyes on me, and I don't know exactly what I'm supposed to do . . . break into tears, scream "Hallelujah!", or faint. The song ends, and I still don't know what to do. So, I just say, "Nice song. Excellent sitar playing. No way am I singing it."

"You have to!" Becca screams. "It's so perfect. He couldn't resist!"

"I resisted him when he did karaoke for me," I point out.

"Yes, but this won't *just* be karaoke," Amitha says, smirking. "We'll all be in saris and Indian costumes."

"We will," Caroline says, more in a statement than a question, and with more than a tinge of "I-don't-think-so" in it.

"Saris are wonderful. They look great on everybody, and my mother has dozens. We can borrow them. And I'll teach you all a traditional Indian dance we can do behind Shelby while she sings. It'll be fantastic! And maybe my brother Naveen can play tabla!"

"I'm assuming that's an instrument?" Elisa asks

"It's a type of drum. That would be wonderful. He's in Academic League, though, so he's very busy. Maybe he can come for just one of the rehearsals at the end."

"Wait!" My voice is louder than I intend for it to be. Everyone stops talking. "As I've already said, I don't want to sing anything." With the realization that their dreams of sari greatness have been dashed, everybody deflates like balloons after New Year's. Amitha especially looks kind of upset. "I'm sorry," I say more gently. "I just can't do it. I'm too shy."

She puts her sitar back in its case, and the conversation quickly turns to something else, but I'm really not listening. I'm thinking about Fletcher again, and this time a vision of him wearing a maharajah's turquoise turban with a big ruby in the middle floats before my eyes. Love sucks, and it makes you stupid.

During the weeks we're practicing for the show, Halloween starts to show signs of emerging. Pumpkins are on everything: pumpkin cream-cheese muffins at the Starbucks, pumpkin-shaped cookies at the cafeteria, pumpkin air fresheners that make the classroom smell like a potpourri bomb hit and we're at ground zero. I know I sound cranky, but come on . . . it's just a glorified gourd. Why the big deal?

After school one day, Becca, Amitha, Amber, and I are walking to my house. For October, it's an unusually hot day, so we're all sweating and feeling pretty rotten, and Amitha is lugging her sitar. We're just talking about nothing and being lazily stupid, when Becca grabs my arm and stops me midstride.

"Don't look," she whispers, staring wide-eyed at the other side of the street. I check Amber's eyes, then Amitha's, and all of them look as if they've seen King Kong in a tutu. "What—"

Ever seen something that hits you so hard you feel like you're in slow motion? The memory of it replays and replays in your head like a movie on the frame-by-frame rewind. That's how this felt. I turn and look across the street, and walking slowly, leisurely on the sidewalk is Fletcher.

With his arm around a girl.

Becca holds my arms with a grip of iron, like she's afraid I might charge through traffic and strangle one or both of them. "Who is she?" Amber whispers.

"Keep walking," Becca hisses as she pushes us forward. "You don't want him to see us!" My eyes are glued to them, transfixed, like people are when a car crashes. Except in this case, it's my life that is totaled.

Too late. He looks up, and our eyes meet. Even as far away as that, I can tell that he's sad about it all, and in that one glance, a whole story flies between us. It doesn't need words, and it doesn't have to be spoken, but I hear it all the same, in my head. Hot tears run down my cheeks, dripping onto my neck, and it feels like I might just cause a flood in the dirty, dusty drainage ditch nearby. And I can feel him watching me as we walk away, and I wonder: Does she mind? Does she even know about me? Was I even worth mentioning?

We get to my house, but I don't remember walking there. When Becca fills Euphoria in on what happened, she offers to get online and zap all the electronics at Fletcher's house, but I tell her that won't be necessary. Everyone is very quiet, as if they're afraid to upset me any more. I'm curled up on the sofa; I'm not even crying, just sort of numb.

"Listen," Becca says, bouncing onto the couch next to me. "Maybe there's a logical explanation for this. Maybe it's a cousin. Maybe it's an exchange student—"

"Maybe a blind exchange student," Elisa offers. "Maybe he's kind of like her guide dog."

"Right!" Becca gestures to Amber to come up with something. She thinks I can't see her, but I can. "Or it could just be a sports injury. Right?"

Amber mumbles and finally says, "Yeah, he could have shattered his . . . elbow . . . and he needed support, so he had it around her neck. For support."

"Stop it!" I hear myself yelling. "You all know that she didn't look like a blind-cousin-exchange-student-elbow-prop. That definitely looked like a potential . . ." I can't even say the word.

"Okay, so if it's his newest hottie, so what?" Elisa says airily. "You didn't need him. You broke it off, right?"

I scream in frustration and bury my head between two pillows to avoid the obvious. She's right. She's right! I absolutely broke up with him. No, I didn't even break up with him. . . . I just sort of disappeared without the benefit of a breakup. And now he's walking with someone else.

"Honey, honey, c'mon, come up for air!" Euphoria whines, grabbing my shirt collar in her steel claw and pulling me back upright. "This boy is just not worth this amount of grief."

"But he is!" I yell, anguished.

The room falls dead silent. Everyone just stares at me and my tear-stained face.

"He is worth it." I stand up, wipe my face, and realize that I've been a total ass. "He is worth it. We're worth it.

And I am going to find out who that girl is. And you are going to help me. And I am going to get him back."

Everybody cheers, slaps hands, hugs.

Then Elisa folds her arms across her chest and says, "Shelby, I'm only saying this for your own good. I think you make a great couple. But maybe he's over the drama, and you must admit, there has been a *lot* of drama. But if you're sure you want him back, we have to be organized. Who's the hottie? We need to do reconnaissance before we can plan a strategy."

"So much to do!" Becca shouts. "I hate to say it, but you're right. Tomorrow, it's Operation Hottie Spotter."

The plan is to totally eliminate me from Fletcher contact the next day (which isn't hard, since we're not speaking to each other), and each girl has a separate mission. We plan to meet at the Rock after school to compare notes.

For most of the day, I just keep thinking about That Girl with Fletcher, thinking about who she might be and why he'd be dating somebody so soon.

I see Becca in P.E. fifth period, and as we're dressing, she gives me an update. "Elisa found out who she is. Her name is Megan Lovett. She's a junior. And Amber text messaged Amitha when she was in geometry with Fletcher, and she was able to check out his binder when he went to sharpen his pencil. No photos of the Hottie." She takes a deep breath and puts a hand on my shoulder. "Brace yourself."

"Why?"

"Because Caroline text messaged Claudette when she saw Fletcher heading toward the library with Hottie, and Claudette was out on a nurse pass because she had cramps, so she followed them, and they were in the hallway having a very serious discussion. And the discussion ended with some pretty intense face sucking. However," she says quickly, staring directly into my eyes, "she was doing the face sucking and he was just passively . . . accepting it."

"Well, that's just great," I mutter, slamming my locker a little too hard. "He didn't object, I suppose."

"To be fair, Shelby, he *is* a guy, and you did kind of blow him off."

"Thanks." I march out of the locker room. "Thanks for pointing that out."

"Hey!" She runs to catch up with me as I try to slip into the stream of girls heading for the field. "Wait! I didn't mean . . . well, I did, sort of . . . but anyway, it's not too late, that's my point. He wasn't that into her. I think she's taking advantage of an opening. We just need to slam the door."

As I jog onto the field, Mr. Cruces, our gym teacher, watches me and I sprint like I'm being chased by the cops. Becca can't even keep up with me. Pounding my feet on the dirt I imagine I am stepping on the Hottie's face, grinding it into the track with each step, willing her to disappear. "Good job, Chapelle!" he yells, sounding somewhat surprised. If he only knew that I wasn't running, but committing virtual assault. . . . I'm not going to tell him.

After school, we all meet at the Rock as planned. Elisa is dancing around Amber and the other girls when Becca and I walk up. "I know who she is, I know who she is!" Elisa sings. She pulls several pieces of computer paper out of her bag and hands them to everyone. "Subject: Megan Lovett. Grade: eleven. Hobbies: stealing people's boyfriends. Weaknesses: unknown." She marches around like a little general, arms behind her back. "Ladies, we need to be sure Ms. Lovett knows exactly what she's dealing with. And we need to be sure we point out to Mr. Berkowitz just what a weasel in a miniskirt she is."

"Is she a weasel?" Amitha asks. "What does that mean?"

Amber waves the paper. "We found out that she's dated the entire football squad, all except Fletcher. We believe that this is a conquest, nothing more. She's just looking to put another notch in her pom-pom."

"But how could he be so stupid that he'd fall for that?" I ask.

"Two words: boobs." Elisa whips out a picture of Megan Lovett in her cheerleading outfit.

I just shake my head. "He can't be that shallow."

Amber gestures toward the parking lot. "Becca, your mom's here."

"Thea said she'd give us a ride to your house. We didn't want to walk in case . . . well . . ."

"In case Fletcher was out walking his cheerleader." Elisa grabs my arm. "C'mon. Let's make you a star."

At first I don't see Becca's mom, because she's not driving the ratty Jeep. Instead, she's perched in the driver's seat of this huge yellow Hummer. "What this?" I ask.

Becca pulls herself up into the cab of the monstrosity. "She's just borrowing. Melvin is doing a shoot down here, and he's rented this stupid thing because he has a very small—"

"Rebecca!" Thea cuts her off. "You won't talk about your father that way!"

"Why not?" She snorts. "It's true. Why else would anyone drive one of these moronic dinosaur eaters?" We can all fit in it, though, and in fact, we could fit a lot more people in there. It's much bigger on the inside than on the outside.

Even though the Hummer is huge and we can see old men's bald spots from above, Thea careens through traffic like she's at a NASCAR race, but we somehow make it to my house without damage. She actually parks and comes in, but I figure if Dad sees the Hummer he will absolutely flip; we are an ecologically minded household, and big gas-guzzling monstrosities are usually not welcome.

"Is your dad home?" Thea asks sweetly. Becca throws her a poisonous glance.

Euphoria meets us at the door. "No, Mr. Chapelle isn't at home right now, ma'am. He's working on a top-secret project that could have ramifications for the entire world."

"It's a new garbage disposal or something," I mumble. "It's not all that exciting."

Thea's face lights up. "Oooh. Sounds fascinating. I'd love to talk to him about it some time. Well, anyway, I wanted to work on the Halloween decorations, and all the supplies are here, so if you could just point me to a table where I could work . . ."

Euphoria takes her into the dining room while the rest of us head for the couch. "Look," Becca says firmly. "You have two choices: You can let it go, or you can fight back. What do you want to do?"

All eyes are on me, and as usual, I don't know what the answer is. My life feels like that most of the time, like everyone knows the rules except for me, and everyone knows what game we're playing, but I am clueless. Then an image flashes in front of my eyes, the image of Fletcher with his arm around Miss Tits, and I suddenly get it. "I want to fight."

Everyone cheers, and Euphoria rejoins us. "Mrs. Becca's Mother is working on some very unusual posters for your party," she comments.

"Ready to rock and roll, Euphoria?" Becca thumps her on the back, which echoes.

"I suppose."

We work on the song for a couple of hours; it's actually dark when we quit. Thea has only come out once and she's smeared with fluorescent metallic paint. "It's just going to be stunning," she says, then stops midsentence. "Why are you all dressed in saris?"

"Never mind," Becca mutters, turning her and shoving her back toward the dining room.

The next day is Friday, and we get a recap of activities at the meeting. The acts we signed up last week are almost ready, and we still have a couple of weeks to go, so we decide to concentrate on getting people to the show (not that I necessarily want that, because I don't want everyone to see me and my robot in saris. That's the kind of thing that follows you around til graduation.)

"Operation GeekFest is underway," Becca says to the roomful of girls. "We've decided that the fifty-fifty ticket split would be better if it were eighty-twenty, with eighty going to the juice bar. That means we need to publicize both getting the juice bar and winning the money, so people see that there's a benefit in both."

"Not to mention the enjoyment of seeing people viciously humiliated," Amber adds, and everyone chuckles, except for the people who are doing the acts.

The whole next week I feel like I'm in a holding pattern; I only see Fletcher once during the week, and sure enough, he's walking with Megan Lovett as an appendage. Knowing that a strategy is planned, I resist the temptation to throw nacho cheese in her hair.

We finally get to the next Saturday, the night of the Halloween party, and Thea has created some intensely strange and interesting decorations. "Where should this go?" she asks, holding up a stylized severed head that looks like it's straight out of an after-hours cheeseburger nightmare.

"Uh . . . the trash?" Becca snipes.

"It's fine," I say, taking the obnoxious head and hanging it over the kitchen doorway. "See? It makes an impact here."

"Yeah, it'll keep you from ever wanting to eat again," Becca mumbles as she untangles a string of pumpkin lights.

Dad walks in, and that's when things get weird. "Oh, hi, Rich!" Thea's voice gets a little higher and sort of strained. "How's it going?"

"Uh . . . fine." He frowns over the top of his glasses at the mess we've made. "Is this . . . for school?"

"No, no, it's for the party." Thea grabs a huge bag sitting by the table and pulls out a prepackaged costume. "I'm going to be Vampira, Temptress of the Night. What are you going to be?"

I truly feel nauseous and so hope that I am misinterpret-ing the whole thing, but I think my best friend's mom is flirting with my dad. "Hey," I say, grabbing Dad by the arm, away from the scary, scary Vampira. "Euphoria is going to tell fortunes at the party. Isn't that great?"

"Uh . . ." He's still staring at the Vampira costume, mesmerized. I want to take a string of pumpkin lights and strangle him.

I push Dad toward the door. If he can't see Vampira, he can't be hypnotized by her charms, whatever they are. "Dad, can you bring the trash cans to the front yard?" He walks out, still looking back as if he doesn't remember he lives here.

After a turbo afternoon of party prep, Amitha calls out from the living room, "What time is it?"

"Four," Becca yells. "We need ice! Shelby, can your dad go get ice?"

I trot out to the garage to find Dad knee-deep in Eugene. "Oh, what happened?"

He shakes his head, and wipes grease on an old rag. "Not sure. Something snapped and he just sort of fell apart."

"Yeah, I know how that feels." He smiles at me, and our eyes meet. I try desperately to forget that he was ogling Becca's moom. "We need ice. Can you run me down to the store?"

We climb into the Volvo and as he backs down the driveway and passes the Hummer, he says, "Becca's mom is nice, huh?"

"Doesn't the Hummer bother you?"

"Oh." He chuckles as he steers the car around the monstrosity. "I'm sure that's not hers. She wouldn't drive something like that. Anyway, she's nice."

"Sure, if you like freaky hippies with nose rings."

He grunts, maneuvers the car around so we're headed in the right direction. "Yeah, she is kind of unusual. But nice."

Desperate to change the subject, I say, "So, I'm doing a karaoke thing to get Fletcher back."

He does a double take and glances over at me, almost running into a curb. "Huh?"

"Yeah. We're all doing it, actually. Euphoria is going to help, remember. So, I'm hoping that he'll see that I'm ready to be in a relationship with him. I'm not so afraid anymore."

"Really." He stops at a light and scratches his head, something he does when he's working out a puzzle. "Not afraid? Were you afraid before?"

"I think I was." I concentrate on the red light changing to green, and it feels kind of like my life. Maybe I'm finally going somewhere.

We get back with the ice and things already look spooky. The girls have put black light bulbs in the sockets, the creepy changing portraits are up, the bald-headed seer is propped on the hall table, and a bloodred cloth covers the dining room table, which is piled with goodies. "Scary, huh?" Claudette says from behind me.

I turn and almost really do scream. She and Caroline are both joined at the hip by some black cloth, and there's what looks like a real heart stuck between them. They also have this icky makeup on that makes them look like their faces are melting off. "Check this out," Caroline says. "Watch the heart."

It starts to pump, and then red stuff oozes out of a tube and disappears back into the costume. "That has got to be one of the most disgusting things I've ever seen." I poke at the heart. "Awesome."

Becca runs in and gives me a hug. "Let's go get our stuff on too. It's nearly five-thirty and people are coming at seven, right? Tunes, Euphoria, tunes!"

Some rock song blares out of the speakers in the house; Euphoria is wireless and can get that going in an instant, and she probably won't play the same song all night. Much better than an iPod, although you can't put her in your pocket.

Becca and I are wearing our costumes from Comic-Con, Vege-tastic and Smart-tastic. We figured, why buy new ones if we barely used those? And I'm pretty sure no one else is going to come to the party as a vegetarian superhero. Elisa has refused to wear hers, though; she says she's developed a hideous allergy to spandex. Instead, she's wearing a Raggedy Ann outfit, complete with red-yarn braids and painted-on freckles. "Returning to the days of my innocence," she says airily. "Plus, it was on sale."

The house looks awesome. Once it gets dark, I know it will really freak people out; we have so many cobwebs it looks like some type-A spider on speed worked all night spinning, and cauldrons of dry ice bubble on the porch. Plus, we've created a huge, misty bowl full of bloodred punch with plastic eyeballs floating in it. They don't exactly look real, but they're kind of gross anyway. Now we just have to wait for people to show up.

Becca and I head out to the porch and swing a bit in the twilight. I see one of our neighbors do a double take when he sees me in my green makeup, but I just wave. Briley, the standard-issue popular girl who lives next door, comes out of her house, glances over at us, and snarls before she crams herself into a black PT Cruiser idling at the curb. "Hey, Briley," Becca calls, waving.

Briley stops and glances at us as if we're museum freaks, which I guess we kind of are. "What are you doing?"

"Just a little beauty treatment. Spinach and artichoke dip," Becca yells. "You should try it."

Briley just shakes her head and slams the car door. "You guys are losers!" she yells as the Cruiser peels out and speeds down the street.

"Yeah," Becca grins, "but you know she's going to come home tonight and smear spinach and artichoke dip all over her face!"

People start showing up at about 7:30 because no one wants to be the first to arrive. We've invited all of the Queen Geeks as well as members of the chess and *Star Wars* clubs, plus a variety of oddballs from school: band geeks, drama geeks, an assortment. Euphoria is cranking the tunes, the food is all laid out, and our eyeball punch is smoking in the kitchen, causing quite a lot of attention. "What's in there?" Amitha's brother, Naveen, asks, squinting into the dimly lit punch bowl.

"Just leftover cow eyes from biology," Becca says. I don't think Naveen believes her, but I don't see him drink any punch.

"What is that costume, anyway?" Becca asks him, yelling over the increasing chatter and noise.

"Oh," he answers, plucking at the brightly woven pirate sleeves and balloon pants. Instead of a traditional pirate hat, he's wearing a jeweled turban made of some shiny purple and green material. "I'm a pirate, but I'm an Indian pirate."

"Did those really exist?" I ask.

"Probably not, but I didn't want to spend money on one of the *Pirates of the Caribbean* hats, so I just used this." He tugs at the front of the turban. "It's kind of tight. . . . It belonged to my grandmother."

Caroline and Claudette move through the room showing off their exposed heart and its amazing pumping power.

Amitha nudges her brother, who frowns at her and says something I cannot understand. "English, please," Amitha says tartly.

Naveen squints at her, and looks like he might dunk her head in the punch. "Your outfit is a bit too revealing," he says, very calmly.

Amitha rolls her eyes. She has come to the party as an angel, but her outfit is far from saintly. She's got this really short white skirt, wings, a halo, and a white sequined halter top that shows off her dark skin beautifully. I always wanted to be dark; you can wear absolutely no makeup and you still look great. If I don't wear makeup, I look like a fish belly with eyelashes.

Jon and Amber cruise into the kitchen. They are dressed as, I guess, tortured poets. They are all in black, with white face paint and stylized black eyeliner snaking in teardrops down their cheeks. "Wow, you look cheerful," Becca comments as she snags a cookie. "Are you going to read some entertaining obituaries later?"

They ignore us and drift into the living room, presumably to discuss how dismal life is in the suburbs.

The biggest shock of the party comes when my dad walks into the kitchen. I'm leaning against the sink, wishing I hadn't worn green makeup, sipping a cold soda, and Dad strolls in wearing a towel. Now, if you've never seen your own father wearing a towel in front of dozens of other kids from your school, it's not something I would recommend unless you are a great actor and can pretend you're not related. To be fair, it is a huge spa towel, and it's clipped at the shoulder with something that looks a little like the hubcaps from Eugene's head.

"Hi, sweetie," he says, kissing me on the top of my asparagus hair.

"What are you supposed to be?"

"I'm a Roman emperor." He twirls and shows off his hairy legs under his towel toga. "Like it?"

"Pool boy, can I have a drink?" Thea materializes from somewhere, and the two of them standing together is electrifying. Not in the exciting, buzzy way, but in the shock-therapy, torturish way.

"Mom?" Becca asks, her voice trailing off into the land of inescapable embarrassment. Thea is wearing the Vampira outfit, but she's painted it with images of fruit, and she's wearing these heels that could puncture the linoleum and drill a hole to China. On her head is a huge hollowed-out coconut with an animated skull that keeps popping out and waving a paintbrush.

"I wanted to be Vampira, but I wanted to make it my own." She ruffles her mango-pineappple-orange-laden skirt. "I'm a fruit bat."

Dad and his towel seem extremely interested in Thea's fruit. I feel extremely nauseous. "Excuse me," I mumble, dashing toward the front door.

Euphoria is stationed in the alcove, bundled up in Becca's fortune-telling gear. As a couple of girls from the club walk through the door, she extends her claw and says, "Good evening. May I tell your fortune?"

The dark haired one nods, kind of astonished that we might own a robot, especially one who's fun at parties. Euphoria grabs her wrist, hums, beeps, buzzes, whines, and then spits out a white piece of paper before saying, "When in doubt about your looks, always remember that humans have evolved, but you still have genetic commonalities with apes."

"Huh?" The girl frowns, grabs the little paper unwillingly, and mutters to her friend as she weaves her way into the party.

Amber and Jon stand side by side. Euphoria moans mystically (something I think Becca taught her), bleeps, bloops, and spits out another white paper. Amber takes it curiously as Euphoria intones, "If you paint your world black and do not see the color, you will most likely run into things when it's dark." Amber rolls her eyes and stands aside so Jon can get his magical reading.

Euphoria waves her claws this time, imitating some spastic, possessed person. "Pest control is never something that can be left to amateurs. Call Terminix today!"

"Huh?" Jon backs away from her, blushing. I suspect she somehow picked up a loop of advertising from some radio frequency, but if it gets Jon to bathe more, I guess it's not all bad.

"Nice fortunes, Euphoria," I say, patting her on the shoulder under her flowing velvet cape. "Want to tell mine?"

She buzzes and beeps. "Gotta change a CD," she says, rolling away. Even my robot knows I'm a loser when it comes to love. Think I'll go eat worms.

Outside it's dark; our strings of ghost globes and purple crystal minilights give the porch a spooky, midnight feeling. Kids are standing under the magnolia tree in front, half in shadows, half lit by the streetlight. Apparently, that's been designated the make-out spot. So, of course I think of Fletcher and just flop down onto the porch swing, first carefully stepping over a couple in salt-and-pepper-shaker costumes who are trying to combine and make a new condiment.

It'd be nice if he'd just sort of show up, I guess; but realistically, that isn't going to happen. I fantasize for a moment that he walks up the street, decked out in a Batman costume or something, and as he gets closer, I can tell it's him from the way he walks. Then I imagine that he walks right up to me, grabs me around the waist and kisses me, kisses me so hard that I can't breathe. But then, I know that's not going to happen. Why should it? What's the use of dwelling on it?

People are still arriving in twos and threes; a cool breeze touches the leaves and makes them moan, a perfect sound for a Halloween party, and a perfect sound for how I feel. But I'm suddenly thrown back to reality when I see a very tall somebody in a rabbit suit walking up my street.

"Becca. Becca!" I hear my own strangled voice as I stumble over the protesting salt and pepper shakers. I rush into the house, elbowing my way through a crowd of witches, teddy bears, cowboys, and oddly, several bananas. Becca's sitting on the floor near the sliding glass door, yakking with Amber, Jon, and Elisa. "Becca. The rabbit guy . . . He's coming!"

She nearly chokes on her punch. "What?"

"You mean the guy from Comic-Con?" Elisa squeaks. "Oh my God, he could be a stalker! Like in *Donnie Darko*! He might be the crazy steel rabbit who is coming to take our souls!"

Becca scrambles to her feet, grabs my hand, and dashes through the crowd. (Being tall, she can actually dash with very little effort.) Followed by Amber and Elisa, we get into my room and Becca slams the door.

"What are you going to do? Should we tell Shelby's dad or something?" Elisa asks, eyes glowing with the possibility of chaos. Like the middle-aged man in a bath towel is going to be able to defend anybody.

Becca primps mercilessly, ditches the blue wig, and forces her blond spikes to stand at attention. "Maybe I'll get to meet him, I mean really actually talk to him tonight!"

Amber, who has had to separate herself from Jon, stares longingly at the door. "Are you ready to go back out?"

"Wait, wait!" Becca yells. "Let me just . . . hang on . . ." She routs around in her purse (which is in my closet) and produces all of the poems the rabbit guy has written her, all sealed in a wrinkled baggy. "I want to make him read these to me."

We march out and are hit by a wave of music and chattering, and the smell of sweaty, costumed bodies. It's all a blur of color, purple/blue/green lights bouncing off surfaces, Euphoria gyrating wildly to some hip-hop tune she's spinning. If I didn't know better, I'd say she was trying to scratch some tracks to go with it.

Off in the dining room, I spot him. "Rabbit, dining room, lead pipe!" I scream, slithering between a couple of

Stormtroopers. We all take different routes, hoping to corner him. What will a cornered rabbit do?

The other kids must sense our seriousness, because the snack table clears out instantly, leaving just us and bunny boy. Munching on a baby carrot through his costume, the guy stops, checks for exits, and realizes he's blocked. Becca strides up to him, rubbing her hands together. "So, Rabbit Man, we meet again, eh?"

He just nods. Becca sidles up to him and traces a line around one of his droopy ears. "Bunnies should be home in their hutches on Halloween. Don't you know that some people like to play tricks and turn them into casseroles?"

He pretends to tremble, putting his paws up to his buckteeth and shaking so hard he practically knocks the cups off the table.

Becca pats him on the back. "Now, now, no need to be afraid. We won't hurt you, will we, girls?"

Everyone says no, of course not, and then I spot Elisa doing a belly crawl on the floor toward him, her red braids inching along with her like two confused garden snakes.

"Maybe you should go outside for some air," I suggest, wondering what weird thing Elisa has planned.

"Oh, no," Becca purrs, putting her arms around the rabbit man. "I want Mr. Bunny to do a poetry reading for all of us, right here." The rabbit shakes his head adamantly. "But you have to! I've been waiting since July to find out who you are, and if you read, I might have a clue." Becca stands on tiptoe and whispers audibly in the droopy ear, "You must have wanted to introduce yourself if you came to the party, honey bunny."

I swear, if a white rabbit could blush, he would have been doing it. Unfortunately, I'd totally forgotten about Elisa, who jumps up from the floor like a minicommando, spazzes into the air, grabs the guy's ears, and yanks, pulling the head sideways at a crazy angle.

The rabbit head pops off, revealing Carl Schwaiger, football moron.

Becca screams, truly terrified, and everyone freezes. Dad comes running in, holding his towel for extra support, with fruity Vampira close behind. "What happened?" he yells. The music has stopped completely.

Becca still stands, mouth agape, eyes glued to Carl Schwaiger and his furry white torso.

Dad grabs her shoulders. "Are you all right, Becca? Did someone do something? What happened? Who's this boy? Did he hurt you?"

"Dad," I mumble in his ear. "Nobody's hurt. Let's just move on. It's just not who she thought it was."

"Oh." Dad studies the situation a moment longer, then yells, "Bobbing for polymers on the front lawn! Right now!" Most of the kids dash out after him, even though *I'm* not even sure what bobbing for polymers involves.

Becca is still staring at Carl, who stares dejectedly at the floor. "It was you?" she finally manages to say.

"Yeah." He booms. "I just think you're really cool. I didn't know how else to get your attention."

Becca glances at me and gives me the "what the heck?" look. I try and help her out by speaking slowly and clearly to the Giant. "So, Carl, you wrote those Alice poems, huh? Because you knew she liked *Alice in Wonderland*."

He looks up, focuses on me, and says, "I'm not retarded, Shelby, just big. You don't have to speak slowly."

Whoa. Slam. I am reminded of what Fletcher said (damn that Fletcher! He will not vacate my brain!) about Carl, and about how he was very smart, and even though he played football, he wasn't just a dumb jock. "Uh, sorry," is all I manage to say. I am very grateful for my green asparagus hair, which conveniently covers my face.

I stumble out to the front porch, where batches of kids are standing around watching my dad and Thea stabbing with their faces at some plastic balls floating in a tub of water. Why am I so stupid? I judged Carl the same way I always criticize everyone else for judging me. When I look back through my screen door, Becca is leaning against the wall, her face softer; she's laughing slightly at something funny that Carl said, and I realize I'm the biggest moron of all.

17

LOVE IS NEVER HAVING TO WEAR A SARI

(or The Screaming Vishnu Revue)

People stay and dance and eat until almost midnight, then Dad kicks them all out. We decide to wait til morning to clean up, much to Euphoria's dismay. "I can't leave the house looking like this!" she screeches, but we just ignore her.

Becca and Carl seem stuck together, and as I trudge into the kitchen to rummage for any last cookies, I hear them talking in the dining room. "How did you know I like Alice?" she says, her voice soft and warm, qualities that I've hardly ever heard in her.

I can't see his expression, but I hear Carl chuckle. "I did a little research. Fletcher was pretty helpful. And, of course, it doesn't hurt that I've read everything on your MySpace page, and that I happen to love all the same things you love."

She giggles (giggles!) and then they start talking about Comic-Con and the poems, and Carl agrees to read one, and as I stumble out of the kitchen, I hear his booming voice reciting poetry to Becca, and I hear her clapping her hands like a kid at Christmas.

At the beginning of the night, I could never have anticipated how things would work out. Of course, I thought Carl was stupid because he was tall, so who am I to predict anything? But as things are wrapping up, I see my best friend and her rabbit admirer, arm in arm, headed for the door. As they pass me, Becca gives me a huge hug. "What's that for?"

"I just think it's so great that Carl showed up and now I know who he is." She glances back at him as he retrieves his huge bunny head that has been propped up in a corner all night, looking like a forlorn piece of a parade float. "Know what he said? He said that I was the only girl in school who had depth, and he knew he wanted to go out with me the first time we met, but he was afraid I'd say no. That's why he did the rabbit thing at Comic-Con. He planned it all out! Isn't that great?"

She's practically glowing with the idea that a guy would think about her enough to plan something out. I, on the other hand, am feeling like so much pocket lint. Now my best friend has a boyfriend, my boyfriend has a girlfriend, and I'm left alone with my asparagus hair.

Carl ambles over to the door and smiles sheepishly at me. "Sorry I couldn't tell you," he says, laughing. "Fletcher told me what you thought of me. No hard feelings, though; I know I look like a dumb jock. Can't help it. But anyway, I hope we can be friends."

Becca pats his back and says, "I'll meet you outside, okay?" He grins at her, and shuffles out on his velvety paws. She turns to me and says, "Listen, I know this is hard for you. I'm sorry, but I promise, it won't change anything."

I know my face must show the disappointment and jealousy I feel, but I try to brighten it up with a big, fake smile. "Hey, I'm happy for you," I say, kind of telling the truth. "Who'd have guessed it was him?"

"Well, now that I think of it, who else at school is that tall?" Becca watches as Carl runs his bunny ears into the low branches of the tree in our yard. "Sometimes what you want is right in front of you, and you just can't see it."

"Especially if it's in a bunny suit." I give her a big hug, a real one this time, and try not to let tears spill down onto her back. I really do feel happy for her, actually; but I feel equally sad for me. She breaks away, gestures that she'll call me later, and scampers down the porch steps.

Jon and Amber walk arm in arm to the door too, smiling contentedly. "See you Monday," she says. "And don't worry about Carl—he's actually really cool. You'll like him. Good night."

Yeah, I'm sure he's cool. But what are we going to do? Double date with three people? I figure my night can't get much worse, but then I walk into the kitchen and Dad and Thea are sloshing down wine (which of course none of us was allowed to have), and giggling like they're about two.

"Uh, hello? Did you know your daughter just left with a football player?" I ask, a bit nastily.

Thea comes out of her winy haze for a moment and focuses on me. "Really? Was he really a football player, or just a guy in a football player costume?"

"No, he was a real football player in a rabbit costume, but what's the difference?" I pick up a rag and violently start to clean the counters. I don't look at them, but Thea silently leaves the kitchen, and I hear her grab her purse and head out the door. Dad follows her, leaving me with the messes in the kitchen and elsewhere.

Amber runs back into the house, panting. "Where's Elisa?"

"Huh?"

"She came with us. I totally forgot. Have you seen her?"

I look around the kitchen, as if she might pop up out of a cupboard. "Well, no. Maybe she got a ride home."

"She wouldn't go without telling me!" Amber darts into the living room. "Elisa!"

Sighing heavily, I check the bathroom, the dining room, and the back patio. No sign of Elisa anywhere. "Crud," I say aloud. Just what I need to end the perfect evening, a missing persons report. I gather up the tablecloth, dumping piles of crumbs on the floor. I keep trying to get Euphoria to consider getting one of the little robotic vacuums, just for floors. It could be like a child to her, and then maybe she'd stop obsessing about me . . . but anyway, I take the tablecloth and some other stuff to the laundry room.

I switch on the light and nearly have a heart attack. Elisa is tangled on the floor, her costume all askew, her hands caressing the back of someone who looks vaguely like a pirate with a turban—

"Hey!" I yell. They both break their vacuum lip hold and slump apart like magnets whose attraction has been sapped.

"Oh, hey," Elisa manages to say as she adjusts her red braids. Her makeup is all smeared, so now she looks like a cartoon character colored out of the lines. The guy she's mauling is Naveen, Amitha's brother.

"So, I guess you didn't hear that the party's over," I say as casually as possible. I continue to load the washer as if they are just tiny dust bunnies annoying me.

"Uh . . . sorry about this," Naveen says, adjusting his crooked turban. "It just sort of—"

"–happened." Elisa finishes, giggling slightly.

"Just get going." I twist the washer dial viciously and dump a cupful of detergent into the water. "Thanks for being part of my lovely evening."

Elisa gestures to Naveen to meet her outside, and she steps up next to me, her yarn hair grazing my shoulder. "Shelby, seriously, I never . . . we never . . . I didn't mean to embarrass you." She giggles again. "But he is cute, huh?"

"How did you two hook up?"

"We started talking about graphic calculators, and that was it." She tilts her head so she can see through the doorway into the dining room. "I mean, he's cute, smart, geeky . . . and he knows Linux. He's perfect."

"Great." I lean against the washer, which has started its vibrating dance of cleanliness. "Hope you two are very happy together."

In one of the few genuine nonjoke-filled moments she's ever had, Elisa turns solemn eyes to me and says, "Don't worry. You'll find someone too."

How sad it is when the only girl in your group who's never dated finally finds the perfect guy. Especially when you're left with nothing but a noisy, cranky washer to curl up with.

When I flip the switch in the laundry room, all I see in the house is the purplish glow of Halloween lights and some stray streamers. Everybody has left, apparently. I walk through the quiet house, as depressed as any superhero has ever been. Nice night for a good cry, I guess, so I head to the porch, where Thea and my dad are swinging and yakking like old school chums. Guess she never followed Becca after all.

"Oh, Shelby," Dad says. He sounds so happy that I want to strangle him. "Come on out. What happened with Elisa? She practically floated off the porch."

"She found true love, I guess." I park on the steps and put my head in my hands.

"Oh, don't be upset," Thea says gently. "In ten years, you won't even remember any of this."

Why do adults always say stuff like that? Who cares about ten years from now? I am in pain now, and I want a solution now. They probably can't remember the pain from high school because they're too darn old. The memory is the first thing to go, you know.

Dad lets loose this cavernous yawn and says, "Better get to bed. I think we'll have a lot of cleanup to do tomorrow. Great party, though. Did you have any fun, honey?"

"I guess." Glancing back at them on the porch swing, I feel a white-hot stab in my gut. Could it be that even my dad is finding someone? That is a discussion for a whole different Oprah show, definitely. As Scarlett O'Hara said, I'll think about it tomorrow. "I'm going to bed. You two don't stay up too late." I stretch, then amble over to Dad to give him a kiss. Thea touches my arm and I recoil without meaning to. "Night."

The white-hot knife thing continues, and washing my face and taking off my asparagus hair doesn't even help. In the mirror, a green-streaked girl stares back at me, and I think she looks pathetic. I turn the knob on the shower and let the water blast away, hot as anything, and I get in to wash away all the crappy events of the evening.

As I lay in bed later staring at the ceiling, I count the constellations of Day-Glo stars, and look for the shape of a heart, but I can't find it. Euphoria can't even make me feel better, even though she tries by playing all my favorite songs. I guess eventually I go to sleep, though, because the next thing I know, it's Sunday morning, and I've awakened to another glorious day in lonerville.

Now that the party is officially over (in more ways than one), I'm back to school, Queen Geeks, and GeekFest as the only things absorbing my time. Monday's lunchtime is truly torturous; Amber and Jon, Elisa and Naveen, and Becca and Carl all hang out under our tree, and I'm left with a bag lunch and a major depression. But where else would I go?

"So, for GeekFest, Carl is going to run the sound system," Becca chirps as she slips a bag of chips to her new companion. "Now, we have to work on Shelby's number so she can get Fletcher back."

"Don't talk about it in front of them!" I hiss, pointing to the guys, who all look confused.

"Well, they are going to help us, so why not?" She turns to Naveen, and says, "Amitha is going to play the sitar with us on Shelby's song. And we're all dressing in saris."

"Should be excellent," he answers. "Except that Amitha is a lousy sitar player. But who will really notice, huh?"

"Do you want Fletcher back?" Carl rumbles. "I thought you broke it off with him."

"She didn't exactly break it off," Amber begins, but Becca finished, "she just didn't keep it going."

"And now he's dating that slutty Megan Lovett," Elisa snipes. "I cannot believe he'd fall for anybody like that."

"I don't think they're dating," Carl mumbles around a mouthful of sandwich.

"Why?" I ask in spite of myself. Like I care if Fletcher's dating. But I do, of course.

"Oh, they had some fight over which car he was going to drive to some party." He laughs as he carefully folds the crusts of his sandwich and sticks them inside a Baggie. "She didn't like his beater mobile."

I'm secretly delighted.

The next couple of weeks are consumed with rehearsal and homework, which I have let slip terribly because of my emotional trauma. At school, I studiously avoid Fletcher, but because I am avoiding him, we seem to run into each other every minute. I come around a corner on my way to math and run smack into him, literally. If it hadn't been about me, I would have laughed at how comical we probably looked trying to pick up each others' stuff without speaking. And then one day at lunch, he happened to come into the cafeteria just as I got into the line.

"Hey," I hear a girl's voice behind me.

"Hi," he answers her, but it's noncommittal. I pick up a carton of milk.

"So, did you make a decision?" She kind of squeaks in that way that cute girls do when they're excited. I have never known if that squeak is genuine, or just something that reveals their evolutionary link to the rodent world.

I am desperate to look back at who it is, but I can't, so I just pick up another carton of milk.

"I don't think I'm going to be able to do it," he says finally, sighing.

I can hear the pout in her voice as she says, "Oh, pooh. I was really counting on it, Fletcher."

By this time, I'm at the end of the line, and the lunch lady says, "You just want five cartons of milk?" I nod as if I absolutely do want five cartons of milk, pay her, and run as if my shoes are on fire.

As I said, the only relief I have from this Fletcher itch is rehearsing for the big show. We practice at my house, and Euphoria cannot get the dance steps right no matter what we do.

"I am trying!" she whines desperately as she clunks her rollers in time to the karaoke CD.

"Stop, stop!" I yell, pulling the tapestried turban off my head. "This is so stupid. Why are we doing this?"

"We want a juice bar?" Elisa croaks.

"You want your boyfriend back?" Amber asks.

Amitha strums the sitar and sings, "Because music is the language of love!"

I've slumped onto the couch, my blue-gold sari hunched up above my knees. "I don't see the point. He will never be interested again, and I don't blame him. I am a mess."

"You are a mess," Becca says, nodding, "but we still love you. I bet he does too."

Amitha, Caroline, Claudette, and Elisa grab me by the arms and drag me back to my place in front of the New Delhi chorus line. I hear the words of the song ringing through my hallway: *Well, how can I forget you, boy? When there is always something there to remind me.*

"Okay, now sway with your arms above your head, like this, one foot propped on your calf." Amitha shows us this exotic move, and I try and mimic it, but instead of looking like a graceful temple dancer, I think I probably look like an epileptic flamingo with one good leg.

The night of GeekFest finally arrives and we're at the theater all afternoon, Carl fiddling with the sound, Jon trying to get the lights to work, Naveen following Elisa around like a sick puppy dog. There's so much love in the room I feel as if I might puke. Seriously.

We rehearse the acts one by one, and each one is pretty good, actually. Caroline and Claudette do a really amazing rap set to classical music and hip hop beats, and then Amitha comes out and plays a solo on her sitar. I think she plays really well, and I think Naveen is just jealous. Of course, he's not even watching the show anyway. He's too obsessed with

Elisa and her Palm Pilot, so they sit huddled in a dark corner, sharing coefficients or something.

Another girl does a comedy routine, and it does make me laugh a little, even though I'm in a rotten mood. Then we have the four-piece orchestra girls who play a medley of *Star Wars* music with a disco beat behind them. Pretty cool. We have an original art movie about the secret lives of coffeemakers, and then Amber gets up to do her poetry about office supplies. Elisa's dramatic reading of "She Blinded Me with Science" is pretty hysterical to everyone except Naveen, who watches lovingly from the front row.

When it's my turn to go, I suddenly get the chills and feel nausea coming on. "I don't think I can do this," I whisper to Becca. "If I can't even do it in front of you guys, how am I going to be able to do it in front of an audience?"

The girls in their brightly colored saris are lined up like tapestry bowling pins on the stage, their bejeweled turbans glowing under the lights. I trudge up the steps to the stage as if I'm going to a hanging, and Becca plops a turban on my head, covering my eyes. Maybe it would be easier to do if I couldn't see anything, after all. . . .

"Here's your mic, Shelby," Amitha says, curling my reluctant fingers around the instrument of embarrassment. "Now, just hold it up about an inch away from your lips."

I adjust the turban so I can squint into the incredibly bright lights. Not so bad. I can't see anything. The music starts, and Amitha starts jamming on her sitar, and the girls behind me do their little dance. Just as I'm getting ready to sing, my dad throws open the doors to the theater and yells, "We're here!"

He has Euphoria strapped to an equipment dolly with multicolored bungee cords, and she's beeping and whirring her indignant protest. He muscles her up the wheelchair ramp and onto the stage, where the girls descend upon her, decorating her like the mice did the ball gown in *Cinderella*.

"I've never had such a rough ride in my life," she sputters, tiny sparks flashing underneath her wheels. "Your father cannot drive a motor vehicle. I just thought you should know."

"I got you here," Dad yells back. "And you're welcome."

"Let's start over," Becca suggests. The tape cues again, and my whole chorus line of living and nonliving backup chicks is in place.

"I walk along the city streets you used to walk—" I am barely audible, which is just the way I like it.

"Turn her up!" Becca screams. She looks like a vengeful Indian goddess in her purple and blue skirt and matching turban, with her little blond spikes sticking out. Nobody will argue with her, which is too bad, because I know this would be better for everyone if no one could hear me.

Now the mic is turned up so high I can hear my own breathing, and when I clear my throat, it's like somebody set off a blasting cap in a coal mine. "I don't think this is a good idea," I moan.

"Oh, c'mon, Shelby," Euphoria says, putting a claw on my shoulder. "Don't mess up my only opportunity for superstardom! I never get out of the house!"

"Is that somebody in a robot suit?" one of the newer girls asks hesitantly.

"Yeah," I nod. "She has a skin condition. Doesn't like to be seen."

"It's almost six," Carl yells from the booth at the back of the theater. "Doors open at seven, so you should all stop and get something to eat."

Everybody whips off their saris (which are Velcroed . . . something I'm not sure Krishna would approve of), and leaves them in an untidy pile on the side of the stage. There's a stampede for the door, where Dad has wheeled in several large pizzas and Thea has towed in a cooler of soft drinks.

Sitting in the alcove eating feels like preparing for a battle. It's my last meal, and I may never eat again. The taste of pizza in my mouth, the gooey cheese, the garlic—

"Hello?" Becca knocks on my head. "What's with the doomsday face?"

"This is just such a lame idea," I begin, but she interrupts.

"You want Fletcher. He wants you. What's the big problem?"

I wipe some stray cheese from my fingers and wonder: What *is* the problem? "I guess I just feel like . . . it will never work out."

"Because you don't deserve it?" Becca whispers in my ear. "It's a gift. You can't earn it or deserve it. It's that simple, really."

She's gone from global domination to philosophy in sixty seconds, and my head is spinning. "Remember Alice," she says as she stands and wipes pizza crumbs from her leggings. "She went down the rabbit hole and through those tiny doors without knowing what was on the other side. You can't ever know what's on the other side. Not really. So, your decision is: Do I stay or do I go?"

I must sit there for quite a while thinking about this question, because when I look up, it's only a few minutes before they open the doors at seven.

"I guess they really want a juice bar," Amitha comments as she peers through a window at the large line of people waiting to get in. "Let's get backstage!"

As we all file into the backstage area, I come to a startling realization: Fletcher probably won't even come to this thing. Why should he? I never invited him. I was about to make a total fool of myself and the reason for my foolishness wasn't even going to be there! I must look horrible, because suddenly Elisa and Amber are on either side of me, holding my arms.

"Are you okay?" Amber asks. "I thought you were going to faint."

"Fine, fine," I mutter, grabbing the handrail.

The theater isn't completely full, but there are at least two-hundred people there, mostly kids or parents. Not too bad. I watch the other acts backstage, listen to the applause, which is mostly genuine (except for when Elisa did her interpretive dance . . . that applause was definitely polite. And confused). I can't help but scan the rows in front to see if he's there . . . but he's not. I don't see him at all. Why should he be here? It's almost time for me to go on, and I feel like throwing up.

Our announcer, a speech club Queen Geek named Danielle, introduces us. "And finally tonight, we have a totally talented group of singers and dancers to entertain you. Shelby and the Screaming Vishnus!"

I glance over at Becca. "Shelby and the Screaming Vishnus?"

"We needed a name." She shrugs. "Amitha's idea."

We take our positions on stage, and the bright lights do block out most of the people in the audience. I do spot my dad, who is videotaping every humiliating moment of this. Great. I can relive my nightmare on DVD for as long as the world turns, and I can pass that on to my nonexistent grandchildren that I'll never have because I'll never be married.

"Break a foot," Euphoria whispers in my ear.

The music starts, and I truly feel I could faint. But instead, I open my mouth and start singing. By the time I get to . . . *"Well, how can I forget you boy? When there is always something there to remind me . . ."* I realize I can't feel my legs! Are they still there? Yes . . . yes. I'm still upright. I go for verse two. And this is where things get really bad.

As I utter the words about wanting to hold him tight, my traitorous tear ducts start flooding the stage. I seriously am going to have them removed. Black mascara is running down my face, and blurring everything in front of me. But I am determined that the show must go on. Plus, Becca is stepping on my sari so I can't run away.

I open my mouth to sing the chorus, but instead of my voice coming out of the mic, it's a guy's voice. It's Fletcher's voice. Right over my shoulder. I turn, and there he is, that stupid freckly face and weird wiry reddish hair, and he's dressed in a dhoti and a turban! And he joins in, grinning at the part about being born to love me. And then we all sing "Always something there to remind me . . ."

And of course everyone loves a happy ending. So when we finally finish the song, there's a massive cheer, and turbans are thrown in the air, and some thumping dance music fills the theater as most of us take our bows. I am not bowing. Instead, I have my arms thrown around Fletcher Berkowitz's neck and I'm crying into his turban, and I'm laughing so hard I might pee my pants.

And then he kisses me, and like in those sappy romance movies, everything sort of fades away, goes into slow motion, and there's only the two of us. And I'm looking into his eyes and he's looking into mine, and for the first time ever, I feel like maybe someone could love me. Maybe I don't deserve it, but that doesn't matter, does it?

EPILOGUE:

ALWAYS
SOMETHING THERE

(or Happily Ever Afterparty)

So, we get through the show. Everybody's happy, even Euphoria, who meets a nice piece of lighting equipment. The weather's turning a bit chillier, so it's perfect for cuddling up on couches with popcorn and a movie. One Friday night, that's just what we're doing. We're all over at Becca's house (because, face it, she has room enough in that mansion for a small army) and we're in her "screening room" watching *V for Vendetta*, a fantastic flick, except that I'm not really watching it closely because Fletcher is rubbing my head. Elisa and Naveen are snuggled in a huge beanbag chair, Amber and Jon sit cross-legged on the floor, Becca and Carl are in back (because they're taller than everyone else). Dad and Thea are even there, and I have to admit that I'm getting used to them being together. Not together in the forever after sense of the word, but together like friends, buddies, and that's all I want to consider at this point.

Fletcher taps my shoulder and motions for me to join him in the hallway. "What?"

"I have something for you. Let's call it an early Christmas present." He pulls a little velvet box from his pocket.

My heart stops pounding for a moment, and my breath stops too. "Uh . . ." is all I manage to say. Very eloquent.

"So, are you going to open it or what?" The box is lying on his outstretched palm. And here I have a choice: I can go back to being the old Shelby, the one who was afraid of everything serious or deep, or I can go down the rabbit hole and see what happens.

Even though I feel panic welling up in my stomach, I take the box. I open it. Inside is a beautiful silver bracelet inlaid with shining blue stones. "Read it," he says proudly.

On the inside of the bracelet, the inscription reads, "Always Something There to Remind Me—Fletcher + Shelby." He's watching me to see if I fling it away, hit him with it, or run crying out of the room. But instead, I just slip the bracelet on my wrist, put my arms around him, give him the biggest kiss I can with my dad in the next room, and whisper in his ear, "I love you."

And then we both just grin like the Cheshire Cat.